11/27/2021

T8 LOU

One More, That's It

Thanks for all
of your HELP !!

Doc

This story is the sequel to the novel
FIVE MINUTES OF BLACKNESS
By Doug Smith

One More, That's It!

Doug Smitty Smith

The Mottled Speck
TAMWORTH, NH

"We are all just walking each other home."
—Ram Dass

To all my sponsors:
Thanks for walking me home.

1.

I REMEMBER THE GUNSHOT.

I DON'T REMEMBER THE AMBULANCE.

I pound my call button. Makeba walks in. My nurse is elegant and sure of herself. She is not grandiose but has an air of royalty. She is cool, calm, and confident.

"Is it time?" I bark.

"Not time yet, sugar." She blows me a kiss. Her rejection is definite. No debate. No negotiation. I sink back in my pillow.

She taps me on the shoulder as she walks out. I hate her touch!

My life is gray. My room is yellow. My pillow is the color of sweat, drool, and mucus.

After an eternity, my nurse comes back. My hopes run high, but I am afraid to be optimistic. Makeba's smile is genuine. Her glistening white teeth glow next to her jet-black skin.

"It's time, sweetheart." She laughs as she clamps off the IV. She injects a cocktail of Dilaudid and Demerol.

I slide into a comfort zone of bubbling warm Jacuzzi jets and smooth, cool, whipped cream. I'm in a full-body blanket of soft silk with the lightness of down feathers. It's the warmth of the sun on a cool spring day. It's as mood changing as the unexpected kiss from the girl at the high school dance. My eyes roll back, and I levitate to a new, comfortable position. Nothing bothers me. Nothing matters. Nothing hurts.

I am suddenly in a different place: a good mood for the first time in forever. Chatty. Effervescent.

"I like your name," I say.

"Named after Mariam Makeba. A South African folk singer." She smiles, taps me three times and walks out. I love her touch!

My days in ICU are a dizzying rollercoaster of pleasure and pain. When I tell Makeba I need a miracle, she frowns.

"You're so cute when you are mad at me, darling!" She taps me.

Makeba is tall, stunning, and professional. She is the only nurse in this hospital who still wears a starched white uniform with long sleeves, even on a warm summer day. There are five tiny buttons at the wrist of each sleeve. Her cap has two black stripes. Her shoes are free of scuffs, her stockings are free of runs, and her face is free of wrinkles. Sometimes, I want to make her smile. Other times, I want to make her cry. My emotions volley between euphoria and clinical depression.

The pain that I experience between my scheduled meds is unbearable. The hollow point bullet that entered me was traveling at two thousand feet per second. My thigh and pelvic bones were shattered.

I can't get comfortable, and when I make an attempt, a new shooting pain blasts into the area I was trying to appease. If I belch, burp, or blink, my body explodes with an instant reminder. The reminder is, *Don't move!* Don't wiggle, don't giggle, don't fart. And, to make matters worse, the pain shifts. Sometimes it's in my back. Other times my upper thigh. But since my pelvis virtually exploded, that's where the affliction is most severe. Nerve damage can be a stabbing feeling, or it can cause numbness and a pulsing sensation. My sciatic nerve was ruined. I'm in agony from the massive bone and soft-tissue trauma. My neurosurgeon says the pain might travel to my genital area.

I am in slow motion. Even X-rays that should only take a few seconds go on forever. Just moving my leg an eighth of an inch is excruciating. I am vocal with my objections. The technician is sick of me. She can't hide her rolling eyes every time I am wheeled into her lab.

The Colorado Community Hospital has 354 beds, and last year over seven thousand patients were admitted. None of them, however, have had as much trauma as me. I should have a separate wing and a team of experts handling my care.

Today, to make matters worse, they want me to get up and walk. Two male nurses hoist me up in a gait belt and drag me down the hall. I complain all the way.

"I want to go back to bed."

"That's why we want you to move," one of them jokes.

Everyone wants to be a comedian!

I am bitter and angry. I have already lost my career. Now I'm afraid I might lose my leg. Or my kidney. Or my pecker.

When a nurse asks a simple question, I say "It's in the chart! Look it up." At meal time, I complain about the food. At night, I bitch about the lights in the hall, or about the patient in the next room who is crying in pain.

I am demanding, demeaning, demoralizing, and demonstrative. I am an inconsiderate, whiny, big-baby jerk. I am an asshole.

I hate this hospital!

I hate everyone who works here.

I hate myself!

2.

LATE ONE NIGHT, MAKEBA WALKS INTO my room. She kills the TV and offs the lights. The room is pitch-black and scary quiet. She drags an old wooden chair next to my bed. It squeaks as it slides across the floor.

"I realize that you are in pain, my friend," she says. "I understand! You don't know this, but I suffer from my own pain, every day." She sighs, and I think she may be choking back a tear.

I shudder.

"You probably don't want to hear my story, but I will tell you anyway.

"One night, in Mississippi," she says, "My father and brother were bound together and tied to a huge cross. It was set ablaze.

"My mother and I ran to them and dragged them away from the fire. In the process, our clothing caught fire.

"In the ER, we found that my mother's hair had completely burned down into her scalp. My father's face was reduced to ashes. His features were never recognizable again. My brother had a huge white scar that ran down the center of his head. 'Grotesque' is the word that was used.

"My arms were shriveled, cracked, and deformed. They look like twigs that were used to toast marshmallows. I have never been in public without a long-sleeve shirt since that day.

"Everyone said my father fell in front of a commuter train. I think he jumped.

"My brother was so full of rage. Big kids picked on him. Little kids laughed at him and called him names. He took up drugs and OD'd.

"But my mother. My poor mother just stopped eating. She lost over a hundred pounds in six months. She sat by the window waiting for her husband and son to come home.

"During that part of my life, I spent many long nights in hospitals. Wherever we were, there was a nurse who made things better. I have worked very hard to earn these stripes." She points to her cap. "It would have been easier to just quit, but I don't believe in quitting. I hope you don't, either!" She kisses me on the cheek, taps me three times, and walks to the door.

"I love you, Jesse," she says.

3.

AFTER OUR LATE NIGHT TALK, MY attitude starts to change. I realize that I am one lucky man. If the bullet had landed one inch higher, I wouldn't be here now. Instead of cursing the pain, I count my blessings.

I am doing this in honor of my nurse Makeba. I am doing this in honor of my wife, Maggie.

My nurse visits me on schedule with magic meds. My wife visits me on schedule, too. Like clockwork. At two o'clock every afternoon, she walks into my room and gives me a hug. She tells me about our rescue dog, Freebee, about our little Colorado country home, and about the weather. She is pleasant and full of encouragement. Secretly, I have a high degree of appreciation and respect for her. She is going through this with me, again. A second time. She is my rock.

I navigate through predictable recovery stages. I sit on the edge of the bed and dangle my legs. I stand by myself. I hobble to the bathroom.

I encourage other suffering patients to make it through the night. I sit bedside with guys who are living in hell. I now do everything in my power to stand tall, both figuratively and literally I will recuperate. I will smile. I will help other people.

My wife beams when I vow that I will never drink again.

4.

MAKEBA STUFFS MY SHOES, SWEATSHIRTS, AND jeans into a suit-case. She puts my meds and get-well cards on my lap and wheels me out to the car. She gives me a gigantic hug and taps me three times.

Maggie drives us to our little house in Boulder. It's been a long time since I have felt the warmth of the sun beaming through a windshield. It feels rejuvenating. I relax. I am buckled into our car. Maggie is in control of this drive, this day, and this life of mine. I feel humble, grateful, and full of joy for the first time in months.

When I get out of the car, I trudge up the front steps on my walker, but within minutes I feel shattered. Emotionally and physically.

The welcome home ceremony is brief. There is a daybed in our living room. My old dog, Freebee, sniffs me. She settles in and takes a nap. I settle in and try to take a nap, too.

5.

AS I GET COMFORTABLE, I FOCUS on a girl named Kiki. She was the God-damned person who ruined my life. What happened to her?

Kiki has been on a killing spree. She has murdered men all over the country. She has tried to kill me twice. She has disappeared twice.

She is someplace with a beautiful smile, a psychopathic personality, and a tiny Kel-Tec pistol.

"Where the hell *is* the girl?"

6.

THE GIRL WAS ON CLOUD NINE.

"Thanks for picking me up," she said. "I was born deaf. I can't hear, but I am really good at reading lips. Can you please look at me when you talk?"

"Of course," he said, as he took his eyes off of the road to turn toward her.

"What's your name again?"

"My name is Kiki," she said. "I was thinking of changing it, but I like Kiki. I really do."

"I like it, too," he said.

"Thanks. It was my birthday present. My mother gave it to me on the day I was born. My name is Kiki." She flashed her best smile.

"I've never hitchhiked before," she lied. "What kind of car is this?"

"Oh, just a little Benz." He smiled.

The SL550 Roadster was new, and Jeb loved it. When he and his ex-wife split, he didn't care if she got the condo. All he wanted was the wheels.

"It's kick-ass," Kiki said.

The first leg of the trip from Boulder to Seattle was perfect. The top was down, and the suntan lotion was in the cup-holder.

Jeb snuck a quick glance at the hitchhiker. She was eye-catching. She was eye candy. Her short, black, pixie hairdo framed her face. She was trim, and her floral summer top was billowing up in the breeze. As it was whipping around, it exposed her tight tummy. He liked her look, but he was thinking that picking her up was probably not a good idea.

"Do you have a girlfriend?" she asked.

"Actually," Jeb said. "I'm engaged to be married."

"Oh shit!" she screamed, as loud as she could. She pounded on the dashboard with her fists.

"Shit, shit, shit. God damn it! It happens all the time. It's always the same thing!"

He looked at her.

"I hate these shorts," she said. "They are too tight. They keep riding up my butt! They look good, but when I sit still for a while, up they come. Up, up, up! They are a pain in the ass!" Then she laughed at her own joke.

"A pain in the ass," she said again. "Do you mind if I change?"

Before he could reply, she shimmied out of her shorts. She threw them as high as she could, right over her head. As the wind quickly took them away from the convertible, he saw them disappear in the rear-view mirror.

"Thank God, they are gone," she said.

She sat there in her undies and looked over at him.

"I hope you like pink panties," she said. "Does your girlfriend wear sexy panties, or does she wear plain old cotton-crotch underpants?"

"She, er, wears . . ."

"I know. You are embarrassed to tell me she is a prude. I bet your girlfriend is prim and proper. Now. I bet she used to be fun, until you got engaged, but now it's starting to change, right? Now she never lets you have any fun. She is trying to change you. All girls do that. I have heard that story from every married man I have ever dated. If you think it's bad now, wait till you get married. You'll never get another blowjob again.

"From her, anyway."

Jeb just stared.

"That's okay. You and I can have fun! Hey, here's a question: Has your girlfriend ever ridden in your car bare-ass? Of course, I would never do anything like that! What kind of a girl do you think I am, anyway?"

She reached in her backpack and pulled out a short, threadbare, jeans skirt.

"How's this?" She smiled, then she lifted her legs, one at a time, and slid into the skirt.

"What looks better? Tan legs or white legs?" She pulled the skirt up to her mid thighs again.

"The color doesn't matter. You have great legs," Jeb finally muttered.

"They go all the way up!" She smiled as she pulled her skirt all the way up to her belly button.

"You getting hot?" she asked.

"You bet. I'm burning up!"

"Maybe I can help!"

Kiki rose up on her knees and turned toward Jeb. She smiled and stared into his cobalt-blue eyes. Her lips were two inches from his. He was trying to look past her face to see the highway. She placed one hand on his shoulder and her other hand on his waist. She playfully tugged at his tank top. He got the idea and let her pull his shirt up over his head. They were cruising along the interstate at seventy-five, but the road was long and straight. So was he.

"I'm going to take care of you while you drive," she said.

She grabbed the suntan lotion and squirted some on his shoulders.

"Oh," is all he said.

She applied lotion to his neck, his shoulders, and his arms. She moved her hand lower. She playfully rubbed his nipples in little circles for a long, long time.

"You probably don't like that, do you?"

"I, er. I love it."

"Hey. Let's play a game. It's called find the belly button, hide the finger." She slid her hand down and stuck her finger into his navel. She wiggled her finger around for a long time. She moved her hands down to his knees, and slid her fingers up and down the insides of his thighs. When she reached the top, his eyebrows rose, and he flashed a big grin.

"Oh. I am so sorry," she said.

"I don't mind, but my fiancée may not approve."

"I'll never tell." Kiki smiled.

"Now I better take care of me," she said, as she leaned back in the passenger seat, lifted her butt up, and pulled her skirt all the way up to her abdomen. She applied sun-tan lotion to her shins and then rubbed along the edge of her legs. When she got to the area near her crotch, she made a face and grimaced. She bared her teeth as if she'd been hit.

"Just shaved. Itchy!"

In order to reach her ankles, she put her feet on the dashboard, then pulled each leg up to the opposite shoulder, one at a time. She lathered up her legs, then pushed her seat all the way back. She let her hand rest between his legs. Her skirt was still up to her belly button.

"Having a fun trip?" she asked.

"You bet!" He smiled and nodded.

She moved her hand further up on his inner thigh and stuck her tongue out. She wiggled it from side to side.

"Hey, let's play charades!" she said as she jumped up on the seat sideways again. She sat on her ankles and looked at him.

"Guess what this is." She stuck her finger into her mouth, licked it all around and got it wet. Then she pulled it out and licked the tip of her finger for a long time. Then she slowly pushed it back in as far as it would go.

"Er, I need to tell you something," he said.

"What's on your mind?" she asked.

"I'm getting married."

"You already told me that! It doesn't matter. Every guy I ever dated had a girlfriend, or a fiancée, or a wife. If I didn't date guys with baggage, I wouldn't date at all." She smiled. "It's no biggie."

Then she looked at the bulge in his shorts. She tapped his groin three times.

"Well, maybe a little biggie!"

"I'm getting married!" he said again.

"God. You're no fun! What's your fiancée's name, anyway?"

"Her name is Blossom."

"Where did you meet her?

"At my restaurant in Springfield, Massachusetts. It's called Bad Boys Burgers. I hired her to wash dishes."

7.

BLOSSOM WAS TALL AND THIN. SHE had a warm, inviting smile. She saved money with thrift shop clothes. Although her outfits were never up-to-date, they were always clean and neat. She couldn't afford makeup, nail polish, or perfume. Her pony tail was dirty blonde and held in place with a rubber band. A few strands always fell in front of her face. Her hair was so fine that any breeze would rearrange her look. If she stood under the ceiling fan, a few random strands would go in several directions at the same time. She unconsciously scrunched her mouth up so she could blow the annoying wisps of hair out of her eyes.

She was a half-hour early for her appointment at Bad Boy Burgers, and the owner, Jeb, asked her to wait.

Who would hire her? She wouldn't hire herself. She had lost so much time at school that she could barely read. She had no marketable skills, and she always applied for the lowest possible entry-level position.

Her father always said she was only good for cleaning toilets, and at her last job, at the Iron Fist Karate Academy, she had been the cleaning lady. It was a minimum-wage job, but there was another benefit: She slowly picked up the moves that clients paid for. She watched students practice, and, through observation and repetition, she began to emulate them. She came in early and stayed late to train. The move that impressed her most was the long roundhouse kick. It required her to raise her center of gravity, tilt her hip, and lean back to swing her leg forward, and she loved the way it made her feel. She worked on the roundhouse every day. Her goal was to deliver a kick that would leave an opponent dripping in blood. Every time her foot connected, she pictured her father's face on the bag.

The sensei was impressed and helped her fine-tune her skills. He let her take a *gi* from lost and found, and she liked it. Loose clothing hid her figure. She hated people ogling at her. What did they see, anyway?

Blossom liked karate, and she could finally protect herself. No man would ever abuse her again. Especially not her father.

When the karate school went out of business, Blossom had to go out and ask a total stranger for a job. She hated asking for anything, but she needed money. She ended up at Bad Boy Burgers.

As she looked around at the bomb site Jeb called a kitchen, she was appalled. *What a dump!* She picked up a broom and started to sweep. Then she filled a bucket with warm water and mopped the floor. One of the employees gave her a dirty look. When Jeb finally came out of his office, he stared in disbelief. The kitchen floor was spotless. He hired her immediately.

She looked at him, blew a six-inch bubble and popped it. Then she smiled. She had a job!

Blossom moved her bucket into the tiny bathroom, where she spent an hour mopping the floor, wiping the walls, cleaning the sink, and scrubbing the toilet.

8.

BAD BOY BURGERS WAS JUST TWO blocks from the home of the Eastern States Exposition. The locals referred to the yearly county fair as the Big E. The restaurant was on a busy traffic circle. There were always fire engines and police cars flying by. The neighborhood was full of trash that had lost its value and people who had lost their hope. The building was old, and the parking lot was a catch-all for candy wrappers, cigarette butts, and take-out packages. Without being asked, Blossom policed the lot before and after each shift.

She commented on service issues, customer satisfaction, maintenance, systems and methods, and she was proud that the place was now spotless. She had no qualms about asking another employee to pick up the trash or pick up the pace. She took pride in explaining how to improve the customer experience.

As she worked her magic, the facility became more welcoming, the staff more friendly, and the service more dependable. Bad Boy became a favorite of locals.

After working together for months, Jeb began to have faith in her.

"Can you lock up, tonight?" he asked.

"Of course," Blossom replied, as she blew a big bubble.

Jeb smiled fondly at his favorite employee and walked out early.

After shutting down the ventilation, activating the security system, and killing the lights, Blossom locked up and walked to the rear parking lot.

She found Jeb in the grips of three muggers. He had been pushed backward against his Mercedes and was bent over, staring straight into the eyes of a huge black man with a gun.

Without a word, Blossom walked up behind the man. There was a tattoo on his neck.

Blossom tapped him on the shoulder, and he turned and yelled at her.

"The fuck you want, bitch?" he shouted.

Within one second, she spun and brought her leg up to the right side of his head. When her foot connected, his neck snapped sharply. The huge man almost bent in half. He hit the parked car with his head and was out cold. His gun went flying.

Without hesitation, she spun again and connected with the second attacker. Since he was taller, she caught him in the neck. He too went down, but he wasn't out. When he hit the gravel, he was still squirming. She jumped as high she could and landed on his back, crushing his rib cage. His scream was deafening. Then there was nothing. The third man ran away.

Jeb dialed 911.

"Thank you! Thank you, Blossom. You saved my life. Thank you! How did you learn to kick like that?"

"Just picked it up," she said with a smile.

Jeb gave Blossom a ride back to her tenement apartment. They sat in her parking lot and talked for an hour. He studied her in the quiet of his small car. Even though he was still shaking, she was calm. She blew a huge bubble and let it pop.

"Tell me your story," Jeb asked.

Blossom told him a little bit of her story, but not everything. She didn't want to scare him.

"You're so easy to talk with," Jeb said. "Why are you washing pots?"

"I missed a lot of school," she said. "I can't get a real job till I get my GED. I'm working toward that now."

"You're going to school and working full time?"

"I want to get certified, but I have to work!"

9.

THE NEXT MORNING, JEB ASKED BLOSSOM to join him for lunch. She looked around the dining room and pointed to a table.

He took out his car keys, held them up, and said, "Let's go."

At a quiet restaurant north of Springfield, Jeb started the conversation.

"I want to make some changes."

Her heart sank.

"You saved my life. I want to repay the favor."

"You don't have to . . ."

He cut her off.

"I want you to continue working on your GED, but let's cut back on your work schedule so you have more time to study. I want to pay you for the hours you are in school. If you need extra help, I will pay for tutoring. I want you to stop washing pots and help me run the restaurant. I want to give you a clothing allowance. And lastly, I will give you a raise."

Blossom stared at him in shock.

10.

BAD BOY BURGERS THRIVED UNDER BLOSSOM'S care. The facility became clean, the windows were spotless, the staff slowly learned how to be courteous. Repeat customer counts were up.

Jeb and Blossom were a wonderful team. The business flourished and they talked constantly. They shared suggestions. They celebrated good sales days. They challenged each other. Jeb spent more time with Blossom than he did with his wife.

After they closed up one night, they sat at a small table in the dark. Jeb put a candle in a cupcake and handed it to Blossom. "You have been helping me for a full year," he said. "Happy anniversary."

That night, Jeb confided in Blossom for the first time. He shared that his wife had been having affairs since the week of their wedding.

"She is a serial adulteress," he said. "I have suspected, investigated, threatened, begged, and cried. She has a sickness. I have caught her five different times. Once she was with a delivery boy, a teenage kid, in the middle of the day. They were both bare-ass, lying on the wooden deck by the pool. I couldn't be as mad at the young, pimple-faced kid as I could at my wife. He was being used by my wife for this fuck fest. I chased him out of the yard. I went back and sat on the chaise lounge and glared at my wife. She was still naked and curled up in a ball on the deck. We both cried. I am so full of shame, embarrassment, and a desire for revenge that I can never forgive her."

"Can't you divorce her?" Blossom asked.

"It's confusing." He sighed. "I have no cash. I would have to give her half the restaurant, and then I wouldn't have a job." The conversation was comfortable, but Jeb felt like the sharing was one-sided.

"I'd like to ask a favor," he said.

"Of course." She smiled.

"Tell me about your life," he asked for the tenth time.

"Ask me anything but that!"

Blossom, I care for you, but I don't know anything about you. There are pages missing from your history book."

"Jeb. You don't need to know what you don't need to know!"

"All I want is to know about you. Your past. Your life."

"All you need to know is that my life was terrible. It was hell. It was like living in a horror chamber. I try to see a bright side, and I don't want to complain. Actually I am happy that my terrible childhood forced me to do the things I had to do to be the woman I am today. But, despite all that I have now, I wouldn't wish my past on anyone. If you can picture a place called Hell, that was my life. And I lived with the devil."

She looked at him and smiled.

"Jeb. Here's the thing. In order to tell you about my life, I will have to bring it up again. Churn it up. Think about it. Relive it. Every time I let myself think about my past, I hyperventilate; I sweat, and gasp for breath. I become clinically depressed.

"If I dwell on my past too much, I have spasms. I know that I will have these feelings, not because I read about them in some medical journal, and not because some doctor told me about them. I know that I will have these incredibly negative reactions because this is what happens. Over and over and over again. It was a painful place.

The memory is like walking barefoot on broken glass. I don't want to go back to that place. Ever again."

After a long pause, she continued. "So, Jeb, if telling you about my past is a condition of my employment, then please accept my resignation."

In the darkness of the restaurant, he could see that she was blowing a huge bubble. When it popped, they both laughed.

11.

BLOSSOM IDOLIZED HER BOSS MORE THAN any man she ever met, but there was a problem. No matter how much Blossom cared for Jeb, it was not right for them to be too close. He was married. As the business grew, they sometimes worked twelve or fourteen hours, sometimes seven days a week. They sat in the same tiny office, had lunch at the same little table, and drank coffee from the same paper cup. They laughed about sharing the same grungy tooth brush.

Occasionally, in frustration, she teased him. She felt a little mean, but she just wanted his attention. What was wrong with doing a quick yoga routine in their little office? What was wrong with bending over and touching her toes? A girl had to stretch, didn't she?

After sitting for a long while, she had to straighten her slip. Make sure that her dress was flat, smooth, and presentable. Sometimes she had to hike her skirt up. It seemed that Jeb was making an effort to look in her eyes, but it was obvious that his eyes sometimes wandered.

Blossom now had a clothing allowance. She shopped with more care and concern. She had her hair done professionally; she used makeup and got her nails manicured. When they traveled to restaurant shows or went on the road to look at competition, Jeb always complimented her on how well she cleaned up. He offered to share his quarters, but she insisted they sleep in separate rooms.

"You are married," she would remind him.

"I may be legally married, but emotionally, you are the person I want to be with. Isn't it obvious?"

It was obvious all right. He invited her to hug him, to kiss him, and to sleep with him. And that's what she wanted, too. More than anything in the world. But he was married.

His offers were genuine, warm, flirtatious, and gracious. But he was married.

She believed that nothing would ever change.

12.

One day, everything changed.

It happened in a short, early-morning conversation. Jeb made two announcements that would transform her life.

First, he announced he had filed for divorce. Officially. With a real lawyer.

Her emotions flew.

"I will give my wife the entire Bad Boy business as settlement," he explained with a grin. "All of it. Every spatula, every salt shaker, every fry basket. The building is leased, but she doesn't understand what that means. She is in for a shock. She has never worked a day in her life. After she bangs every employee in the place, she will go out of business. She will end up with a leased, third-rate building in a run-down, fourth-rate location. I should feel bad, but payback is a bitch."

The second announcement was not as exciting. "The owner of a small fast-food chain in Seattle is a friend of mine. He used to work with us here, but he moved out west to follow his own dream.

He is a big gambler, and he is in trouble. He bet his entire payroll on a craps game. Lost everything. I think he might owe money to some bad people. Now, he can't buy product, pay the mortgage, or cover salary. He just wants to dump everything, and he is offering four separate locations for no money down. Just pay him back over time. I can't pass it up. I am going to buy it.

"It's perfect for us, but we have to move quickly. We can set up a new corporation but keep our business name. It will now be Bad Boy Burgers of Seattle." He looked her in the eyes, held her hand, and said that he would leave for Seattle in the morning.

"You mean the Seattle on the other side of the country?"

"I want you to work here for two months. Please spend time with the lawyers and go through the transfer. Then I want you to join me out there. By that time, my divorce will be official. He knelt down and held Blossom's hand, right in the restaurant.

"Blossom will you marry me?"

She just stared.

"Blossom, I want you to marry me, but first I am asking you to help with the transition."

That night, they made love for hours. She was so happy.

Then she quietly wept for hours. She was so sad.

Blossom helped Jeb load a few things in the small trunk of his Mercedes, and she kissed him goodbye. It was by far their most passionate and loving kiss. She would treasure that memory as Jeb drove to Seattle.

On the other side of the country.

13.

I WAKE UP IN MY DAYBED instead of a hospital bed for the first time in a year.

I smile and tell Maggie I am grateful she is still with me. I tell her I love her, and I tell her I will never drink again. She seems happy.

Drinking was why I had bar-room fights. Drinking was why I went to jail. Drinking was why I lost my job as an FBI agent. Drinking was why I was on probation as a San Diego Police Detective.

Drinking was the reason Maggie left me in the first place. Now that we are together again, I have two orders:

"Never pick up a drink, and never wear a cop uniform. Even on Halloween."

Maggie and I have quiet dinners in front of the fireplace and make plans for our future. When I am well enough, we will travel. Maybe we will buy a small motor home. We discuss trips and look at brochures from campgrounds in faraway places.

14.

As I FINISH UP MY DISCHARGE meds, I search for a local doctor to track my progress and administer my aftercare prescriptions. I call several offices and pick a family doctor who doesn't have a long wait. His name is Dr. Knox, and his office is in a huge, renovated Victorian, complete with original woodwork, sanded floors, and scattered oriental rugs.

When I meet my new doctor, I understand why there was no wait. I am in the care of the world's oldest practicing physician. He might be in his early eighties.

Dr. Knox wears a soiled, white lab coat over a blue, button-down oxford shirt. One button is undone. His unruly white hair is thin. His wire-rim glasses are perched lopsided on the top of his balding head. He walks slowly and uses the table to steady himself. He removes his glasses from his head and perches them on his nose. After reading my chart, his eyes close for a brief second and his head drops an inch. Then he opens his eyes wide, shakes his head, and tilts it back. Then, as if by sheer willpower, he is awake. He taps the top of his head. Then he looks at the table and at his desk. He touches the pockets of his lab coat three times.

"Where the hell are my glasses?" he asks no one.

"Maybe on your nose?" I say.

He gives me a dirty look.

"Who put them there?"

He asks questions about my pain and my sleep patterns. He wants to know about my bathroom habits. Then he asks about my relationship with alcohol.

"I don't drink anymore, doctor."

"Well, that's good news." He smiles. "I sure as hell won't prescribe any booze!" Instead, he prescribes a ninety-day supply of Oxycontin.

"Oxy is a painkiller that will make you warm and happy," he says. "It will make you feel like you just got laid.

"But," he adds, "it is addictive, so please just take as prescribed."

Since my wife, Maggie, is busy, I become my own caretaker. On the first day, I take the prescribed dose, but getting around is hard. I look at my huge bottle of Oxys. I have always believed that if one is good, two will be better. I take an extra tab.

On the second day, I take a few extra pills. Within no time, my personal requirements have doubled. Then tripled. After three weeks, I call Dr. Knox.

"I've accidentally dumped my pill bottle down the toilet."

"I've done that myself." He laughs.

He calls in a new script, and I relax.

"This is too easy," I say out loud.

I stop counting, and in a heartbeat I've gone through another ninety-day supply.

15.

"DR. KNOX, I WAS ROBBED."

His phone voice sounds different this time. Very stern. "We need to talk."

I think he will give me a lecture and a new script.

When I get to the office, he introduces me to his new associate. My old doctor has sold his practice to a much younger Dr. Garcia, who will take over all patient care.

Dr. Garcia is about five feet tall. He is also about five feet wide. He has a dark completion and wavy black hair. He has a wart on his nose. His glasses are two inches thick.

"I will help you through this pain," he says. He doesn't smile.

Since Dr. Garcia is newly graduated, he has a better handle on addictive medication than his predecessor, who graduated before Purdue Pharma shipped their first dose of OxyContin. Unfortunately, addiction is not strictly a medical issue. Pills can stop the pain, but they won't be able to stop the addiction.

After a brief talk, Dr. Garcia knows I am hooked. We review my history with alcohol. I tell him about my time in Alcoholics Anonymous.

"I am so happy to be sober," I say.

"You are not sober!" he barks. "You have switched from one master to another!"

Without hesitation, he says. "We need to make a change in your script."

Even though I am sitting, I feel faint.

"From now on, no ninety-day supply!"

I hear him say this, but I have trouble understanding.

"Starting today, I will only give you a one-month supply at a time. Then you must come here in-person each month for a refill. We will discuss your progress, and, if required, I will then give you a new script. Our goal is to taper you off these meds completely."

I am in a state of shock. I feel faint. This is totally unacceptable. I grimace as I walk out of the office.

During the next week, I try to cut back from three or four pills a day to one. My body shuts down. My leg starts to shake. A dull pain slowly develops in my arms and lower back. It spreads and intensifies. Because of the back pain, I can't get comfortable. I can't sit still; I can't move; I can't sleep. My meds are the only thing I can think about. This obsession is worse than anything I ever experienced with alcohol. I have hallucinations; I am paranoid; I have chills and cold sweats. My mouth is dry. I am chewing on my gums. I can't sit still. I am confused. It's difficult to breathe. I am dizzy and lightheaded. I can't eat. I can't shit. I am obsessed with my pain. I am obsessed with OxyContin.

I am dope sick!

I know about doc shopping. When I was a cop, I busted many people for buying scripts from multiple doctors. Most of them were trying to sell the extras. I check into local regulations. Colorado has a law that requires a physical exam before a controlled substance can be prescribed. I wouldn't mind sitting through another exam, but since my wife, Maggie, is my main source of transportation, she would catch on in a heartbeat. Back to square one.

I have been taking triple or quadruple the original dose, and I can't imagine surviving on less. Instead, I want more. I am hooked. I don't know what to do. I break down and cry.

"I will cut back!" I say to no one, but no one is listening.

I am pissed at myself for getting into this predicament. My wife is pissed, too.

"Look at you!" she yells. "You are sweating. You are bloated. You are disgusting! One of the reasons I married you is because you were a stud. Now, why would I want to live with you? Why would I ever want to have sex with you? Why don't you just kill yourself and get it over with? You are acting like a zombie. I don't care if you are drinking it, snorting it, or sticking it up your dubuzzy. You are addicted to something, and it doesn't matter what it is! If you can't get this under control, you will have to move out! Period! I am not taking care of you again."

Unfortunately, my wife is serious. I understand her position, but it might be too late.

The fact is, I am addicted. The fact is, I am trying to cut down. The fact is, my body doesn't want to cut down.

16.

My old friend Hem picks me up and we head to a noon AA meeting. During the meeting, I share about unintentionally swapping one addiction for another.

A guy in the back row says, "The chains of habit are too weak to be felt until they are too strong to be broken."

As we leave the meeting, a good friend says "Jesse, you look like shit. Try to get some sleep." He pats me on the back.

As we make our way to Hem's car, a stranger slowly walks up.

"Hi," she says quietly, almost in a whisper. She is probably twenty-five, towering tall and Tiny-Tim thin. She looks like a broomstick that's been on a diet. Her face is gray. There is no eye liner, no makeup and no lipstick. She is shivering, but it's not cold. Her hair is short, spiked, and uncombed. Her forehead is shiny. There is no eye contact. She offers her hand. It's clammy. "What's your name, again?"

I tell her.

"My name is Layla. Like the song," she says.

"Clapton?"

"My parents were groupies. I heard you share that you were in a lot of pain," she says. "I've been there. It's terrible."

"I don't know what I am going to do." I shake my head.

"Would a few Percs help?"

I slowly smile and start to relax. *Perc is* short for the drug Percocet. It's an opiate. A painkiller. Perc 30s are a fair substitute for Oxy. I know that Percs will give me the relief I need.

I am amazed how people in recovery help each other!

"Thirty bucks."

"What?"

"Each."

"What?"

I stare at her in disbelief. She reacts to my hesitation.

"Never mind," she says. "I was only trying to help!" She starts to walk away.

"Wait!" I empty my wallet. It happens so quickly. What did I just do?

Layla gives me two tabs and scribbles her cell number on the back of a convenience-store receipt. I stuff her number in my pocket and rush to the restroom. There are no cups, so I fill the palm of my hand with a puddle of water and pop the first pill. This is all within minutes of the purchase. I calm down. I feel better even before the oxycodone and acetaminophen hit my blood stream. I take a big breath. I hear myself exhale a huge sigh of relief. Before I leave the bathroom, I take the second pill.

If one is good, two will be better!

I see Layla almost every day. I don't even think about the money. I only think about relief. If I don't take these little pills, I will be in a world of pain. I wish I could eat tranquilizers for breakfast.

The Percs, at thirty dollars each, take a slow, steady toll on our retirement account.

"I'll stop tomorrow," I say to myself.

On the way to our daily meeting, Hem pulls through the ATM line, and I hit our account again. He doesn't ask.

In no time, I am up to four, five, or six pills a day. This is in addition to my prescribed amount.

I am in a daze, but my wife doesn't seem to notice. She is only happy because it seems that I have stabilized.

At an average of a hundred and fifty bucks a day, our funds spike southward, but Maggie hasn't checked our savings account in months. Why would she?

17.

"Hello?

"Yes, this is Maggie.

"A review of our account. Why?

"Excuse me?

"Suspicious activity?

"Just me and my husband.

Yes, his name is Jesse.

"Right here!

"Yes I will! You're damn right! You are damn right I'll look into it!"

The phone slams down.

She screams from the kitchen.

"What the fuck?" yells my wife, who almost never swears.

She storms into the living room and stops two inches from my face.

"What the fuck is happening to our savings account?"

I start to cry. I'm busted. It is hard to explain the withdrawals of over four thousand dollars a month.

"Please try to understand," I beg.

"Understand what?" she finally shouts. She is waving her fists. She throws her cup at me. Fortunately, she is a lousy shot. She charges out. The door slams behind her. I hear tires churn up the gravel.

The next day, I hit the ATM, but our account has been closed.

I am desperate and call Layla. She comes to the house with an emergency delivery. I offer our small kitchen TV. She takes it, but says from now on, no more trades. She needs the cash.

18.

MAGGIE WALKS INTO THE LIVING ROOM with her stone-cold face on. It is puffy, stretched, and white.

"We had a deal," she says. "You drink, or use drugs, you are out! So, you have to leave!"

She can't be serious, I think. *This will blow over.*

Two minutes later, she is yelling into the phone.

"Fig, your friend is hooked!" she screams. "He's using drugs! Over twelve thousand dollars are gone from our retirement account. Our TV is missing, and he can't explain it. He is lying, cheating, and stealing! He can't stay here. Either you come and get him or I am dumping him at a homeless shelter! I am done with this marriage! I am done with this relationship! I am done with him!"

I sit in the next room and sob. *How did this happen?*

19.

THE NEXT DAY, THE SKY IS black. Just like my life. There is a pile driver pounding between my ears. My mouth tastes like a pickle that has been marinating in sewage. My best friend, Fig, from the San Diego police force, shows up. He has flown over a thousand miles to be here. He, too, is pissed.

"Here's the deal, Jesse," he says. "I have a bed reserved for you in a detox and then a long-term recovery center in California. We are going now." Maggie opens the hall closet and produces two huge garbage bags filled with everything I own. The fight in me is gone.

I try to hug her, but she backs away as if I stink. She points to the door. I feel like a kid who has been sent to his room.

Maggie is blank and stoic. No eye contact. Not even a goodbye.

In the rental car, I look at my friend, Sam Newton. He has had the nickname Fig since high school. At five-six he reminds me of a hungry bulldog. He has a crooked nose and broad shoulders. His biceps bulge. His crew cut is salt-and-pepper. One of his front teeth is chipped, and he has never bothered to get it fixed. The scar on his face is long. He is a great cop, and, when he was my partner, he literally saved my life. Today, he is here to save it again.

Fig drives toward the airport. He asks the hard question.

"With everything that you know about addiction, how could you get hooked again?"

"It wasn't easy."

He doesn't laugh.

I am choking from remorse, but also the jitters of withdrawal. My mouth tastes like a camel has died in there.

To lighten the situation, he reaches into a bag on the back seat. He hands me a warm beer.

"This is probably against some AA tradition or step. I don't care. You will be resetting your sobriety date anyway. I don't want you to have a seizure.

"You can have a beer now and order another one on the plane. One more; that's it. Then you will quit again, cold turkey. But this time, my friend, you will be under the care of a medical team.

I grab the warm beer and guzzle. Liquid runs out of my mouth and onto my shirt. I choke and gasp for breath. Then I drink the rest.

20.

"I GUESS YOU CAN BLAME IT on the girl," Fig says. "How did she just happen to show up? And why did she fill you up with hollow points?"

"Only two."

"I should have been with you, instead of sitting on the other side of the park."

"Don't blame yourself," I said

"I do, but I am so glad she's a poor shot."

We are still for a long time.

"So, here we are again," he says, quietly. "We know her name is Kiki. We even have a picture of her. She shot you in New Jersey, and she shot you in Colorado. This is getting to be a pain in the ass."

"Easy for you to say!"

"Don't know if she drove away, flew away, or just walked."

21.

DEAR DIARY_____

I know I will find peace if I just sit still and journal. Things have been so crazy that I don't even know who I am anymore. I just got up and looked at myself. I am still beautiful. I love being naked, but I really prefer some accessories. White heels and a wide, black-leather belt complete the picture. And what a picture.

"My name is Kiki. It's Kiki. I am the same girl, but I am a new lady. Hello Kiki. You are beautiful."

I love my new haircut. A number-two buzz on the sides with a number-four buzz on top. "High and tight" is what the barber called it. It is jet black. I look like a lady jarhead. Maybe I look like Grace Jones. It's a good cut for Seattle, Washington.

I am anonymous again. New city. New girl.

That San Diego cop, Jesse Collins, will never find me now.

The man I love, Jeb, has invited me to live with him. Before he goes off to work each day, he tells me I have to leave. He says he can't see me anymore. When he comes back home at night, he wants to see all of me.

I love to open the motel door in just a half slip, or a pair of panties, or a pair of heels. He is such a prude, but he loves to see me naked. The next morning, he says he can't see me anymore.

We almost never go out, but when we do, it's not to make me happy. It is for a business reason. He wants to check out the competition. Sometimes we go to Pike Place Market. I get to see Rachel the Pig. I rub her snout for good luck. Then he wants action in the car. He wants me to sit on him. Right in public. Right in the middle of the parking lot. But it's okay. I love Jeb! Before he has a climax, he says he loves me.

The next morning, he wants to break up.

It's another gloomy, rainy day in Seattle, but then, aren't they all? It has rained every day for the three weeks I have been here. The locals laugh about the hundred and fifty days of rain every year. They call it clean and green, but I don't care. My life is almost perfect. I am happy to be journaling for the first time in months.

The fact that Jeb picked me up while I was hitchhiking is a miracle. I was so lucky to get out of Colorado after that little mishap with my pistol. I really didn't mean for it to go off. Funny how those things just happen. I don't know if I killed Jesse Collins or if I just hit him again. But if he is alive, he won't be line dancing for a long time.

I'm afraid to admit this, but I am in love with Jeb. He is handsome, fun, and generous. Every morning when he leaves for work he asks me if I can move out. Every night when he comes back, he asks me if he can slide in.

Isn't it obvious that he loves me more than her? He sees me every night. He never sees her.

He is taking care of me. And I am certainly taking care of him!

22.

FIG DROPS ME OFF AT A detox. I am tapered off the Percs with something called Suboxone.

I have no energy. I am anxious and depressed. I feel like a gigantic snake has slithered into my ass and bitten me from the inside. I am nauseous, weak, and sweating. I have a massive headache and constant diarrhea. I can't carry on conversations. I nod off five times a day and lie awake all night.

After seven days in detox hell, Fig picks me up again, and we head to a recovery center called "The Last House on the Road."

As I open the front door, a giant of a man stands up from a desk and walks toward me. He is dressed impeccably in a dark-blue business suit and a white, starched shirt. His shoes are shined.

This man is probably two hundred and fifty pounds, but he moves like a gymnast, or a dancer, or a yoga instructor.

"Hello. You must be Jesse," he says. "They call me Big Jim, but I don't know why. I am the director here." Then he engulfs me in a bear hug. I almost lose my breath.

He looks at me and says, "I understand."

What does he understand? I wonder.

As he steps back, a trim, attractive woman in her thirties walks by. She is fashionably dressed and still has a young girl's figure. Her smile is contagious.

"Hi. I'm Callie." She gives me a big hug, too, and says, "It's okay. I understand."

Other staff members appear, too. They all hug me. Everyone tells me they understand. The maintenance man says he understands, and the chef says she understands.

I find out they are all in recovery. They all seem proud of their ongoing sobriety. When they share, it's easy to realize that they understand, first hand, what every new resident is going through.

The Last House is in a small town an hour northwest of San Diego. It's a huge, dilapidated old building, but it is clean. Beds are hand-me-down donations, but I sleep well. Living-room furniture is threadbare but comfortable. The food is good, and the coffee is strong. There are gardens. There is a stream and an old barn. There are Monterey pines surrounding the building.

Residents range in age from eighteen to seventy-eight. I'm in the middle. Our drugs of choice range from booze to heroin. We all took whatever made us feel better.

"It doesn't matter what we use, how much we use, or how often we use it," Big Jim says. "What matters is why we keep going back to this thing that is killing us."

My roommate, Cody, is much younger than me, but we have the same master. We were both hooked on Percs. Unlike him, I had been an alcoholic first.

"I had so many blackouts!" he shares.

"Blackouts?" I laugh. "I missed the eighties. I don't even remember who was president."

After my first week, I wonder if a recovery center is necessary. I think I can just go home and stay clean by myself. Then I hear someone talking about a relapse, and I remember why I am here. I am so raw, and still in so much pain, that if I weren't here, I would pick up in a heartbeat. On the other hand, I never want to use again.

On my third night in the house, Cody closes our bedroom door and whispers, "Wanna get wasted?"

"What?"

"Stoned, loaded, wrecked."

I'm still queasy from my detox, but I'm paralyzed by his offer.

"The fuck you talking about?" I ask.

"My girlfriend just came for a visit. She smuggled me some oxy." He holds out a handful of tiny white pills.

I am staring at him dumbfounded, trying to think of a reason to say no. I'm trying to think of a reason to say yes. My pulse quickens, and I feel lightheaded.

I am in a recovery center to get off the prescription meds that almost killed me, and now I am offered a chance to go back to my misery. My mind is racing between relief and pain.

Maybe I could just have one, I think. Then I feel nauseous. I might be sick.

One pill promises me everything. That same pill will take everything away. I become dizzy.

I take one of the powerful little pills, put it to my lips, and then, just as quickly, spit it out. I make it to the bathroom before I heave.

Our bedroom door slams opens. The overhead light is snapped on. Big Jim bellows, "Cody, we hear you have some stash. Get down to the office for a UA now!

"Jesse, since you are his roommate, we will piss-test you, too!

"While you guys are down in the office, we will rip this room apart. And we will give each of you the most invasive strip search you ever had."

During the search, they find oxy in my roommate's pocket and in his system. They find one lone pill on the floor in our room.

Later that night, after Cody is kicked out, my heart is pounding. I count my blessings. If another two seconds had gone by, I would have been dirty. If I use again, I may never be able to stop.

"We have burned our bridges and pawned our feelings," Big Jim says, later, to the group. "We hocked everything of value. We have lied, cheated, and stolen from family, friends, and neighbors. When we come into a recovery center, we are broken souls. Our need to be accepted is so strong that even the threat of being kicked out won't stand in the way. The sad part is that at this early stage in our recovery, we are more fragile than we have ever been in our life."

I make it through ninety days, one day at a time.

23.

DEAR DIARY_____

Jeb told me he had a girlfriend. A few times. Okay, maybe a hundred times. He even told me he wanted to marry her. But I didn't take him seriously. He only told me about the girlfriend after he fucked me. And God, did he fuck me. Over and over and over again. He couldn't get enough. But then after he finished, he felt guilty. Just like every other man in the world. Guys are such assholes. Tonight, he said, "We have to talk!"

That's what they all say.

He stammered and stuttered. "I have had a wonderful time with you, but . . ."

Of course he had a wonderful time. He did me in the shower. He did me in his convertible with the top down. He did me in the restroom of the library. He got a hand job in a movie theater. He got a BJ in the dressing room of a department store. He is such a sick bastard. He used me and abused me. Just like every other guy in my life. Now it's over. I am sore and mad as hell.

"You wanted a ride to Seattle," he said, "and now you are here. I am going to open a new branch of my company, and my girlfriend is coming out to help. This is not new news. This is the same story I have told you since the day we met. So, now we have to go our separate ways."

He paid for the motel room for a month in advance and gave me a hundred dollar bill. He said goodbye and quickly walked out. I feel like a prostitute!

I followed him out to the parking lot, bare-assed but who cares. I stood there naked, pounding on his car. I picked up a lawn chair and heaved it toward his windshield.

That's it? It's over? Once again, a guy does me and dumps me. This is my life. What am I supposed to do, now? I tried to talk to him. I yelled at him. He drove away.

I am alone again, but I have been through this before. Maybe I just have to regroup. I still have my backpack full of cash. Over one hundred thousand dollars from my dear mother's estate. And I have my Kel-Tec pistol. And I love to get even!

I don't just want to kill Jeb like I have killed the other men in my life.

I develop a much better plan.

24.

DEAR DIARY_____

A new day. A new chapter in my life. It's hard to find a place to rent when you have a disability. I could certainly afford a place of my own, but I can't fill out applications without revealing who I am. I am sure my name would send up huge red flags. But I have finally found a room to rent.

My new landlord calls herself Candice.

"Not Candy," she says. I have mistakenly called her Candy eleven times. She has corrected me eleven times.

"It's Candice," she says again, with a fixed smile. "I am on antidepressants and cannot have chaos in my life. Please call me by the name my mother gave me. Also, we need to discuss the schedule. The kitchen will be available to you until 7pm. There will be no cooking, snacking, or even microwaving after the kitchen is closed. I expect all dishes and silverware to be washed, dried, and put away after use. Nothing out of place, ever.

"And we will have a strict lights-out policy. The house will be dark at 10pm."

As I tried to pay attention, I glanced around the kitchen. I saw a book called Paleo Diet *and another called* Extreme Weight Loss.

I suspect Candy may have recently gained a few dress sizes. Maybe because of her medication, or maybe because of her lack of willpower. Her pants were stretched tight, and a huge, over-sized shirt covered her stomach.

Later that morning, I walked to the local convenience store and bought a box of Brownie Bites.

When I got back, I found Candy in the kitchen playing with her digital scale.

I stood in front of her and popped a Brownie Bite.

"Bet you can't have just one!" I smiled as I walked away. I left the food on the counter and counted the seconds until she caught up and jumped in my face.

"We will put our food away in its proper place!"

"Hey, that's a good idea, Candy. Go for it."

She hyperventilated.

Candy is the world's biggest neat-freak. Plastic slip covers are on couches and a plastic covering is tacked down over the living-room carpet. I asked about the braided rope between the kitchen and living room.

"We can't go in there," she said. "I want to save my furniture for when I get married."

"Do you even have a boyfriend?" I asked.

She glared at me.

"Hey, it was just a question. Get over yourself Candy. Or Candice."

We each have our own bedroom, but we are forced to share a tiny bathroom. If there is a splatter of toothpaste on the mirror or a pubic hair in the toilet, she goes ballistic.

"We have to do a better job at keeping our living space clean," *she scolded me after our first day together.*

"Sorry, Candy."

"Candice!"

25.

On my third morning in the house, I incurred Candy's wrath. A crumb from my Brownie Bite fell to the floor and was not cleaned up properly.

Later that day, she stood at my bedroom door and handed me some paperwork. It was a homemade booklet, five pages long. The title page said: "Our Book of Rules."

"You're kidding me, right?" I said. "You want me to read a 'Book of Rules?'"

"I expect you to read this important document, and also abide by all of these principles!" she said. "The last page requires your signature."

"You're shitting me, right?"

"We will refrain from using profanity in this house!"

"Is this a fucking joke?"

Her glare intensified.

I took the book and opened it to the first page. It was an introduction.

It said: "My name is Candice, not Candy."

I put the book on my dresser.

"I'll clear up my schedule and try to find a few days to digest this information."

I closed my door in her face. I have some work to do that is more important than her stupid book. I logged onto the internet and looked for the type of retail store that would help me.

My real goal is to get even with Jeb. This will be a long, slow, wonderful process.

26.

AT 10PM, MADELINE ELLSWORTH CLOCKED OUT of Bad Boy Burgers. She smiled to herself. "They remembered my birthday. Seventy-five years young."

Her co-workers at the Capitol Hill branch of Bad Boy had given her a card. They even sang her a song. Since her husband had passed away, the kids at work were her new family.

"How is your new kitten?" she would ask.

"Was your test as hard as you thought it would be?"

"Is your baby feeling better?"

Mrs. Ellsworth was happy to have her job, but she was also glad when her workday was over; she was beat.

She said goodnight to everyone and walked to her old Ford Escort. The back lot was dark. She should mention this to Jeb.

As Mrs. Ellsworth climbed into her car, a young girl with an oversized hoodie walked toward her. The hoodie was pulled down to the girl's eyebrows and tied under her chin. The girl was wearing an oversized pair of dark-rimmed glasses. They looked like something you might wear on New Year's Eve. The girl was carrying a rolled-up yoga mat. She was smiling. She was average height and thin. The girl was asking a question. Mrs. Ellsworth rolled her window down and smiled up at the stranger.

The gunshot to her face was the last thing Mrs. Ellsworth ever saw.

When police arrived, they found an elderly woman slumped against her steering wheel. The driver's window was down and the bullet that passed through her head had lodged in the passenger door. The birthday card was still clutched in her hand.

27.

"SHE'S DEAD!" JEB SHOUTED INTO THE phone. "Mrs. Ellsworth is dead!"

"Who? What?"

"Dead!"

What are you talking about?" Blossom asked from three thousand miles away.

"She's dead!"

"Who's dead? Slow down, please."

"I can't slow down. I can't fucking slow down!"

"Jeb!"

"She's dead!"

"Who's dead?"

"Mrs. Ellsworth! Sweet little old Mrs. Ellsworth."

"What are you talking about?"

"She's dead! Mrs. Ellsworth is dead. Killed. Shot! She clocked out at ten. Two minutes later, she was dead. Shot to death! Right in our parking lot. Right behind our restaurant. Right in the face. Dead!"

"Jeb!!!"

"The cops are here! I gotta go."

"Jeb?

"Jeb?"

Within minutes, police were everywhere. The property was roped off. Fifteen minutes after that, a panel van with a magnetic sign on the side and a professional news-truck parked in front of the building. Spotlights lit up the street. They started interviewing customers, passers-by, and neighbors.

Much later that night, Jeb called Blossom again.

"She's dead! Mrs. Ellsworth is dead."

28.

After ninety days in the "Last House on the Road," my friend Fig picks me up. He has found me an apartment in my favorite little seaside town. I love the beaches and the long boardwalk. I love a town where most people live outdoors. I love Mission Beach. I am so happy to be back in Southern California. My apartment is on the first floor overlooking the pool.

Every morning, as the sun rises, there is light reflecting from the pool onto the kitchen ceiling. Usually the image is calm, but if someone is in the pool, or there's a breeze, the light ripples around my apartment in thousands of little triangles. The bougainvillea plants look terrific. There are no stairs, and I have a feeling of power. I can get around on my walker. I am still in pain but have vowed to take my meds as prescribed.

My home is also just two miles from the "Giant Dipper," the recently restored wooden roller coaster at the best beach in the world. When I lived in San Diego years ago, this was my Happy Place. Now my goal is to be able to walk to Mission Beach by myself.

My future seems bright. I see Fig and his wife, Libby, each week. We enjoy a Padres game or order Chinese. We play cribbage. We watch old movies. Fig and I talk endlessly about detective stuff. Since

Fig and Libby both work full time, I have the days to myself. There is an early morning AA meeting nearby, and a friend picks me up.

29.

BUSINESS AT BAD BOY BURGERS WAS returning to normal. There were lots of newsworthy disasters in the world, and the media forgot about Mrs. Ellsworth's unfortunate murder in the parking lot.

Jeb rotated his time among his locations. After the killing in the Capital Hill store, he spent time in South Beacon Hill. This store was near the former home of Amazon. The town is on a hill and there are views of downtown. When the weather is good, Mount Rainier and the Olympic mountains are visible.

"The mountain is out," the locals say.

South Beacon Hill was voted "Best of 2012" by *Seattle Magazine*.

Staffing is always an issue at a fast food restaurant. Since Mrs. Ellsworth's passing, hiring was an even bigger challenge. Fortunately, most candidates, especially the younger staff, believed that the killing was a one-time thing. A fluke. A mistake. Can't see it from my house. Someone else's problem.

Jeb said good night to his newest and youngest employee, Duffy Longmeadow. Duffy was a good worker but reserved. He was thin and about five-ten, with straight, shoulder-length hair parted in the middle. He seldom offered eye contact or even said a word unless spoken to first. He was guarded and cautious but always on time.

Most nights, when he finished up, he asked if there was anything else to do and then punched out. No fanfare.

Five minutes after Duffy left, a customer ran in waving his arms. "Someone's on the ground. Not moving. Call 911."

Jeb ran out to see Duffy in a heap with blood puddled around his face. His bicycle was still chained to the fence next to the dumpster.

"Blossom! It happened again!" Jeb screamed. "Another one!"

"Another what?"

"Another murder! Another fucking murder!"

"What?"

"Another one. A kid. Dead. Police. Newspaper guys. Gotta go."

"Jeb?

"Jeb?"

Police were on the scene in a heartbeat. They found the young employee face-down with a single gunshot though the temple. There was no sign of a scuffle.

When reviewing the security tape, the police saw someone who looked like a technician or maybe a middle-aged repairman wearing a gray shirt with a wide, black stripe across the chest. Average height, average build, with a large, gray, handlebar mustache, dark-rimmed glasses, and greasy hair hanging in front of his face. He was wearing a Seattle Mariners hat pulled down. Covering his eyes. He had a one-inch wide, flesh-colored bandage across his nose. Maybe Mohs surgery. He was carrying a small, black toolbox. The technician walked up to Duffy and seemed to be asking for directions. He was pointing with his hand and smiling. Then he put his finger up, as if to say *wait a minute*. He reached in his tool box and came out with a pistol. The blast filled the screen and the back of the boy's head exploded. The technician calmly walked away.

Once again, business at Bad Boy Burgers came to a screeching halt. There were press videos showing police tape, dogs, spinning red lights on top of cars, road blocks, and a sign on the front door that said, "Temporarily Closed."

The lead story in the papers was about a second cold-blooded murder at a second location of the newly opened Bad Boy Burger chain.

Later that night, Jeb called Blossom. He was sobbing. He was very drunk.

"If this continues, I will go crazy. If this continues, I will go out of business."

30.

I AM ADJUSTING TO SINGLE LIFE, and I take my meds on schedule. I like living in Mission Beach again. On my trips in and out of my condo, I notice a small restaurant about two blocks away. The old, two-story brick building on Cohasset Street is well maintained, and a hand-carved wooden sign simply says, "JASPERS." In smaller letters under the name, it says, "Superior Breakfast, Speedy Lunch, Sensational Dinner." Fortunately for me, Jaspers is on the first floor.

Two blocks on a walker is a huge undertaking, but the exercise will do me good. I walk slowly, with a fixed smile. Halfway to the restaurant, I stop to refresh my body and renew my resolve. My trip takes forever, but I am determined. When I get to the restaurant, I am shaking and dizzy. My shirt is wet, and my head is throbbing.

As I walk into Jaspers, an attractive, thirty-something woman jogs toward the entrance and holds the door open.

"What took you so long?" She giggles.

"The bridge was washed out," I reply.

"My name is Flower," she says. "Welcome to Jaspers."

"Hi, Flower," I say. Her smile is magnificent.

She leads me to an oversized, upholstered red booth in front of a huge, picture window. The bench is comfortable, and the wooden table is spotless. There are daffodils in a tiny, milk-glass vase, and

I hear instrumental music playing. I have a good view of the street activity. The hostess acts as if we have known each other forever.

She brings rolls, butter, and a local newspaper. As she hands me a glass of ice water with a slice of lemon perched on top, she apologizes.

"I'd take your drink order, but we don't have a liquor license."

"Well, I would like to have a drink," I reply, "but I really need to be home by Christmas."

"I know that feeling!" She laughs.

Flower stands perfectly erect, her head held high with an air of grace and sophistication. She looks comfortable. She has probably had a life of nannies , private teachers, and mentors.

I like Jaspers, and I like Flower. Her voice is refined, almost like music. She is about five-five with fine, short, blond hair. She has sparkling white teeth, and her dark-blue Bambi eyes are wide open. She has a constant smile, and her nose is wiggling.

If she were a train, I would say she has a well-maintained engine, headlights on high beam, and an adorable little caboose.

I wonder if she is trim from a strict diet or from rigorous exercise. Whatever the reason, she looks great. Instead of walking, Flower seems to glide. She reminds me of a line from a Neil Young song:

She used to work in a diner. Never saw a woman look finer. I would order just to watch her float across the floor.

Flower introduces me to my waitress. Jamie has a genuine smile, wears almost no makeup, and her blond hair is short and curly. Or messy. I don't see any earrings or other jewelry. Jamie wears a plaid men's shirt, tan chino slacks, and comfortable black sneakers. As she takes my hand, I notice her fingernails have been bitten. She is the girl next door. No pretense. I feel like I have known Jamie for years.

"Hi, Jesse." She smiles. "You are going to like it here at Jaspers."

Between the two of them, my needs are met. I order something called a "Mission Beach Salad." It's a healthy serving of romaine topped with tuna salad, chicken salad, and cottage cheese. Dressing on the side. After I pay my bill, I wave to the two girls and start to walk out.

Flower runs to the door and opens it for me.

"If you don't come back to Jaspers, you will break my heart." She smiles.

It's a no-brainer. I don't want to break Flower's heart. I go back the next day. The food is tasty, the price is right, and I need the exercise. Also, I have a new best friend. Flower is always polite, attentive, and pleasant. She is well-dressed but never flashy. She is articulate and well spoken. She is classy and contemporary. Her makeup is minimalistic, her teeth sparkle, and her nails look professionally manicured. She seems happy to see me.

In between greeting customers, Flower always seems to be reading something as she stands erect at the hostess station.

Flower and I become the king and queen of small talk. The weather is fine, the traffic is bad, the tourists are happy, and the business is good. After weeks, I know absolutely nothing about her.

"Do you live nearby?" I ask.

"Not too far away," she answers.

"How long have you lived in Mission Beach?"

"For a while."

"Do you have a big family?"

"I am blessed to have people in my life who love me."

"Do you have any hobbies?"

"I have lots of fun things to do."

"Are you an outdoors kind of gal, or are you a bookworm?"

"I would love to sit outdoors and read a book."

By this time, Flower knows a lot about me. I've told her about my failed marriage, my career in law enforcement, and the reason I am on a walker.

"Shot in the line of duty," I lie.

But of her, I know nothing.

"What's your favorite kind of food?" I ask.

"I'm easy to please," she says.

"Do you believe in love at first sight?"

"If I found someone like you, Jesse, I would fall in love in a heartbeat, but let's face it. There is no one like you!"

As time goes on, I run out of questions. Maybe she is married and just being nice because I am on a walker. Maybe she wishes I would stop asking stupid questions. Maybe she wishes I would go away.

But I don't go away. When I walk into Jaspers, I am treated like a celebrity.

The waitresses say, "Hello, Jessie."

The bus boy yells, "Hey, Jess."

The cook shouts, "Jessie is in the house." He hits a frying pan with his spatula.

I know every employee. I know where they live, and I know the names of their kids. I know everything about everyone who works at Jaspers.

Except Flower.

Although I know nothing about her, she always greets me at the door with a smile. Sometimes I get a hug. She acts as if we were long-lost cousins.

"What is your happiest memory?" I ask.

"The day you came into Jaspers." She laughs.

"If you could go on only one vacation, where would you go?"

"Your house."

"What is your favorite song?"

"I love you, a bushel and a peck!"

When I think about Flower, I realize I am in trouble. She is a Miss Goody-Two-Shoes. A rule-follower, a heart-breaker, and probably a tear-jerker. I think I care for her more than I should care for a hostess in a restaurant.

One day I get up the courage.

"Flower, would you have dinner with me?"

"Oh, wouldn't that be nice!" she says, as she offers a big smile. She places her hand on my shoulder as she walks away to help serve a large group. The topic of a date never comes up again. On the way out, she squeezes my arm very tightly and giggles. We are becoming friends. Sort of.

I love seeing her every day, because her mood is always bright.

31.

ONE DAY, HER MOOD IS NOT bright.

When I walk in, I am barely acknowledged. Flower offers a mini wave but seems focused on something at the hostess stand.

As Jamie takes my order, I nod toward Flower.

"What's up with her?"

Jamie raises her shoulders. "No clue. She's been staring at that newspaper all morning."

"Can you tell me what newspaper she is reading?"

Jamie comes back with my salad and whispers, "Seattle Weekly"

32.

DEAR DIARY_____

I have been hurt so many times. Being deaf is not an easy road. Going to that private school to learn lip reading was so demanding.

Trying to understand why my father walked out of my life left me bewildered and confused. I blamed myself. If I wasn't deaf, my father would have loved me. If I had been a better daughter, he wouldn't have left.

Then there was that living nightmare with my Uncle Emmett.

He was chubby and soft, and he always had a red face. He smelled funny. "Get your uncle a little nip," he would say, slowly.

My uncle paid attention to me. He would read to me and tickle me. He would lift me up and have me straddle him so we could sit face to face. I liked that because I could read his lips. We would play patty cake. He loved me. Sometimes he would say, "You have been a bad girl." He would put me across his knee, pull up my skirt, and pat my fanny for a long, long time.

I just wanted someone to talk to me. I wanted someone to play with me. I wanted someone to pay attention to me.

When I was at Uncle Emmett's house, we had fun, but we had secrets. He would give me ice cream for breakfast and tell me it was our secret. He would give me candy for lunch and tell me it was our secret. No one would ever know our secrets.

And when we started playing games, he said, "This will be our biggest secret." How old was I? Was I four years old? Was I five?

It was fun in the beginning. Then it was so confusing. Then it was scary. He had me touch him, and he would touch me. Finally he was fucking me. Weekend after weekend. I didn't want to go back. I cried and dragged my feet.

"He is your weekend babysitter," my mother would yell. "You have to go!"

Years later, there were all those boys. I wanted to have friends. The boys would use me and then abuse me. They all belonged to the same club: The 4F Club. Find 'em, Feel 'em , Fuck 'em, and Forget 'em. They each left me lying in a heap and crying.

They all thought they got away with it, but they weren't happy when I came back into their lives many years later. I didn't mind killing any of them. After all, it's much easier to kill someone who really deserves it.

Now my focus is on Jeb. He used me. He abused me. He kicked me out. I will get even. In a different way.

33.

As Flower walks around the dining room, she carries the coffee pot. Everyone gets a "freshen up." She chats with patrons. I love her attitude.

When she gets to my table, she fills up my cup and sits down next to me. Our elbows are touching. She smiles.

"Hi, Jesse."

"Hi, Flower. How are you?"

"Pretty good."

"What's happening in Seattle?" I ask.

"Seattle?" Her eyes open wide. "Nothing is happening in Seattle! I don't even know what you are talking about. Why would you ask me about Seattle?" Her voice becomes weak. She glares at me. "How do you know about Seattle?"

"I'm a detective."

She gets up and walks to the kitchen. She doesn't come back.

34.

I CONTINUE TO GO TO JASPERS every day, and Flower gives me the cold shoulder.

We are in a new phase of our relationship. I am the customer, and she is the hostess. No smile. No eye contact.

I am sure my feelings for her are greater than her feelings for me, but I can live with it. Just seeing her calms me down.

After a long, awkward week, she sits at my table. Not next to me, but across from me. She squints.

"Please do not ask me about Seattle."

"Okay. Got it. What are you doing tonight?" I ask.

"Cleaning my lint trap."

35.

Two weeks later, I walk into Jaspers and find Flower standing at the hostess station in tears. Her head is down, again. There is a newspaper open in front of her. Again.

I look across the room at Jamie. She shrugs her shoulders.

I walk up behind Flower and touch her arm.

She jumps. "Oh, Jesse! I'm sorry. I was just, er . . ."

She looks embarrassed, like a kid with her hand in the cookie jar. "Nothing is wrong!"

She quickly crumples up the newspaper and stuffs it in the trash. She tries to smile.

"Really! Nothing is wrong," she says again.

As I sit at my favorite booth, I stare at the folded newspaper. In law enforcement, we say that the cover-up can be worse than the crime. Her cover-up is terrible.

Before I leave, Flower carries a tray of dishes into the kitchen. I grab the newspaper and leave the restaurant.

When I get home, I read the wrinkled *Seattle Weekly* from cover to cover. The page that was folded open was the News & Comment section. I read a submission by Mr. Lawrence L. Longmeadow.

Two residents of Seattle have been murdered in cold blood. The perpetrators of these horrendous crimes are scum-sucking bottom feeders with no self-esteem, no morals, and no ethics. *Despicable* is the word I will use. You killers are oozing, open sores. We think that you are sadistic, thoughtless pieces of filth who execute for fun. You are festering heaps of compost. You murderers have wasted your life looking for acceptance on Social Media. Well, rectums, whoever you are, you are not going to get a "Like" from me.

The first victim was a semi-retired elderly woman who was working for a minimum wage. The second victim was a high-school student who was saving for college.

Our heart goes out to the friends and family of Mrs. Madeline Ellsworth. She was a pleasant retiree who had a special relationship with all her co-workers. On the day you killed her, she was celebrating her seventy-fifth birthday. Happy Birthday, Mrs. Ellsworth.

Our heart also goes out to the family and friends of a young man named Duffy Longmeadow.

Victim number two was my sixteen-year-old son. Duffy was shot in the face. An open casket service is out of the question. I am stricken with grief. His mother is despondent and under sedation.

Duffy Longmeadow was a hardworking, dedicated young man who was saving for a college education. He dreamed of a career in animal medicine. When a job opening was posted at Bad Boy Burgers, he asked for our blessing. His mother said *no*. I reluctantly gave my permission. Now I will live with my decision for the rest of my life. Our family has been torn apart. His mother blames me. She screams, she cries, she throws dishes. She is now in a medical facility. No amount of counseling will ever repair the damage.

Mrs. Ellsworth and my son have been murdered. The people who did this are swine pigs with untreated mad-cow disease.

From now on, I will refer to you as *Blattodea,* but I suspect you assassins are too stupid to know what that means.

I urge this newspaper organization to encourage some old-fashioned police work. As they say in the airport, *if you see something, say something.*

We will find you, cockroaches. We in this community will step on you and watch you squirm beneath our boots.

36.

"FLOWER, WHY ARE YOU SO OBSESSED with killings that are taking place a thousand miles away?"

"Not!"

"What?"

"Not obsessed with nothing."

"Anything."

"That, too. And if I was obsessed, it would be none of your business, now would it?"

"But."

"No butts! No cuts! No coconuts!"

"What?"

"Forget it! Drop it. Dump it. Please and thank you!"

"But."

"You just don't get it, do you, Jesse? This is none of your business. Just let it go! Mind your own business."

She walks away.

She turns, comes back to me, and gently places her hand on my shoulder.

"Please mind your own business."

37.

I SPEND TOO MUCH TIME FOCUSING on Flower. I can't figure out why she is so charming some of the time, and so elusive other times.

Although I am skilled at interviewing, I can't get a bit of personal information. It's becoming a joke between us. I have been obsessed with many things in my life, but now I am obsessed with a girl. I have tried every trick in the book, but I still can't figure out where she lives, who she lives with, or what she does with her life. I also can't figure out her obsession with killings in another town.

I look online and find a last-minute, low-cost, late-night flight to Seattle. I reserve a car from Rent-A-Wreck and book a room at the cheapest motel in town.

I attend the funeral of a young man named Duffy Longmeadow. There are at least a thousand people in attendance. The crowd spills out to the street. The whole block is roped off.

I don't know what I'm searching for, but I look into every face. I visit all locations of the Bad Boy Burgers chain.

As I head back to San Diego, I try to justify my trip. It was an impetuous idea. A ridiculous, costly, ill-founded adventure. On the one hand, I am counting my pennies. The cost of a hotel, the airfare, and a car add up. It is more than a retired man should pay for an unnecessary trip. On the other hand, as an ex police detective, I am interested in justice.

Maybe I am trying to find information that I can share with Flower.

Maybe I am trying to get into her good graces.

Maybe I am trying to get into her pants.

"Have you been away?" Flower asks.

"Quick trip."

"Where did ya go?"

"Went to check up on a guy named Duffy."

"A friend?"

"A friend of a friend."

"You never told me about him. What's he do?"

"Not much now."

"Is he in-between jobs?"

"Something like that."

"I hate those transitional periods."

"Me too."

"What does he want to do?"

"Work with animals."

"That's nice. Where is he?"

"I don't want to talk about it."

"What?"

"There are some things you don't want to share with me, and some things I don't want to share with you."

"Yeah, but—"

"No buts, no cuts, no coconuts."

38.

I'VE BEEN GOING TO MORNING MEETINGS of Alcoholics Anonymous for months. Although I have a lot of stable friends who enjoy long-term recovery, I miss the chaos, excitement, and white-knuckle sobriety that are usually found at evening groups. Evening meetings are scheduled at 8pm to help newcomers make it through the night without a drink or a drug.

I'm strong enough to walk to an evening meeting, but it takes longer than I planned. The meeting has already started, and I tip-toe in. There are at least a hundred people in this church basement, and I see an empty seat in the middle of the last row. I squeeze in. Since I am still shaky on my feet, I annoy and bother everyone along the way. I get a few dirty looks from strangers, and a few pats on the back from friends. The open seat is right behind an old friend. Tall Paul is the most enormous cop on the San Diego police force. I can't see the girl who is talking.

Tonight's speaker is on the verge of tears. The room is very quiet, and I can hear people breathing. As she is sharing her story, she pauses a lot. I wonder if she is finished or if she will continue. She's talking in slow motion. Her voice is almost a whisper.

"The thing I remember most about my childhood," she says, "is that my father beat us. He was a drunk. A pathetic, loser asshole."

Her breathing escalates. "He was abusive, both verbally and physically. We lived with a monster!

"He was not only an alcoholic, but he was mean. At any given time, I had a black-and-blue mark or a welt. My father was savvy and only hurt me where the bruises wouldn't show. A punch in the stomach. Cigarette marks on my butt. An Indian burn on my upper arm.

"'This is for your own good,' he would say. 'I am just teaching you how to have respect.'

"One Christmas, my mother gave me a cheap doll. I went to the bathroom and used her mascara pen to paint a huge circle on the face. I thought all little girls had black eyes, just like me.

"As time went on, his punishments became more severe. I will never forget the time I thought my father would kill my mother. I guess I was about ten or eleven. I tried to stop him, but he laughed. He hit me across the face and, while I was down, handcuffed me to a radiator. All I could do was watch as he slapped my mother over and over again. I remember screaming, but we lived in the woods. I yanked on the handcuffs so violently I had scars on my wrist for a long time. After that night, my mother changed. She became quiet and lived in a fog. No appetite, no smiling, no talking, no crying.

"One day, after school, I found my mother on the floor. She had swallowed a bottle of sleeping pills. She was lying in a pool of vomit and urine. She died in my arms.

"I never even thought about calling the police, because my father was a traffic cop.

"'We take care of our own!' I heard them say. Whenever the police were involved, they would have a talk with him, suspend him for a day, and then cut him loose.

"I was fourteen when I ran away. I was sitting on the sidewalk, crying, and two girls invited me to climb into their rusty old pickup truck. They took care of me. Taught me how to survive. Drinking was a big part of our lives together. The girls taught me something else, too. They taught me about drugs. I was so full of fear, rage, and resentment, that I couldn't find any peace unless I was over the line. I have been hooked several times, and once I start I can't stop.

"I have tried to break the cycle. I have tried to change my life. I have tried to rearrange the deck furniture on the Titanic.

"Nothing worked for me except AA and NA. The people who stay sober go to a lot of meetings. I want to stay sober, so I go to a lot of meetings. Getting sober without meetings is like having half an orgasm.

"There were many times that I tried to stop without twelve-step meetings. I could white-knuckle it and go a few days, but then someone would offer me a free sample. Without the support of my friends in recovery, I would go right back to the shit.

"I have been going to AA meetings for three years now. My life is so much better. I have a job, a nice place to live, and wonderful, supportive, friends.

"Getting sober was the second hardest thing I have ever done. The hardest thing is staying sober. If I can stay in today, and forget about my past, I am good."

As she ends her story, she starts to cry. A girl tip-toes up and hands her a tissue. Everyone starts to applaud. After the meeting, people crowd around the speaker and offer their encouragement. I wait till the group thins out, and then I walk up to the girl who just told her story.

39.

"Hi, Flower," I say, gently. She sees me and shrieks.

"Jesse!" She jumps up and squeezes me tightly and then steps back to look at me again. She starts to shake and giggle. She crushes me again. I think this is the longest, most satisfying hug I have ever had.

"Oh my God. What are you doing here?" she asks. I just smile.

"I have wanted to tell you my story," she says, "But I was afraid you would walk out of my life. I was afraid I would never see you again."

"That won't happen."

She smiles and hugs me again.

While other people wash the coffee cups, sweep the floor, and put away the chairs, we sit and talk. When they are ready to lock up, we leave the room.

She asks, "Did you walk here? Come on; I'll give you a ride."

When we get to my apartment, she is happy to come in.

"So," I say. "I learned more about you tonight than I have in months of seeing you at your restaurant. How did you end up at Jaspers, anyway?"

"My Aunt Carrie owns Jaspers."

"Bless you, Aunt Carrie!"

She gives me another long hug.

40.

I SHOW FLOWER AROUND MY APARTMENT. It takes two seconds. She likes my little deck overlooking the pool. We share nervous, meaningless conversation.

"Flower, I have a thousand questions, and I don't want to overwhelm you. Will you let me ask one small, insignificant little question?"

"What would that be?"

"Do you believe in love at first sight?"

She laughs.

"If I found someone like you, Jesse, I would fall in love in a heartbeat, but let's face it. There is no one like you!"

We laugh, and it breaks the ice.

"So, tell me your story." It's a lighthearted, conversational request. People in recovery share their stories. It helps us get grounded. We believe we are unique, but in actuality we are all pretty much the same.

She smiles and then becomes very serious. She quietly stares into space.

"My story! Oh no. I am afraid that it will scare you away. You will never come back to Jaspers."

We just sit quietly. When I was a detective, I practiced an interview technique called silence. People hate silence. If I say nothing, then the other person is encouraged to say something. Usually, before I start an interview, I write the letters "SU" on the top of each page. "SU" stands for *Shut Up*.

I say nothing. She says something.

"After my mother died, it was only me and my father. For the next two years, I feared for my life. I spent a lot of time couch surfing, but I still had to go home. I had no food, no clothes, no skills. I had missed so much time from school that I could barely read or write.

"One morning, after spending a week at a friend's house, I came home to find my father snot-dripping drunk. Falling down, throwing up. He was staggering and had to hold on to a chair to keep from falling. His head kept jerking backwards. Then he got his second wind. He was mad at me for staying away. He was mad at me for coming home. I thought this was the day I would die.

"He found his legs and chased me into the kitchen. When he slipped on newspapers, he smashed his head on the door jamb. I cringed, waiting for him to kill me. When I realized he was out cold, I shouted at him and called him names. I got up the courage and kicked him.

"Are you sure that you want to hear this?" Flower asks. She is on the verge of tears again. I quietly nod but say nothing.

"My father was down. My lifetime of fear and rage came back. He beat me. He was responsible for my mother's death. You have no idea how much I hated him. I had one eye on him and my other eye on the door. There was no movement. I got madder and braver.

"Oh, Jesse. I can't go on. I have so many secrets. I am so full of shame and guilt. I have been through so many horrific things. A counselor told me I have PTSD.

"I am so exhausted." She starts to cry again, like she did at the meeting.

I don't say a word. After another long silence, she continues her story.

"I don't know where this idea came from, but I lit a match and threw it at my father. It was my feeble attempt to punish. The pile of old newspapers burst into flames. I was horrified, and I raced from the house. I ran for a block and looked back. I saw smoke. I kept running until I couldn't run anymore. I crumpled down on the curb. I remember crying hysterically."

She stops talking and looks at me. Eyes misty and bloodshot.

"Jesse, I have only known you for a few months, but I really don't know you at all. I feel that you are a calm, gentle soul, and I don't want to burden you with this stuff. I should really go." She starts to stand up, and I grab her wrist and lovingly pull her back down. She flops next to me.

"If I keep talking, you will walk out of my life. I will never see you again. If you don't come back to Jaspers, it will break my heart." She smiles.

I fight to keep my mouth shut.

She leans into me. Maybe the beginning of a hug, but it's awkward. She is vulnerable, and I want to be the big guy who saves her. All of a sudden she comes out of her fog.

"What time is it?" she asks.

"One in the morning," I say.

"Oh my God. I have to get home before the bikers get there. She jumps up, bends over, and gives me a quick kiss on the cheek. She races out the door.

41.

THE NEXT AFTERNOON, WE MEET AT Mission Beach. There is a Santa Ana breeze blowing in from the desert, and the temperature is unusually warm. Flower is wearing a pair of tailored, white, cotton shorts and a white lace top. The pink camisole underneath is a subdued fashion accent. Her hair is swept up in a bun. Her tan arms and legs seem to glow. She is so natural that I can't imagine her surviving in her previous life. She is cute and clean-cut. She is wholesome. I sense there is more to her story, but I give her space. I will let her continue when she is ready. We sip iced coffee and sit alone together.

Although it's about eighty degrees, there is a gentle breeze coming in from the ocean. It is like a quiet, circulating fan passing over our bodies every few minutes. It's hard to explain this weather to someone who lives in another part of the country.

There are tourists looking at the ocean. There are locals looking at the tourists. There are homeless people looking into brown paper bags.

"Were you busy at lunch?" I ask, trying to make conversation.

"Very."

"What was the special of the day?"

"Leftovers from yesterday."

"Last night you mentioned bikers. What's that all about?" I ask.

She looks toward the ocean and starts to talk. It's almost like a new conversation, but she is just answering my question.

"I have always wanted a place of my own," she says. "But I'm a single girl. I have no cash and no deposit. Not even a reference."

"A regular customer at Jaspers told me about his small house. He said he was in financial trouble. Way over his head. His balloon mortgage was going to bury him. He was expecting a foreclosure but wanted to do the right thing. He said he would rent his house to me and just send my payment to the bank.

"'It will take years for the bank to repossess,' he said. 'In the meantime, you can move in and call it home.'

"There was no paperwork, no forms. Only a handshake. I moved in the next day. It was good for him. It was great for me.

"Now, I am thrilled to live in a community of small starter homes. I painted the bedroom and bought a lawn mower at a yard sale. I have a rocking chair on my porch. It's my very happy place!

"My next-door neighbor was also in trouble, and when a cute young girl answered his ad, he didn't check references. He was excited to introduce me to his tenant who was about my age. She was attractive and well dressed. He introduced me to Jennifer Toadette.

"'Call me Toad,' she said, quietly, under her breath. She looked hard. No smile, no eye contact.

"All went fine for the first few hours until she had company. Her visitor arrived on a huge Harley Davidson. He was a mess, but Toad ran out into the yard and gave him a long, sloppy kiss.

"That evening, as they walked out of her house, I couldn't believe the transformation. She had changed from a stylish, mild-mannered young lady to a slutty, low-life biker bitch. She wore low-rider, tight, ripped jeans. Her thong was up high on her waist. She wore a tiny, cutoff, tank top that was working hard to hold her body in place. There was a bandana and black lipstick. Also, now I could see tattoos that weren't visible when she was masquerading as a lady. They left the yard in a storm. I have never heard such loud pipes.

"A little after two in the morning, they came back, but they weren't alone. There were about twenty other bikers who parked all over her lawn. Bikes were on the sidewalk and on the street. The music was ramped up. The amps were loud enough for professional-grade gigging. Neighbors came out of their houses and looked. Then just as quickly, they went back inside. There was a fight between two guys, and they tumbled from the steps. The madness went all night long. There was screaming and swearing. The next morning, they left, one by one, but the yard looked like a combat zone.

"I called the owner of the house, and, although he was horrified, he didn't have the strength or financial resources to fix the problem. He was going to lose his house anyway.

"The next night, they came back again. A little after two in the morning. This time, there was a much larger crowd. There were probably fifty bikes. They not only took over Toad's yard, they also took over my yard, too. I was petrified."

42.

I CALL MY FRIEND FROM THE San Diego police force and relate the story.

"Hey, Fig. Why would a bunch of bikers come into a neighborhood at 2:15 in the morning? What happens at two?" I ask.

"Bars close?"

"Duh!"

I look at Flower.

"I can get rid of them, but it will take a few nights."

"You can't fight them all. There are fifty of them."

"Let's go shopping," I say.

On the way to her house, we buy two cases of Karo Syrup.

"Are you having a pancake breakfast?" She laughs, nervously.

"We are going to have a picnic," I say.

"Who will come?"

"Every ant within two miles."

As Flower explained, the neighborhood has been trashed. There are used motorcycle parts in the yard. Beer cans everywhere. Tire ruts have ruined the lawns. There's a broken window. I look at the huge Harley sitting by the front door.

Later that night, after Toad and her boyfriend drive away, I sneak through the back yard, stepping over beer bottles and trash along the way. I pour a heavy line of Karo syrup around the perimeter of the house.

On the second night, I go back and pour several bottles of Karo around the inside perimeter of the house.

On the third night, I sneak back one more time and pour more of the sweet liquid under the carpet and under the couch.

I drizzle the syrup along the edge of the beds, behind the toilet, and under the kitchen sink.

After the bikers come back that night and ramp up their party, someone screams. Then everyone is yelling. The music is too loud to hear the dialog, but fifty bikers and their women run out of the house, slapping their pants and shirts and running fingers through their hair. They fire up their bikes and leave in a heartbeat. Within twenty minutes, the neighborhood is quiet. The house is empty. The bikers are gone. For some reason, they never come back.

Once again, the neighborhood is peaceful.

43.

As FLOWER AND I MOVE ALONG in our life together, we seem to fit into each other's routine. We are friends. No groping. No grubbing. Gentle hugs and a kiss on the cheek. We are taking our relationship slowly. We have each lost a lot, and we are afraid of losing more.

"Flower, the world would be a better place if there were more people like you."

Her eyes mist.

"Are you crying?" I ask.

"No, I just put in my eye drops."

44.

ONE NIGHT, WHILE WATCHING A MOVIE, Flower sits very close. My arm is around her, and she is leaning into my chest. We are enjoying our very strange relationship. For some reason, we never get close enough to have a real kiss. So close, but so far away.

Out of the blue, she says, "I can't sleep with you!"

I sit up straight and look at her. I turn around and look over my left shoulder. I turn again and look over my right shoulder. Then I look behind me.

"Are you talking to me?"

"Yes." She laughs.

"Oh my gosh," I say. "I am so sorry. I don't remember asking you to sleep with me."

"You didn't ask me to sleep with you."

"Then, what?"

"Jesse, can't you read a girl's mind?"

"I flunked mind reading."

She hits me. "You are my best friend," she says. "What we have now is wonderful and beautiful. We are here tonight because we want to be. If we sleep together, one of us will end up being hurt, or pissed, or heart-broken.

"Jesse. We have no relationship, no rings, and no rules. We have no rules!" she says again. "We alcoholics hate rules. We don't want to be told what to do. We despise being tied up. We despise being tied down.

"One night in bed with you will be fabulous, but it will ruin everything.

"I am afraid of hurting you. I am afraid of losing you. I don't want to ruin our relationship. I cannot sleep with you."

"Let me see if my hand still works," I reply, as I hold up my fist.

She hits me and walks away.

Two seconds later, she walks back and stands in front of me.

"Good night, Jesse." She smiles and gives me a kiss on the cheek.

45.

A FEW DAYS LATER, FIG'S WIFE, Libby, drives me to my doctor's appointment. She is taller and thinner than Fig. She is down-to-earth, no nonsense, no bullshit. Libby feels comfortable wearing a striped blouse with checkered slacks. Her socks don't match. Sometimes they are rolled down. She never wears makeup and doesn't care about fashion. She has two rescue dogs and is always covered in their hair.

Libby is more interested in the sports channel than the cooking channel. She has probably never had a perm, a pedicure, or a Brazilian bikini wax.

I have known her a long time, and I call her my friend.

When Libby and I get back to my condo, we sit on my little deck overlooking the pool. We have ice cream.

"I like your new girlfriend," she says. "Flower has so much spunk, and she has totally reinvented herself."

"I like my new friend, too," I say, "but I can't call her my girlfriend. We are just friends."

"Yeah, right!"

"Libby. We're addicts. We have each lost many things. We have each been in recovery centers. Because of our checkered pasts, we are afraid to make a commitment. Neither of us wants to lose this thing we have now. She is my buddy. I have confided in her, and she has told me secrets. When she spends the night, we sleep in our PJs. We are best friends! Really!"

"Really?" She laughs. "Well, if this doesn't work out, I want you to meet my friend Valantina. She is spectacular!"

"Libby, I don't need your matchmaking services."

"Yes, you do."

46.

IT'S A SOFT, COMFORTABLE, EASY SUNDAY morning. Flower and I are lounging in my condo. We are home alone, together, and we haven't felt the need to talk for hours. This is the kind of peace I imagine normal people enjoy.

I am slouched in my easy chair reading a James Lee Burke novel. Flower is reorganizing my kitchen cabinets. There are piles of dishes, silverware, and serving bowls everywhere.

An oldies station is playing softly, and I hear songs I have either never heard before or conveniently forgotten.

Flower is in another world, and I am happy, because she seems happy, too.

Out of the corner of my eye, I see her moving in time to the music. The song changes, and I think she might be dancing, but I have never seen her dance. I stare. She is doing a little routine, up on her toes and down in a squat. She spins. She holds her arms up to the sky. She bends and rises up to complete a pirouette. At the exact second the song ends, she stops with both hands extended. She bows.

She sees me staring and smiles.

"I love that song," she says. "When I was dancing, it was one of my favorites. It's called 'Don't Rock the Boat' by The Hues Corporation."

"Dancing? You mean like ballet?"

She comes out of her fantasy. Her eyes open wide.

"Oh. I'm sorry. Never mind." She looks concerned. "It's really nothing."

"It's really something. A dancer? Irish Step?" I ask. "Tap?

"Jesse, I'm sorry I brought it up. Let's just forget it."

"You started a conversation, so maybe we can finish it." I get pushy. I hate it when I get pushy.

She stares at me.

"What kind of dancer, Flower?"

"Oh Jeez," she says.

"Ballroom? Square? Belly?"

"It doesn't matter."

"It kind of matters."

There is no answer, and she slowly shakes her head. She is definitely sorry she brought this up. This girl, this friend of mine, is becoming defensive.

I give her plenty of space and plenty of time. We stare, but I can't stuff it forever.

"What kind of dancing, Flower?" I ask again.

After another long silence, she glares at me. She gets mad. She answers out of desperation.

"I was a dancer in a club."

"You? Club? Spotlights?"

She looks at me, but she is not smiling.

"You don't want to know."

"I want to know!"

"You won't like me anymore."

"I will always like you, but I may not be with you."

She has heard this line before, but today it's not funny.

"I don't want to shock you."

"You can't possibly shock me."

"My story will shock you."

"Nothing you can say will shock me."

"Okay. You'll be sorry."

There is a long silence.

"I danced for dollar bills."

I try to hide my shock.

"See, I told you this would shock you."

"I am absolutely not shocked," I lie.

We change the subject, and I stuff it. I become uneasy. She becomes defensive.

After some major two-way discomfort, she decides to cut our day short. She quickly cleans up the kitchen, makes a feeble excuse, and heads for the door.

After she leaves, I stare at the space she had just occupied. I told her I was not shocked, but I am shocked. I am so shocked! I am dumbfounded, flabbergasted, and yes, shocked.

Flower is poised, self-confident, graceful, and well-spoken. She is respectful and responsible. How could she possibly be a dancer? What is a dancer, anyway? She said she was a dancer. She didn't say she was a stripper, but what else could it be? If she was a stripper, was she naked? Of course she was naked, stupid. Strippers are naked. That's why they call them strippers. Was she also a hooker? Did she walk the street, or did she have a pimp sending men to a hotel room?

"No problem," I said to her. But it is a problem. It's a huge problem. I just don't know how big of a problem it will be.

Nothing has happened in this instant right here, right now, today. Our present relationship has not changed. But our past has changed. Maybe our future has changed, too.

My pride is fucked. I am out of control. I pound my self-sabotage button. It kicks in. My low self-esteem is exploding with electricity. I experience chaos, crisis, and calamity.

If I wasn't bonkers before this revelation, I am bat-shit crazy now. Now, I am in a blind alley. Am I in a rabbit hole, a pot hole, or a black hole? What else will she tell me? Is there anything else?

I always wondered what her jobs had been. I imagined her working in a bookstore. She likes to read. She might have been a cashier. She is good with numbers. Maybe she worked in a women's boutique. She is always well-dressed, well-mannered, and attentive. Or maybe she had always worked in a restaurant.

She never wants to talk about her past. Her previous occupation is a closed-door topic. I want to see into her past. How many times did I reach out?

"What kind of work did you do before you worked in Jaspers?"

"It was so boring. It was mundane. It was routine. If I explained it, you would fall asleep. I really don't want to bore you with it."

Ha. She had me fooled. What a jerk I am. What a sucker!

How can I have a relationship with a stripper? What would my friends say?

I realize I don't have any friends.

Never, in my wildest dreams, did I ever picture her up on a stage. I try to stifle it, but I know this new bit of information will keep me reckless, irritable, and discontent for the next million nights.

Her admission answers one question. Her admission opens up a thousand new questions.

I trust Fig more than anyone I know. He is my buddy. He knows my deepest, darkest secrets.

I share my concern about Flower's previous occupation. He is surprised, but as a detective he has heard every story in the book.

"What can I do?" I ask him.

"Why do you have to do anything?"

"Her past is a problem."

"Was her past a problem yesterday?"

"No."

"Why did she even tell you about her past?"

"I asked her. Over and over again. I begged her to tell me."

"So who can you blame?

"Fig, you never take my side!"

"Oh, poor baby! Do you love her?"

"More than anything."

"Well, it is what it is."

"What is it?"

"It's only rock and roll."

47.

FLOWER AND I TALK IN GENERALITIES about her career.

"I had no other option," she says.

I ask questions about working in a club, about dancing, and about being naked on a stage.

Her answers are one-word replies. Or less.

Flower is the queen of secrets.

"You don't need to know what you don't need to know," she says. It's her new favorite comeback.

My life can be as good as I want it to be.

My life can be as bad as I let it be.

I think about our relationship. We are not lovers, but we are friends. We don't have sex with each other, but we support each other. She instinctively knew this bit of information would crush me. If we had been lovers, it would have ruined our relationship. Now, it's just another chapter. I wonder how many more chapters there will be.

I like her. I like being near her.

I decide to circle the drain. I will forget the past and try to live in today.

I buy a book called *The Power of Now* and start reading.

"What would you like for dinner?" I ask.

48.

DEAR DIARY_____

It's 3am, and I'm still awake. I can't stop my mind. If my father hadn't left me, I might be a different girl today. If my uncle hadn't been such a perverted, pedophile predator, I might be a different woman. If every man I have ever loved hadn't used me and abused me, I might be a different person.

I feel like I'm on a rollercoaster. I hear the gears clacking as we slowly creak up an old wooden scaffold into the clouds. The little car sways, and I think we might go off the rusty track. There is no hand rail. There is nothing to hold onto. There has never been anything to hold onto. Nothing has ever been secure and stable in my life. As soon as I get accustomed to the height, we drop at a million miles an hour. I almost lose my breath At the bottom of the downfall, we enter a pitch-black tunnel. I have no idea where we are, or where we're going. I am tossed around as we jog to the left and jerk to the right. I am looking for some- thing to grab onto. Anything to secure my footing. We come out of the tunnel. It becomes very hot and blinding. Then we drop underground again and it is freezing cold. I vacillate between blinding lights and total blackness. There are screaming voices laughing at me. Yelling at me.

I am exhausted. Mostly I am in a constant state of confusion. It seems to be getting worse, not better. I am in too deep. I wonder if my spasms are visible to others.

I spend half my time thinking about yesterday. I spend the other half thinking about tomorrow. I know that my past and my future are more terrifying than my present. I laugh at myself when I think about how many hours I've wasted worrying about what was said, or what wasn't said. I cry when I realize how much energy I have put into trying to change my past.

I wonder if I might calm down if I take some kind of action. I might relax if I had something to focus on. Maybe then I can leave yesterday where it belongs. I might be able to feel good about myself. When I finally even the score with someone who has hurt me, I may be whole.

I believe the things I do are not my fault. I am not to blame. How can anyone blame me? If I hadn't been dragged through the fire, I wouldn't be smoldering in the ashes right now.

I think about a Buddhist principle called The Second Arrow.

49.

THERE IS AT LEAST A HUNDRED-PERCENT employee turnover in the fast-food industry. Now, after recent killings, there is a new challenge. Almost no one in their right mind would even apply for a job at Bad Boy.

Jeb is spending twelve to fourteen hours a day covering all his shifts. He is cooking, serving, cleaning, ordering product, and tallying business receipts at the end of each day.

When Ferguson Jenkins applied, Jeb had his doubts. Fergie was about thirty-five, tall, and very thin. He had scars from childhood acne and rough features.

Fergie's last résumé entry showed that he was laid off. Before that, he explained that he was working for a friend. Previous to that, another entry just said, "Let go."

Fergie was quiet, nervous, and always looked down when spoken to. During the interview, Fergie volunteered that he had four kids. His wife couldn't work because of the babies, but she took in mending.

Fergie was not the kind of guy Jeb would hire under normal circumstances, but these weren't normal circumstances. Jeb needed an employee; Fergie needed a job. Jeb's only requirement was that Fergie show up.

Fergie did show up, and he did the tasks that other employees avoided. Pots were scrubbed, the urinal was washed, and the grease trap was cleaned. One night, after lugging two huge garbage bags to the dumpster, Fergie never came back.

50.

PARKING LOT VIDEO SURVEILLANCE SHOWED AN unsteady, obese woman waddling up to Fergie. She may have weighed two hundred and fifty pounds. She was wearing an oversized winter coat over a worn house dress that hung down to the ground. She appeared not only overweight but handicapped by her girth. She was bent over, and her face was barely visible to the camera. Her cheeks were puffed out, and there were huge bags under her eyes. Her long, gray hair was unruly. She had a bulky scarf around her neck. Her nose was large and pointy like a witch's.

Maybe she was homeless. Maybe she was lost. Maybe she was crazy. There was a lot of hand waving as they stood by the dumpster. It seemed that Fergie couldn't understand her. Was she asking for directions or a hand-out? She held up a finger as if to say, *Wait,* and then she reached into a plastic bag and came out with a pistol. As the explosion flashed, Fergie's head jerked backward. He went down and instantly hit the pavement. The rotund woman slowly waddled away.

51.

THE COVERAGE OF FERGIE'S DEATH WAS even more damaging than that of the previous victims. The deceased man was leaving a family of five with no income. The wife would be in a home for the destitute. The children would be put into foster care.

The media loved this kind of story. News teams were flown in from around the country. A *GoFundMe* campaign was established to assist the family. The governor of Washington State was chastised by the opposing party for allowing this kind of problem to exist in the first place.

"Why don't you take care of your constituents?"

52.

DEAR DIARY_____

I have had so much fun learning about facial recognition soft-ware. I am a much better student than I ever realized I could be.

It's really simple, when you think about it. The YouTube videos on facial recognition were so helpful. Just alter a few key fea-tures. My nose, my chin, my eyebrows.

A year ago, I couldn't even spell nodal points, but now I know all about them.

Just cover my eyebrows, change the size of my nose, the shape of my cheekbones, and the length of my jaw line. Hats, hoodies, and big, wraparound sunglasses help, too.

I have used nose putty, scar wax, and cotton balls. A wig hang-ing in front of my eyes always screws up the camera.

I have a few other things going for me: I have not had a driver's license for the last six years; I have never filled out a job appli-cation; I have never applied for a passport, a credit card, or a loan application; I do not have a Facebook account; I have never been in a yearbook, part of a team, or in an Alma Mater group picture; No one has ever taken a selfie with me in it.

Damn it!

53.

"WHERE DID THE FAT LADY GO?" everyone asked. The mayor asked. The newspapers asked.

A TV reporter asked, "Did the fat lady stop singing?"

54.

DEAR DIARY_____

I have this down pat. I amaze myself at how good I am at hiding, reappearing as someone else, and then hiding again. Two days before each killing, I check into a local transit motel, pay cash, and then settle in. I am good at waiting. I have been waiting for something good most of my life.

On the night of the killing, I change into my new outfit and spend hours on makeup. Every detail is checked off my list: Clothes; shoes; hair; accessories. I have photographs of the person I want to be. I love to do my research. After the unfortunate incident, I go back to the motel and clean up. I take a long shower and change back to my regular clothes. Then I clean the room and order a pizza. I place my costume into the pizza box and walk to a dumpster.

Boom! The evidence is gone.

55.

I WALK INTO JASPERS, AND FIND Flower sobbing at the hostess station. Again. Same deal. Different day. There is another Seattle newspaper on the hostess stand.

"What's up?"

She crumples the newspaper and throws it into the waste basket.

"What's up," I ask again.

"None of your fucking business!"

I physically push past her, grab the newspaper, and leave the restaurant.

She screams my name as I walk down the street. I want to see the story she was obsessing over. The headline reads: "Another Employee Killed at Bad Boy Burgers."

I go back to Jaspers, and she pounds on my chest. Then she hugs me. Then she cries. She almost collapses, and I hold her up. Flower is shaking. I hand the newspaper back to her, and she hits me again.

"You had no right to steal that paper from me!" she shouts.

She is powerless over the situation and powerless over her emotions. I am powerless over her.

She is punching. I am her punching bag.

56.

FOR MOST OF MY MARRIED LIFE, my relationship with my wife was strained. No mystery there; I was the sole cause of the stress. I was either drunk, emotionally abusive, or distant. On and on. Over and over. Jekyll & Hyde. Happy or sad. Up and down. Drunk or hungover. In the way or out of sight.

Now, my relationship with Flower is strained, but this is different. Something is happening a thousand miles away, and I am in the dark. Flower won't discuss the issue, and she turns cold when I bring it up.

Even though I am using my interviewing skills, I get nothing. I am not even scratching the surface. The conversation is always the same.

"I'd like to ask . . ."

"Don't ask!"

Today, she changes the subject and asks me endless questions to divert her frustration.

"What's your favorite movie? Would rather be rich or famous? Are you a Republican or a Democrat? Do you want to open the door with the lady or the tiger?"

I tap her on the side of her head. "Is anybody home?" I ask.

She gives me the finger.

"I just want to know," I say.

"I don't want you to know. Jesse. If I've told you once, I have told you a hundred times: This Seattle thing is none of your business. You are becoming really pushy about this. Actually, you are becoming a royal pain in my ass. I wish I didn't have this royal pain in my ass!"

Time freezes as we face each other in a staring contest. We don't say a word for two minutes. We fix our eyes on each other. We are both hyperventilating.

I turn around and walk out of her restaurant.

57.

I CAN TAKE A HINT AS well as the next guy. Instead of going to Jaspers for lunch, I sit by my pool and eat junk food. It's been weeks since I've talked to Flower.

Our relationship is in the *off* position. The fact is, I have no idea what position our relationship had been in.

I practice CBT. My therapist called it Cognitive Behavioral Therapy.

A girl that I used to date called it Cock and Ball Torture. I put all my thoughts onto a piece of paper; I see a downward spiral. My therapist would outline it like this:

- Low self-esteem.
- Fear of losing.
- Lack of control.
- Self-sabotage.
- Leaving the situation.

More specifically, in my case, it probably goes like this:

- Flower is busy.
- She doesn't need me for happiness.
- She doesn't need me for anything.
- She doesn't love me.
- Let's forget the whole thing.

We each suffer from abandonment issues. We each suffer from depression, rejection, and neglect.

We have never talked about a life together. We never talked about our expectations. I have never asked her what she wants in a relationship. We never discussed kids. What about fun? What do we like? The beach? The mountains? Ice cream?

I have absolutely no hobbies. For most of my working life, I was either too busy or too drunk. Now that I have time, hobbies seem like more work than play. Tennis is too hard to learn, golf takes too much time, and bird-watching would put me to sleep. I don't want to be a ham radio operator or play the accordion. I am too old for martial arts, and spear fishing can't be done in a pool.

I have never asked Flower what she is most proud of. I have never asked myself that question. But if the question were asked now, I would say that I am most proud of my sobriety. It is my biggest single accomplishment! What about her? Except for the rocking chair on her porch, I wonder where she goes in her mind to be happy.

Flower told me she likes to read, but we never discussed her favorite novel. I asked a thousand questions but never got an answer.

We never talked about music although we both need background noise. She has endless instrumentals on her Pandora. She's mentioned the names. Maybe Buckethead and Emancipator. I listen to Pink Floyd and Jackson Browne.

We never talked about the "end game." What if I won the lottery? Or what if her Aunt Carrie sold the restaurant? Everything would change. But would our friendship change? We are so concerned with living in today that we can't even think about tomorrow.

We never tried to define our relationship. We never talked about the future. We never talked about marriage. Were we moving forward, or were we stuck in reverse?

We were never lovers, but I care more for Flower than anyone I have ever met.

It's probably all about my ego, but really I don't have an ego problem.

I'll be damned if I will lower my standard. I will not reach out. I will not call her.

But it's not a big deal! We be cool. No problem, mon. I am good! Life goes on. I don't care about her. I don't need her.

I probably won't even answer the phone if she calls, but I glance at my phone twenty times a day. No messages. In the middle of the night, I check my battery to see if it's charging. I look at my internet status to see how many bars I have.

Can you hear me now?

58.

STREET FAIRS ARE A REGULAR EVENT in southern California. There is a fair almost every weekend in a different direction. It's hard to ignore these mini festivals.

When a town hosts a fair, people come from miles away and spend money and eat junk food. There are always yoga demonstrations, face painting, Christmas decorations, and music.

Today, I am wasting time at a street fair in Carlsbad. I am all by myself.

I walk in front of a vendor selling wheat grass. It's hard to pass his booth. He positions himself in the center of the aisle right in front of me.

"You should try wheat grass for a month," he says.

"Why would I do that?"

"Because of all the benefits."

"What are the benefits?"

"Too numerous to mention."

I look at this unshaven, overweight man. He is wearing a filthy Hawaiian shirt. He has green teeth, a skin rash and horrendous breath. He has hair growing out of his nostrils,

"Name a few benefits," I challenge.

He holds up a pamphlet and reads:

"Repair damaged cells. Rejuvenate tissues. Enhance fat metabolism. Regulate bowel movements."

I try to push past him again. When I move right, he moves right.

"Sum it up in one sentence," I say.

"If you take wheat grass, you will be healthy, like me!"

I physically push him out of the way and walk to the food vendors.

"Two hot dogs, please."

59.

I HAVE TIME ON MY HANDS and a crick in my back. I am moving slowly. I shuffle, hunch, and grimace. I give up sitting and try to take a nap. As I wait for peace, I think about my parents. I wonder if I am the person I am because of the people they were.

My father was a workaholic. He had to commute to the city, and spent three hours a day sitting on a train He would suit up and show up to a job he didn't like. He managed a huge staff. He was tired, distant, and full of anxiety. He suffered from high blood pressure and ulcers. At the end of his long day, he was exhausted. He didn't say *hi*. He didn't smile. He didn't ask how my day was.

He was proud to say he didn't bring the stress of his job home. What he didn't say was that, when he got home, he had to deal with the stress of my mother.

My mother was an immaculate housekeeper. She changed the sheets every day and ironed our underwear. She constantly rearranged furniture. She was the boss of our house, and she was the boss of my father. It was easier for him to go with the flow. He was always exhausted.

My father put everything into his career. My mother put everything into her parties. After a long week, they were on different ends of the seesaw. My father wanted peace and quiet. My mother wanted company. She won.

Every weekend there was a cocktail party, a cookout, or a formal dinner.

I have memories of them, but my memories are crowded, noisy, and congested. There are always people in my memories. They all like my mother, but my father was just there.

When the music got loud, men danced with someone else's wife. A neighbor had his hand on my mother's ass, but she didn't seem to care. The person who was feeling her up had a big house and a yacht. In her eyes, that made him a good person.

On Sunday mornings, my mother would get up to see if I had a clean shirt on for church. Then she would go back to bed. The only thing that mattered was how we looked to the outside world.

My folks couldn't help with homework or come to school plays.

When I came home from a week at Boy Scout camp, I sat at the bus stop and watched other kids reunite with their parents. My folks were two hours late. I was the last of the Mohicans. I was the last man standing. I was the last kid on the block. They were too drunk to get out of the car.

My mother rolled her window down.

"Look at how filthy you are! What will people think?"

My father sat behind the wheel and said nothing.

One night, when she was inebriated, my mother said I was unworthy and ungrateful. Another time, I overheard her say I was unplanned. She never asked me what I thought. In our family, we never discussed feelings.

I will never forget the night my father sat in the big, living-room chair, crying. He was drunk, of course. He gave me an unrequested review.

"You are failing in high school, you have no idea what you want to do when you got out of school. If you ever get out of school. You have no interests, no hobbies. What are you going to do with your life?"

I constantly let him down and was so ashamed when I did. I lived with the guilt.

He had no time or energy for me. Instead of encouraging me, he ignored me. He was there, bigger than life, and I was there, smaller than life.

I don't remember a ball game, a boat ride, or a beach.

When something good happened to me, they never noticed. When something bad happened, they always noticed.

"He will never amount to anything," I overheard my mother say.

"Don't blame me; he's your son," my father said.

As a result, I am just like my parents. A people pleaser to the max. Looking for acceptance. I seek attachments to anything that makes me feel better. I look for instant gratification in relationships, in work, and in booze.

I have spent my life looking for forgiveness and peace of mind. I tortured myself for years. I still feel anger, hate, resentment, and loneliness. My mother never said yes to my father. My father never said no to my mother. No one ever said boo to me. I never heard either of them say, "I love you."

Some people think I am a grizzly bear. Others have called me a teddy bear. I wonder which group I am fooling today.

60.

"Hey, what's the matter man? I'm going to come around at twelve with a Puerto Rican girl who's just dying to meet you."

"Should I bring a case of wine?" I laugh.

"Let's fool around, you know, like we used to."

"Hi Libby," I say to my best friend's wife.

 "She is spectacular!"

"Who is spectacular?"

"Her name is Valantina. I told you about her before. She is Puerto Rican, and she is just dying to meet you."

"I'm not looking for Miss Right!"

"How about Miss Right Now?" she asks.

"Libby!"

"Valantina lives in your building. Actually, she lives on the second floor, directly above you. She is your upstairs neighbor. Be neighborly! She just wants to introduce herself. I've given her your info."

"Libby!"

"You'll love her! She has all the right parts in all the right places!"

"Libby, I don't need help with my love life."

"Yes, you do! Your wife divorced you, and your girlfriend dumped you."

"She's wasn't my girlfriend, and she didn't dump me. It was a mutual decision."

"You sound like a politician."

"Yes. I would appreciate your vote. But I don't want your match-making services. Please hold a minute, Libby. There's someone at the door."

"Hi. I'm Valantina."

I am blown away. This girl is spectacular. She has materialized out of thin air, and she is standing in my doorway. The light from behind her shows through her thin skirt. I love her skirt. My eyes adjust to her effervescent glow. She is probably five-nine with a full, rich, jet-black ponytail. She is trim and pleasing to look at. She has an overbite and a smile.

"Libby, can I call you back?"

Valantina holds up her hand. "Before you even speak," she says. "I want to apologize for barging in. It was Libby's idea. She has been telling me about you, like, forever! Relentless! She has been trying to hook us up since you moved to Mission Beach, but I'm not looking for a new relationship. Especially not with a cop. So, now that you and I have met, I can tell her that you are not my type. We have nothing in common. It was very nice to meet you. Goodbye."

She turns and heads in the direction of the stairway that will take her up to her apartment on the second floor.

"Wait!

"Wait, wait, wait! Valantina. Don't go. Do you like messy apartments? This one gets a prize. Come on in, and let's sit on the porch. I'd offer you a drink, but I am fresh out."

"I almost never drink."

"I like that in a girl. How do you know Libby?"

"Her real estate broker."

I suggest something to eat. "I have Zebra Cakes and Mountain Dew."

"No thank you. I need to go, but I'll tell you everything about me. I live upstairs, but I am a quiet neighbor. I have a job, but I'm looking for a new one. I have a Facebook account, but I never post. I like to bake cookies, but I don't eat sweets. I like music, but I can't dance. I like sex, but I don't want to have sex with you."

Valantina seems wired. A hot button waiting to be pushed. Eyes moving back and forth. Hands fidgeting. Forehead shiny, very nervous. After she leaves, I am jittery, too. It's contagious.

"Libby, I don't get it. She says she is shy, but she seems like a Nervous Nelly."

"Maybe you make her nervous."

"She is well-spoken, but she doesn't want to talk. She is gorgeous, but she doesn't date much. Does she like guys?"

"She likes guys, and she loves you!"

"Thanks for introducing us, but there's a piece of the puzzle missing."

At eight o'clock on Saturday morning, Valantina is pounding at my door. She is balancing a tall, pewter pitcher on a large, gold-and-silver serving tray. There are stem glasses and red napkins. The outside of the pitcher is covered with frost, and it is sloshing with an orange liquid. Lots of cubes. Valantina is wobbly, and I think she or the pitcher might crumble.

"Good morning," she says with a fixed smile. "Just wanted to treat you to some freshly squeezed orange juice. And a little champagne. Best way to start the day. She leans back against the wall. Maybe to steady herself."

"Have you had a few hits this morning?" I smile.

"Hits?"

"Drinks?"

"Oh no. I never drink this early. Not really drinks. Just a little taste test. Or two." She giggles. "Different category. Not really drinking. Just testing."

"I'm on my way out. I gotta go."

"Can't you just have one little mimosa with me, first? I hate to drink alone."

"Me too."

I close my door and start to walk away.

"Where are you going? We just met, and you are turning your back? You are walking away from me? You bastard. You are so rude." She throws the contents of the pitcher at me. I am covered with cold, sticky, orange liquid. I smell like a barroom rag.

When I get to my morning AA meeting, my friends laugh out loud about my OJ shirt.

"Libby, how do I get orange juice out of a shirt?"

"She just called me all in tears. What did you say to her?"

"One word."

"What word?"

"No."

Two nights later, I hear thunder from above. There is bouncy, noisy music from professional-grade speakers. The vibrations are so loud the glasses in my own cabinet clink. At nine o'clock, I walk up and pound on her door.

It takes a long time for her to answer. I look past her, and she is alone.

"How's the party?"

"Fuck you!" The door slams in my face.

The hammering goes on till three in the morning.

The next night, Valantina is at my door. I look through my privacy peep hole. She is crying. She is rotating her head. She is squinting. She exhales loudly.

I open my door, but instead of inviting her in, I step out into the hallway. I close the door behind me.

She has a card for me.

It says, "Sorry."

She walks toward the stairs.

I have such a double-standard when it comes to women.

If she wasn't so gorgeous, I would ignore her.

"Libby, what do you know about this girl?" I ask

"Nothing. She sells houses. But there is one unsettling part. Sometimes, she is on top of the world. Other times, she seems so down in the dumps. I feel so sorry for her. I like her, but I really don't have time to spend with her."

"That's why you sent her to me?"

"Just be nice."

Two days later, Valantina visits me. It's about 6pm, and she is on her way home from work.

Today, she is very professional. Magnificent. Dressed in a well-tailored, two-piece, dark-blue business suit. Her skirt is pressed. Her starched, white blouse has a stand-up collar. Her heels probably cost a fortune.

"Jesse, I would like to ask a favor. It's very important to me."

I try not to roll my eyes, but she looks different today. Reserved, calm, gracious.

"I've invited my staff to join me for an after-work get-together. None of them are flamboyant, so it will be a quiet evening. It will be on Thursday night at a place called Diego's. Do you know where it is?"

"I was thrown out of there once."

"Three girls," she continues. "I just want to get to know them. They are all married or have boyfriends or whatever. I have no one. I would just like to introduce you as my friend. That's it. Please stop by, meet the girls for a few minutes, and then you can leave. As I said, it is a favor, and I would really appreciate it."

On the night of the party, I take my time and finally get to the club. *This is a favor,* I say to myself. I expect the girls will have gone home by the time I get there.

Instead, I see Valantina on the dance floor with two men. She is shouting the words to a song. Her captives are trying to get away, but she is holding on to their hands tightly.

Her staff is staring in disbelief. They are all younger. A few of them are taking videos of the debacle on the dance floor.

Valantina sees me and runs in my direction. She wobbles in her high heels and catches herself on a chair. She screams my name and tries to pull me toward the dance floor. I pull away and she starts swearing. As I walk to the door, she yells:

"Don't you dare walk out on me! You asshole!"

On the way out, I talk to the bouncer.

"That your girlfriend?" he asks.

"NFW," I say.

"Good for you. She is a professional-grade loser," he says. "Came in drunk, got drunker, and now trying to get everyone in the club drunk. On nights like this, we lose so many good customers."

The bouncer is a good guy. We talk for a while. He understands my situation. He lets me back in through a side door, and I sit out of sight. The show gets worse.

On Friday afternoon, I visit Valantina's office. The receptionist walks me to a small, stark cubicle, and the girl who was so bubbly last night looks like death. Her face is pasty, and her hands are shaking. The smell of alcohol is in the air. She reeks. She squints and acts surprised to see me.

"I was hoping you would come to Diego's last night."

"I did."

"You did not."

"Do you ever have blackouts?"

"I've heard that term, but I don't know what it means."

"Do you remember calling me?"

"When?"

"Last night?"

"I didn't call you last night."

"Four times."

"That's ridiculous."

"The last message at three in the morning was scary. You kept telling me I was an asshole." I play the message, and she is horrified.

"I don't believe I left that message! That's not me! But if I did, it was because I was drunk. I do lots of stupid things when I am drunk. Don't pay any attention to it."

"What about the videos?"

"What videos?"

"Your girlfriends all took videos."

"Videos of what?"

"A lot of people in the club were taking videos, too."

"What are you talking about? Videos of what?"

"Flashing your underwear."

"What?" She glares at me. "What are you talking about? That is an inappropriate comment. You should leave the building."

She stands up, glares at me, and slams down again. She stares at me.

"I have never flashed my underwear in my life. What are you talking about?"

"Your friends all took pictures, but they won't show you. You're the boss. I bet they've posted the videos. Probably gone viral by now."

"I don't know what you are talking about." She is afraid of what I am talking about.

"Lime green? Pink lacy trim?"

She starts to look sick.

"Do you remember the young guy you were hitting on?" I ask. "Sports jacket? Crew cut? He was with another well-dressed man. Older. Maybe his father. Maybe his boss. The young kid looked so embarrassed. He was pushing you away, trying to get you to stop grabbing him. He wouldn't dance with you, so you pulled your dress up to your armpits. Everyone in the room was watching. Laughing. Taking videos. You straddled the poor kid, face first. He was pushing you. Punching you. The older man pulled you off, and you fell backwards. How is your head?" I ask.

She squints and rubs the back of her head.

"The young guy and the older man walked out. All of your friends left the club at the same time."

"I don't have any friends."

"So, Valantina, here's a scary question: How did you get home?"

She shakes her head and explodes into a tearful, sobbing, emotional breakdown. Her head goes down to her desk.

She looks up at me over her crossed arms. Crying eyes.

"I think I drove, because my car was in the garage this morning. But, last night someone crashed into my car. The whole front is damaged." Her head falls down to the desk again. Without looking, she reaches for the tissue box, but it is empty. I hand her my handkerchief.

"Maybe I should go to an AA meeting for a day or two. How would I even find one? Do you know anyone who goes to AA? Anyone who can take me?"

"I know someone."

When we get to the meeting, a few of my pals say *hi*. A friend pats me on the back. A girl comes over and gives me a hug. Someone waves from across the room. Valantina looks surprised.

My associate from work, Erica Ringline, sees us and walks over. She introduces herself to Valantina, and takes her hand.

"Hi. Let's go to the ladies' room and freshen up."

During the meeting, Valantina sniffles quietly.

At the end, she doesn't move.

"I'll take her home," Erica says.

During her first few months of recovery, Valantina changes so much. She becomes a woman of grace, dignity, and self-respect. She is optimistic and attentive. She and Erica become inseparable. They have coffee with other girls before meetings. They walk on the beach with her new friends after groups. She smiles a lot. Valantina may feel like she belongs for the first time in her life. Her friends are a powerful example. She is an example of power.

After three months, Valantina tells me about her new job.

"They have asked me to take over a larger office. I will report to a new boss. He is so nice," she says.

She starts to skip meetings, and I am concerned. Her sponsor, Erica, is concerned, too.

"Way too busy with my new staff," Valantina tells me. "Spending a lot of time with my boss. No time for AA. Oh, and by the way, my new boss asked me out. He invited me to dinner, and I think I will go. He's a big drinker, but that is not a problem for me, because I quit drinking."

Valantina stops going to meetings altogether.

"I can't tell you what to do," I say, when I see her in the parking lot, "But I will ask one favor."

"What's that?"

"Don't take the sucker drink."

A week later, the 6am call jars me.

"Oh Jesse," Erica's voice is low. I think that she is crying. "Did you hear?"

"Hear what?"

"The news."

"The news is usually bad."

She cries. "You are right. It's bad news."

"Tell me."

"Three o'clock in the morning. Eighty miles an hour. Bridge abutment. Instant."

61.

FOR MOST OF MY CAREER, I have been in good shape. A hollow-point bullet changed all that. Now, I am stiff, weak, and immobile. I suffer from insomnia and dizziness. I am nauseous. I have dry mouth, bad breath, and hemorrhoids.

More than that, I'm suffering from a broken heart.

I haven't talked with Flower in over a month.

Why would I? She told me to get lost.

To keep busy, I walk to the new gym. It's called "Why Weight." I don't have a weight problem. I have a wait problem. *I'll do it tomorrow* is my motto.

I start my trial membership and climb onto a treadmill. Not running but shuffling. I might look like a dork. What a waste of a treadmill. I am moving slower than anyone else in the club. I bump up the speed to a meaningless number. It says I am walking three miles an hour. Is that good or bad?

I flip my mind off and flip my Pandora on. Sam and Dave are singing "Hold On, I'm Coming." I sing the song to myself. I tap the speed button up again, so that I'm walking in time to the beat. Perfect three and a half miles an hour.

I am probably the oldest guy here, and I certainly don't fit in. *What a loser,* I think.

I should just go home and kill myself. I could easily commit SBC. Suicide By Chocolate.

Out of the corner of my eye, I see someone climbing onto the machine next to me. A tall, thin girl starts walking. She is very attractive. She taps her speed button up a few notches, and then slows it down a bit until we are walking in sync as if we had practiced. Her arms are moving in long strides. I glance at her. She smiles. She is graceful, as if on a fashion-show runway.

Sam and Dave's lyrics brighten my mood.

"Reach out to me. For satisfaction. Call my name for quick reaction." I try to keep my singing to myself, but I just can't do it. It's impossible to be grouchy when this song plays. My smile increases. My mood improves.

I look at my neighbor. She flashes a conservative smirk. She winks.

I acknowledge her. She starts to chuckle, and I wonder if she is putting me down or beaming me up. Either way, we are marching together.

The song switches to an Otis Reading classic. Otis sings with Carla Thomas. I slowly notch up the volume a little bit at a time. Now it's louder. Then much louder. Then blasting in my earbuds.

I sing along. Of course I know the words. I grew up with this song.

I am sure the look on my face changes from a grin to a wide-eyed smile.

I shout out loud with the music. No one cares. No one notices. Except my neighbor. She seems very interested. She smiles again.

"Oh, it's like thunder and lightnin'. I gotta tell you the way you love me is frightenin'." Then the good part of the song comes up, and I pound my fists on the machine three times. I scream, "Knock, knock, knock on wood, baby!"

The girl looks quizzically. She smiles with eyebrows raised. She mouths the words, "What are you listening to?"

I remove one of my earbuds and lean in toward her. We are walking at 3½ miles an hour. I hand the bud to her. She leans in, gently takes it and pops it in her ear. Her head jumps when she feels the volume. Then it's okay. She smiles. I am now connected to this beauty.

I hit the replay button, and she laughs. We walk together with more of a commitment than before. Almost like Florida love bugs. We are both smiling and singing at the top of our lungs. Even though she is younger, she knows the words. Everyone knows the words. When the good part comes, we both pound our fists on at the same time. We shout: "Knock, knock, knock, knock, knock on wood, baby!"

Some people may think we are crazy. Other people may be jealous.

My walking mate is about five-nine. She is incredibly thin and has absolutely no curves. In high school, we would have made fun of her shape, but today no one is making fun of her. She is very tan and full of energy. Her short hair is a striking shade of neon blonde, swept up on the sides. Maybe they call that a bob. I wonder who Bob was. She has a favorite color. It's black. She has black shoes, black capris, a brief black tank top. The black bandana tied up in her hair accents her neon blonde do. As she walks, she bounces, and her hair bounces, too. She smiles again and winks. Again. This girl isn't sweating, she is glistening.

The song changes. We each flash a big smile. We laugh. Of course, we know the words. We sing together:

"What you want, baby, I got it. What you need, do you know that I got it."

Then the good part comes along and we pound on our treadmills. "Re, re, re, re, re, re, spect."

After the song stops, I touch my speed button and gently slow down. She slows, too. We step off our treadmills within seconds of each other.

"That was fun!" She returns my earbud and takes my hand.

"Hi," she says, "My name is Alexis Jane."

"Does anyone call you AJ?" I ask.

"My mother calls me AJ.

"Hi, AJ."

I give up my name.

We talk about the gym, the traffic, and the weather.

We talk about Aretha.

She is poised, refined, and engaging.

She seems rejuvenated from thirty minutes on the machine.

I am exhausted from thirty minutes on the machine.

After a long, double handshake, I say goodbye and walk toward the parking lot.

AJ catches up and walks alongside me in perfect cadence. Again.

"Nice to meet you," she says.

We approach a tiny, two-seat BMW Z convertible. It's sparkling white with tan leather seats. The top is down.

She jogs ahead and cuts in front of me. She opens the passenger door.

"I have a favorite coffee shop near the beach," she says. "Hop in."

Since I have absolutely nothing to do for the rest of my life, I hop in.

I love her little Z. It seems like my butt is only four inches off the ground, and we look up at everyone who is riding by. Her surround-sound speakers are in the dash, the doors, and the head rest. She blasts Bob Marley. We both like music, and we sing every word together. Again. We harmonize. "No Woman, No Cry."

We laugh. Life is good.

At the coffee shop, our little patio table overlooks the boardwalk. We sit on small, metal café chairs. It's crowded, and AJ moves in close. Very close. Our knees are touching.

We glance at two women at the next table. One of them is holding her hand on her pregnant friend's stomach. Maybe listening for a heartbeat or feeling a kick. AJ smiles gently, and I wonder if she has ever had a baby.

"I live at The Bella Vita," she says. "It's a residential home for eating disorders, and I've been there for eight months."

I am about to congratulate her on her weight loss.

"I am so happy," she says. "I have gained twenty-nine pounds."

She orders a milk shake, two English muffins with peanut butter, and a sliced banana.

"I like your tan," I say, trying to make conversation.

"Oh, thanks," she says. "When I lived in New Jersey, I was so white. My skin was the color of printer paper. I have never had tan lines before, but now that I live in California, I have tan lines. I love them. I wish I could show you my tan lines!"

My eyes open wide, but she doesn't seem to notice.

As we talk, she is constantly touching. Like best friends. Tapping my hands to emphasize a point. Caressing my fingers when there is a brief silence. With every new sentence, she moves her hand to another spot of my wrist, or forearm, or elbow. She squeezes my fingers one at a time, as if she is giving me a hand massage. Or a hand job. She is looking for attention and getting it.

We talk nonstop for an hour.

She slides in even closer and puts her hand on my knee. We are almost within kissing distance. When she whispers in my ear, her breath is warm.

"I am going to get breast implants," she confides.

"What?"

"You know. A boob job?"

"What?"

"A guy I know wants me to enhance my breasts, and he is going to pay."

"I'll be right back," I say, as I abruptly get up and walk to the men's room. I grab a paper towel, load it up with soap, and walk back to the table. I straddle AJ and slowly move the soapy paper towel towards her mouth.

She looks horrified and slaps my hands.

"What are you doing?" she screams.

"I am going to wash your mouth out with soap. Just like my grandma used to do to me."

She pushes me away and looks into my eyes.

"Are you saying I shouldn't get implants? I thought guys loved girls with big boobs."

"Not true!" I say. "I don't believe you should get fake breasts. I don't think you should get fake anything. I don't believe in elective surgery. I wouldn't admire anyone who had an unnecessary operation.

"AJ," I say. "You don't need to change any part of your body to please some stupid guy. You don't need make-believe boobs. You don't need make-believe anything."

She looks at me and slowly shakes her head. Her mood has shifted from happy to hurt. Her eyes start to mist.

I emphasize my point. "AJ, if you do this, and I see you in a restaurant, I will leave the building. If you call me, I will hang up. If we pass each other walking down the street, I will cross to the other side."

Her eyes squint, and she shakes her head. Now she is really crying.

"Jesse, you don't know what it was like. Growing up."

"What was it like?"

"I am so flat. All through school, I had a nicknames. In grammar school, they called me Twiggy. In high school, they called me Olive Oyl. You know, Popeye's girlfriend?"

"AJ. Any guy in the world would love to have you as his girlfriend," I say. "Any guy in the world would love to have you feeding him spinach out of a can."

She slaps me, but it's a playful tap.

I get up to leave, and she jumps up, too. She squeezes my elbow. As I walk out of the coffee shop, she walks, too, right in step. Her misty eyes are locked on my face. She moves her hand to my wrist, and awkwardly tries to hold my hand.

I stop, turn towards her, and take both of her hands. I smile and give her one last thought.

"AJ," I say, as compassionately as I can. "You are a beautiful, exciting, intelligent, vibrant woman. You look amazing. You would be fun to live with. Just the way you are. Stop letting guys fuck with your mind."

"Oh, Jesse." She engulfs me in her arms as if we have been friends for years. "Thank you!"

The bear hug lasts for a long time.

I smile and say, "I gotta run. See ya."

I leave her on the boardwalk.

As I get free, I realize I may have hurt her feelings, but I have told the truth. It's a new concept for me.

62.

ON THE WAY HOME, I WALK past Jaspers Restaurant. I could go in. I could reach out, but screw that! Flower and I each have gigantic egos. Our pride will keep us apart. I am not going to lower myself. This is all her fault. If this is going to get fixed, she will have to fix it.

I don't see her in the big picture window, so I keep walking. As I reach the corner, I hear my name being screamed.

"Jesse, Jesse, Jesse!"

I turn around and see Flower running toward me. She almost knocks me over.

We hug for a long time.

That night, Flower and I talk till three. We rejuvenate our friendship. We rekindle our relationship. We rededicate our feelings, whatever they are.

Flower fixes our relationship. Our routine changes, and we tip-toe through touchy topics.

"We can talk about anything you want. As long as you don't want to talk about killings."

Our exchanges are guarded. It's like walking barefoot through a room full of rat traps. I go back to Jaspers every day. Flower and I go to recovery meetings. We have dinner dates. We walk on the beach. We are a pair, but not a couple. At my age, and in my current medical condition, this is good. I am happy to be wherever she is. She pumps me up, calms me down, and smooths me out. I am half empty, and she is half full. We are made for each other.

When she spends the night, she raids my closet and comes out wearing my faded Chargers t-shirt. It is frayed at the sleeves and stretched at the neck. It has been washed so many times that it is paper thin. I have never worn pajama bottoms, but I own a pair. On Flower, they look like a clown costume. She ties the drawstring high up on her waist and rolls the pant legs up to her knees. She also wears a mismatched pair of my worst sweat socks. Our relationship is all attention but no action. We hold hands but are hands-off.

Early one morning, after I step into the shower, I hear the bathroom door open. The shower curtain quietly parts, and she steps in. She is naked and has a bar of soap in her hand.

"Don't look," she says, as I stare at her beautiful body.

She turns her back to me. "Sorry I'm in such a hurry. A waitress called in sick." She grabs a second bar of soap from the edge of the tub and hands it to me.

"Can you do my back? Top. Not back side. And don't get your hopes up. I can do the front all by myself."

Within two minutes, she steps out, vigorously wiggles her tiny butt, and grabs a towel. She runs out of the bathroom as quickly as she came in. I stand there with a bar of soap in one hand and my dick in the other hand.

The weeks go by, and our routine stabilizes. We are kind to each other.

"What's your schedule on this beautiful Sunday?" I ask

"Absolutely nothing."

"Me too, but I have an idea."

"So what's up your dirty little sleeve?"

"Let's spend the day with your Aunt Carrie."

"What? Really? You would do that? Jesse, you will make me cry."

"I'd rather make you smile. Let's take Aunt Carrie on the San Diego Trolley tour. Hop on. Hop off. All over town."

"Really? You would do that, Jesse?"

"The trolley stops at Seaport, Gaslamp, and The Zoo. We will see Old Town and downtown. We can be tourists today."

Flower starts giggling.

When the trolley stops at the Del Coronado Hotel, Aunt Carrie treats us to ice cream sundaes.

We enjoy the day. We enjoy the weeks that follow. We carelessly muddle through the disorderly confusion that is our life.

63.

THE CALLER ID SAYS SHARP MEMORIAL Hospital. Flower is hysterical.

"Aunt Carrie!"

"What?"

"Aunt Carrie!"

"What about Aunt Carrie?"

"She's in the ER, all black and blue, a huge bump on the back of her head."

"What are you talking about?"

"Aunt Carrie was walking her dog. A jerk came out of his house and shouted at my aunt. 'Don't walk your dog in front of my house,' he said.

"Then, he pushed my aunt down. She hit her head on the sidewalk. Then he kicked her. This fucking fat asshole kicked my poor little old aunt! In the ribs! She's all black and blue and so sore."

A week later, when Carrie is feeling better, we take a ride. She points to a small, run-down, brown cape, with a broken basement window. The lawn has never been cut. The dirt driveway is full of potholes. The rusted tan pickup has oversized snow tires. One hubcap is missing. The passenger door has been sprayed with flat green primer.

The name on the mailbox says "W. Pickles."

I call my ex-partner Fig with the address and the name. He comes back with the story.

"Wallace Pickles! What a handle." He laughs. "Wallace just got out of jail: Penal Code 596-597."

"Fig, I'm retired over here. Please stop showing off with the penal code stuff!"

"Pay attention. Maybe you'll learn something." He laughs. "'Maliciously and intentionally maims, mutilates, or tortures a living animal. It goes on to say . . .'"

"Fig. One sentence. Please."

"Doesn't play well with animals."

"Thank you!"

64.

I CALL MY FRIEND FROM AA. "Hey, Bob. I need to ask a little favor."

Bob's father beat a neighbor to death. Since that day, Bob's whole family has been traumatized. His mother committed suicide. His sister has gained two hundred pounds and watches "God's Learning Channel" all day long.

Bob has been trying to right his father's wrong. He got sober. He boxes for a hobby and runs for fun. He never passes up a chance to help the underdog.

"A little old lady was beaten up by a lunatic," I say.

"Let's go," he says.

We park in front of the run-down cape and pound on the door. A sad-sack of a man in his underwear opens the door. He needs a bath.

We push against the door. He pushes back.

"I'll call the police," he says.

"I am the police!"

The man behind the door has a pasty, pudgy, piggy face. His pot belly is impressive. He may have the nickname Beach Ball Man.

"Quit your knocking!" he yells. "You're upsetting my dog."

A little puppy starts barking.

"Are you Pickles?" I shout.

"Fuck you!" He tries to slam the door, but Bob's foot is wedged in the jamb.

The smell of poop leaks out of the house.

Wallace looks at us and shouts again.

"Quit your knocking! You're pissing me off."

He looks at the little dog and shouts:

"Quit your barking! You're pissing me off, too."

Then Wallace kicks the little puppy. Right in the flank. The dog flies backward, whimpers, and hides behind a chair.

As we push Wallace into his house, he falls backwards.

I kick him in the flank, just like he kicked the dog. Wallace whimpers and hides behind a chair.

As Wallace starts to cry, Bob picks up the puppy. We walk outside and climb into his truck. Our plan is to drop the dog off at a shelter in another town. Another home. A new life, far away from Wallace Pickles.

I have a second thought.

"Bob, be nice to the puppy for a minute. I'll be right back," I say.

I walk back in the house and find Wallace still lying on the floor. He is sobbing. He stares up at me in horror. I make a fist and threaten to hit him. He covers his face. Instead of hitting him, I lift my foot as high as it will go and stomp down on his ankle. I may have cracked a bone. His scream is electrifying.

"If you ever kick a dog again," I say, "I will remove your foot at the ankle. Might be a good time to sell your leash and donate your Kibbles 'n Bits."

Back in the truck, Bob raises one eyebrow.

"I just politely asked Wallace to refrain from kicking dogs."

As we drive away, I call 911.

"A man named Wallace Pickles broke his ankle. In a lot of pain. Delirious. Doesn't know what he is saying. Also, I think his dog just ran away."

Bob smiles at me and starts to focus on the puppy.

"Cavalier King Charles!" he says.

I hadn't really noticed the dog, thought about the breed, or considered her condition.

"Probably only one or two," Bob continues, "but so skinny. Wonder if Wallace ever fed her? And scratching like crazy. Think she has fleas?"

"The shelter will groom her. I'll pay them."

"But I love the black and whites. Don't you?" he asks.

We drive for a while and park in front of a shelter. The puppy looks back and forth between us. She licks Bob's hand and then licks my hand.

"Changed my mind," I smile. "I'm going to rescue her."

The dog licks Bob on the hand again and then jumps onto my lap. She barks softly and licks me on the face. Her tail is like a vibrator on the super stud setting.

"Gonna name her after a women who changed my life," I say.

"Who's that?"

"Bob, meet Mia."

"Who?"

"Sister Mia."

"Who?"

"Sister Mia hit me so hard with her ruler that my knuckles still hurt. After the third time, I walked out. Never went back. I'm still a recovering Catholic, but she got me out early. I can never thank her enough.

65.

"JESSE, I'VE BEEN CALLING AND CALLING. Where have you been?"

"I've been busy, Flower."

"Busy. Like what?"

"I've been taking walks."

"Walks? You don't take walks! Who are you walking with?"

"Just a friend."

"A friend? What friend?"

"Just a new friend. I don't want to make a big deal of this, Flower, really, but my new friend, you know, she needed a place to stay."

"She?"

"I am just trying to make her feel at home."

"Home?"

"Everything is different, Flower. My friend has, you know, kind of changed my life!"

"Well! I don't believe this," she says. "What is your friend's name?"

"Well if you must know, her name is Mia."

"Mia? Is she like, one of your AA friends? Needy? Homeless?"

"Sort of."

"And she is there now?"

"Actually, she's in the bedroom. I don't want to wake her."

"She's sleeping in your bedroom? On your bed?"

"She kind of moved in."

"You've got to be kidding me! What does she look like?"

"She's trim. Well, actually, you might say that she is thin. Long hair. Big eyes. Cute little nose. Great personality."

"And?"

"I like her. She is so easy to talk with. Her eyes follow me wherever I go."

"I don't fucking believe this. Is there anything else?"

"Just one other little thing."

"Yeah, what's that?"

"Well, if you must know, she's kind of affectionate!"

"Jesse, have you told her about us?"

"Not yet!"

"Well, I will!"

The phone slams down.

Thirty minutes later, there is a loud pounding on my door.

"Flower, meet Mia."

"Flower looks at me. Then she looks down at the little black-and-white Cavalier King Charles. Tears well up in her eyes. She drops to the floor and starts the hugging and kissing. Back and forth. They become very affectionate.

Then she looks up at me and punches me in the gut.

"You are such a jerk!"

She bends down and continues to hug. Mia loves every minute of it.

66.

WE ARE ALL WALKING ON THE beach. Mia is in the middle. It's a good time to walk. It's a good time to talk. We stop to let Mia sniff, and I get serious.

"Flower, why are you so interested in a crime that is happening a thousand miles away? In Seattle, Washington?"

"Jesus. Jesse. For the hundredth time, I don't want to talk about it!"

"So, we are not good friends after all?" I ask.

She is quiet, and her eyes close. Her face scrunches up. She is not good at hiding emotion.

"We are very good friends, Jesse. You are my best friend in the world. If I didn't know any better, I would say I am in love with you!"

"Then what?"

After a long pause, she turns and stares at the ocean.

"It's none of your business! I keep telling you! This is none of your damn business!"

"You are two different people, Flower," I say. "One of them is open and honest. The other one keeps secrets. I cannot have a relationship with someone who keeps secrets."

I take the leash away from Flower, give Mia a nudge, and we start to walk away.

"Oh shit!" Flower screams louder than I have ever heard her scream.

"Okay! All right!" She stomps up next to us. "Damnit! God damnit! God damn you, Jesse. If you must know, I will tell you! But it's none of your business."

There is a long, painful silence.

She takes a big breath, glares at me, and shouts.

"That chain where people are getting killed? That Bad Boy Burger place? My sister works for that chain. She will be moving to Seattle, and I am scared shitless. Now! Are you happy?"

"Your sister? You have a sister?"

"Yes, I have a sister!"

"Why haven't you ever told me about your sister?"

"My sister dumped me. She ditched me. She walked out of my life. I hate my sister! I despise my sister! I never want to see my sister again. I disown my sister! I miss her so much! I love her more than anyone in the whole world! Every single day, I think of my sister! Every single day, I pray for my sister. Damn it! Damn her! Damn you, Jesse! Mind your own damn business."

She flops on the beach and curls up in a fetal position. Mia licks her tears.

"Oh fuck! Fuck her! Fuck you! It's none of your business!" She starts shaking. I sit on the beach next to her and gently place my hand on her back.

After a long silence, she talks. "My older sister was my hero." She talks in a very husky monotone I can barely hear over the ocean roar.

"I idolized my sister. She was my best friend. I wanted to be just like her. She helped me. She stood up for me. She protected me from our father. She was only two years older than me, but she was so much stronger. One morning she was gone. She disappeared.

Walked out! She never said goodbye. She left me and my mother alone with that lunatic. How could she just leave?"

Flower sobs and shakes. She beats the sand with her fist. I sit still.

"Why didn't she tell me she was leaving? Why didn't she say goodbye? Why didn't she take me? Why didn't she come back and get me? My world was torn in half. My mother started to sob about my sister, and my father punched her in the stomach. She fell to the floor and stopped crying. My father came toward me with that look in his eye. He started to take off his belt, and I knew what that meant.

"What happened to . . ." I started to ask.

"'Don't you ever ask me about your sister!' my father shouted. 'Don't ever mention her name again. From now on, you never had a sister. She is gone. Good riddance. I am so glad she is out of here. Fuck her! Fuck your sister. You don't have a sister!'

"I was so devastated. I was heartbroken. I had a void in my heart. I was so sad. I was so mad at her for leaving me. I was confused and couldn't imagine why she would just walk out. I loved her. I thought she would shelter me, or at least salvage me, but she never came back. I wondered if she was dead. Then I hated myself for thinking that. We haven't spoken since."

"How do you know where she is?"

"Aunt Carrie keeps me informed. Aunt Carrie lets me read her letters. Aunt Carrie shows me her pictures. Now she works for a restaurant chain where people are being killed. I am afraid I will never see her again. I should call her! But she dumped me! Why would I call her? Fuck her. I miss her so much."

After a very long silence, Flower speaks again. "I'm sorry, Jesse. I've been living with turbulence my whole life. I think I'm still in a cyclone. I know I am a lot of work. Even though I am sober, I am still crazy. I have a pilot light flickering inside me, just waiting for a tiny spark. I am living under a bridge in my head.

"But." She smiles. "There are a lot of people who would love to have my worst day. I have you as my best friend, and now I have Mia as a surrogate sister.

"Life is okay, but it really sucks."

Mia is pulling us toward a parking lot to see a stray dog. Flower and Mia are inseparable, and I let them go. I am happy to wait. I am happy to soak in the warm air and the cool breeze.

Out of nowhere, AJ appears. The girl from the gym. All dressed in black. Her neon blond hair is glowing in the sun.

"Jesse!" she screams. She flings her arms around me. She almost knocks me to the ground.

She continues our relationship right where we left off. This tall, thin, beautiful girl with a radiant personality has both arms around me. She is squeezing so hard.

"Oh, Jesse, I am so happy to see you. I was waiting for you to come back to Why Weight. You never came back. Are you okay?"

"Me? I'm good."

She pulls back and looks at me again. She kisses me on the cheek. She giggles.

"I want to thank you. I took your advice," she says. "I decided not to have that boob job! I told the guy with the money to take a hike! My self-esteem has improved since that day. Because of your suggestion! Because of that decision, I am who I am. Take it or leave it. I am not going to lower myself just to please some stupid guy. How can I ever thank you?"

She moves in, slowly, and then it is a full-force hug.

She plants a firm lip-lock. One hand on the back of my head, the other hand on my neck. Her head is tilted. Arms all around. Glued together for a long, long kiss.

Flower's scream from thirty feet away is louder than the ocean waves. She scares the hell out of AJ. She scares the hell out of me, too.

My introductions are awkward.

On our way home, Flower gets in between Mia and me. She holds my hand all the way back to the apartment. She keeps looking up at me.

"Jesse. We can talk. I want to talk with you. I want to be open. I don't want to have any secrets from you. Where do you want me to start? I'll tell you anything. I'll tell you everything."

"To start with, what is your sister's name?"

"Her name is Blossom."

"What is she doing now?"

67.

BLOSSOM WAS PACKING FOR A LIFE-CHANGING trip. She was moving three thousand miles away. She would travel from Springfield, Massachusetts, to Seattle, Washington.

She had so much to do just to get ready. Counting down to an early wake-up call in a few short weeks. Another time zone. What would the weather be like? Should she bring everything she owns or just essentials? Where would she live? Would Jeb still want her? Did Jeb still love her? Did Jeb even remember who she was?

Jeb was so distant now and hard to talk with. He had changed so much since the killings. He sounded depressed. Gravelly voice, short of breath. The murders had brought him down. Way down. On their nightly calls, he sounded desperate and despondent. He gagged and choked. Did he remember that she was joining him? She should just blurt it out and ask him the question: *Do you still want me? Do you still love me?* If he said *no*, then what?

He never really hung up, but he often said, "Gotta go now," and then quickly ended the call.

Blossom had to face the fact. Life has ups and downs. Jeb was having a down. But he was the man she loved. She would be with him come what may. They would work together. They would live together. This is what they both wanted. Nothing would ever come between them. They would love each other forever.

68.

I CALL MY OLD PARTNER FROM the San Diego Police Force.

"Fig," I say. "Need a favor."

"What's new?"

"Three people have been killed in Seattle."

"Little out of my neighborhood."

"Yeah. Like I said, it's a favor."

"Do I even need to know why?"

"Flower has an estranged sister who works for Bad Boy Burgers."

"Really? I'm so sorry. What does estranged mean?"

I ignore his question.

"Bad Boy. I repeat. That chain where the killings are happening. People are getting whacked. Flower's sister is moving to Seattle. I really like Flower, but she is fixated on this killing spree. Can you ask around?"

"I'll call Upchuck."

"Who?"

"My friend at Seattle PD, Charles Upton. In high school, he made the mistake of changing his first name to Chuck. Been Upchuck ever since. He is now the Chief."

69.

The Seattle Weekly.

This is a response to a ridiculous article that you published in your news and comment section

Yes, I may have shortened a few lives, but please consider this one fact: It's not my fault. You have no idea what I have been through.

I struggle with depression. It is an illness that afflicts people all around the world. It interferes with my concentration, my motivation, and my attitude. It disrupts sleep, and it messes with my head. It's hard to understand depression, but there is one thing that makes me feel better: My solution is revenge. When I get even, I feel better. Period. Even-Steven.

After years of therapy, I have come to terms with my past. Things were done to me by many bad people. I have been hurt over and over again. My father left me. My uncle molested me. Every lover I ever had took advantage of me. I was flattened, crushed, and trampled. I was pissed on when I was a kid. I was crapped on as an adult.

And the insults just keep happening. People have aimed many theoretical arrows at me.

The arrows kept coming.

I just stood there and let the arrows penetrate my body. It all affected me. I didn't just suffer from anxiety, I became a carrier.

I have never stood up for myself. Until now. The people who have hurt me deserve to be punished.

And if extinction is necessary to cleanse myself, than that's what I need to do. My therapist would approve. After all, it's so much easier to punish someone who really deserves it.

I have no regrets. I will finish my mission and leave this town. An arrow has been shot.

Don't blame me. This is just the second arrow.

70.

WHAT'S ALL THIS STUFF ABOUT THE second arrow? I ask Erica.

"It's a Buddhist thing," she says

"Tell me."

"The Buddhists say that when something bad happens, there are two arrows. The first arrow is the bad thing that happens. The second arrow is the thing we do because of the first arrow.

"Do you want me to go on?" Erica says.

"Let's go all the way."

She hits me.

"Buddhists say that when we are hurt, we have an amazing ability to punish. We continually self-sabotage and relive pain. Sometimes the pain is directed to other people. Sometimes we shoot ourselves with the second arrow. It happens all the time.

"The killer is shooting with anger and frustration. Trying to appease the pain. This person feels justified in killing others to make themselves feel better."

71.

FIG ARRANGES A CONFERENCE CALL WITH Chief Upton.

"Call me Upchuck," he says. "Everyone else does."

He brings us up to date. "We got nothing. The letter to the editor was mailed from a remote county mailbox with no security cameras. The stamp was purchased in bulk. There were no fingerprints on anything. The paper was bought at a Walmart. Any Walmart! Same with the envelope. The font was Times New Roman, size 16. Any printer.

"Finding this killer will be a long shot. A long shot." He laughs. "Bad choice of words."

"There is another bombshell I need to drop." We listen to the chief.

"The three killings were committed with the same handgun. Maybe by the same person."

"What?" Fig and I say into the phone at the same time.

"Same caliber hollow-point!"

"What about security cameras?"

"Security cameras lie!" he says.

Fig and I stare at each other.

Upchuck continues. "We don't know if these killing were committed by a man or a woman. But we are now only looking for one person. We think it was probably a guy. None of us can imagine that a woman would be capable of such cold-blooded devastation. And, whoever we are looking for is a master of disguise."

We are both shocked into silence.

"One last thought," Upchuck says. "The victims were random. The killer was standing there waiting for a target. Any target. If a different employee had walked into the back parking lot, a different employee would have been shot."

"How do you know this?" I ask.

"On the night that the elderly lady, Mrs. Ellsworth, was murdered, she was allowed to leave work early. It was her birthday. It was a last-minute decision. The other employees told her they would finish up for her. Also, Jeb tells me that on any given night, any of his employees might have left early, depending on customer traffic."

Fig and I look at each other.

"Hollow point?" I ask. We stare at each other.

"Are you thinking what I am thinking?" he says.

"Impossible!"

"Too much of a coincidence!"

"Stupid!"

"Ridiculous!"

"Excuse me, boys. What are you talking about?" Upchuck asks over the speaker phone.

"Sorry, we are just obsessed, paranoid, and suspicious."

"About?"

"Everything."

Fig says, "Did someone steal her gun, or did she team up with someone else?"

"Who?"

"Why would she be targeting strangers? That's not her M.O," I say

"Whose M.O?"

I speak first. "I feel like I'm having a root canal."

Fig pipes in, "I feel like I am sitting on a cold toilet seat."

Okay. What's up? Upchuck asks.

We slowly tell him the story about Kiki. Nothing in the story connects to a burger chain in Seattle.

72.

AT 10AM IN SEATTLE, WASHINGTON, THE temperature is up to 54 degrees. It's drizzling. It's always drizzling. Except when it's raining.

Jeb is with the police, again. They are looking at videos, again. They are going over the same old story, again.

"Three months ago, a young girl with a fuzzy hat and a yoga mat killed a little old lady. Then a middle-aged technician with a toolbox shot a high school boy. This time, an obese bag lady killed a family man."

Chief Upchuck is pissed. He shouts at Jeb. "What is going on, Mister?"

No answer.

"The first attack was sad, for sure, but we all thought it was a one-hit wonder. Just a fluke. Now it's a real story.

"Here's the juicy part! The media lives for this shit. This story will be on every news channel in the world. The news dogs will interview every employee you ever had. They will interrogate any customer who has ever bought a bag of fries. They will call your providers. They will talk with your competitors. They will find your grandma. You have no idea how big this story will get! This is an easy way for a competitor to put you out of business," the police chief says.

Jeb bends forward in his chair and puts his head between his knees. He hyperventilates.

"I'll tell you what, mister!" Upchuck says as loud as he can without screaming. "If you know something, you better say something. Now."

73.

"HELLO."

"Hello, Blossom. This is your fiancée, Jeb, calling."

"I know it's you, but your voice sounds so husky. Are you okay?"

"Sure. I'm fine. Well, not really fine. You know. I don't know."

"Have you been gargling with martinis?"

"I might have had a little social beverage. Or two. Can't remember."

"Talk to me."

"I just want to tell you that I love you."

"I love you, too."

"No matter what happens, I love you."

"Okay. Thanks. The feeling is mutual."

"Blossom, whatever you hear, whatever you think, whatever you find out, just remember, I love you."

"Jeb, you're scaring me. What's going on?"

"I don't know. Blossom. Listen . . . er."

"I'm listening. I am listening to every word you say. My eyes and ears are glued on you. What are you saying?"

"Nothing, really. I just want you to know that, regardless of whatever people talk about, whatever you read in the paper, whatever it is, I love you. You know?"

"No. I don't know. What is this story you are you trying to tell me? What is happening? You are freaking me out!"

"Blossom, on the road of life, there are speed bumps. Sometimes there are pot holes or frost heaves. But the destination is always the most important part. The final outcome is what matters. Do you know what I mean?"

"No. I don't know what you mean. Jeb, what the fuck are you talking about?"

"I love you."

"I love you, too. I think."

"Gotta go."

Blossom took her suitcase off the bed and put it back into the closet.

74.

Sometimes, I have good days. Other times, not so much.

Today, I feel weak and tired. I am lonely and vulnerable. The physical pain of a gunshot and the emotional pain of my life drags me down.

I call my sponsor, Jigger Jack. Since we only use first names in AA, a lot of us end up with nicknames. Some handles apply to a career, some to an attitude, and some to a hobby. In my group there is a Sleepy Tom, Grateful Bob, Weepy Dan, and Kayak Dick. Jigger got his handle because of his size.

Jigger is five-two. When he was drinking, he bragged that he could drink more, spit further, and yell louder than any other man. Now that he's sober, he cares more, helps more, and listens more than any other man.

Early on, Jigger suggested I keep track of my roller-coaster mood swings.

"Start a DRC," he said.

"What the hell is a DRC?"

"Daily Reality Check." He laughs. "A journal. Just a line or two every day. The good part is that you can assign a number rating to each day. Track your disposition. Try to track your realism."

"My what?"

"A one would be the day you want to jump off a bridge."

"That may happen soon," I say.

"A ten is the day you've just gotten laid four times."

"That will never happen!"

Today, Jigger asks me about my DRC.

"I have never had a DRC I could rate as a one or a ten," I say. "But today is a two. Today is the pits."

"Did you drink today?" My sponsor asks.

"No."

"Give yourself a nine!" He laughs.

Flower senses my miserable mood and suggests we plant our feet in the sand after her shift at work.

"Meet me in front of Dog Beach Deli," she suggests.

Ocean Beach is my favorite tacky, trashy, touristy little seaside town. The locals refer to it as OB. I refer to it as skivvy beach. I've seen lots of high-school kids hanging out in their underwear. It's a California thing.

I like OB. I remember the day I drove my first motorcycle, a rusty old Yamaha, to Ocean Beach. As I parked in front of a locals bar, a homeless drunk yelled at me.

"You have a hell of a nerve bringing that piece of shit to this town!"

I couldn't agree more. That was the day I decided to upgrade to a Harley.

Today, because of the gunshot, I am having trouble walking in the sand.

I try to act regular, but that's a term used to describe bowel movements.

I pass eleven drunken college kids. I remember a line from the movie *Animal House*. "Being fat, drunk, and stupid is no way to go through life, son."

These fat, drunk, and stupid kids are on their way to annihilation. To celebrate their achievement, they are stacking empty beer cans in a huge pyramid on their blanket.

Rap music is blaring from a boom box, but I can hear the shouting as I limp past their blanket.

"Look at that old loser," one of them says.

I get mad.

"He's dragging his foot. He's either a drunk or a cripple."

I get madder.

"He's all alone. He'll live alone; he'll die alone."

I get madder than mad. I become bullshit.

"He couldn't get laid if his life depended on it."

They all laugh at me.

I throw my blanket on the sand. I am pissed because of my age. I am pissed because of my disability. I am pissed because these self-absorbed, privileged kids are assholes. In the old days, I would have made an issue of this, but today, the best I can do is sit still. I face the ocean with my back to the jerks.

My mood swings are on a constant, ever-changing cycle. Sometimes they evolve slowly, and I can feel them fluctuating. Other times they explode.

I remember a terrifying, turbulent airplane flight. Every few seconds, the plane would drop violently and then, just as quickly, jerk up again. When we plunged, it felt like a free-fall. Like the floor was being pulled out from under us. We would hit a plateau, and then everyone would scream. Or cry. We would stabilize, and everyone would breathe a sigh of relief. For a second. Then we would bounce up again, like on an elevator. Some of us became dizzy. We would flat-line and then plummet.

Some passengers were white-knuckling the bumps. Literally. Other people were praying. Hands clasped, heads bowed.

In the midst of all this, a young boy was enjoying the roller-coaster fun. Every time we dipped, he shrieked at the top of his lungs. He laughed. He shouted, "Wheee!" People close to him started chuckling. It was contagious. Soon people near him were laughing. Then, the whole plane began shouting "Wheee!" like a group of happy dancing monkeys or flying hippos. Our mood changed in an instant. It became a "Wheee!" kind of day.

Today, I am looking for an excuse to shout, "Wheee." I come back to reality.

As I stare at the ocean, I hear cat-calls. I hear inappropriate comments.

Someone yells, "Bitchin' babe!"

I slowly turn around and see Flower walking toward me. She is floating as if she is on a runway. Graceful, long strides in the sand. She is cool. She is hot. As she passes in front of the kids, they start screaming degrading comments and obnoxious suggestions. She just glides past them and doesn't say a word. No eye contact.

I stand up and watch her saunter toward me. We smile. When the kids realize she is walking towards me, they become confused and surprisingly quiet.

One of them sums it up. "What the fuck!"

Flower is wearing a short, black skirt and a tan tank top over her bikini. A red Willie Nelson bandana is tied around her forehead. She walks right into my arms. This beautiful young girl hugs the old cripple. The college guys become quiet.

She is facing the ocean, and I am facing the drunks.

"These kids need a lesson." She smiles.

Without a word, we start to kiss. We have never kissed before, and I think I like it. We are making out in public. Heads tilted. Her hands on my lower back. It's a performance we didn't rehearse. We should get an Oscar.

The kids stare. As we hug each other, I reach up under the back of her blouse and unhook her bikini top. I expect her to stop me, but she doesn't. Instead, she pulls away and the top falls from under her shirt. I dangle the bathing suit, and it waves in the breeze. This has become a very colorful day.

The college kids are silent. No more shouting

"Do we have their attention?" she asks.

"We have their undivided attention!" I answer.

She drops to her knees and plants her face firmly in my stomach. Her arms circle my waist.

Shortly after that, the kids pack up, abandon their beer can pyramid, and leave the beach.

I shout at the top of my lungs, "Wheee!"

75.

AFTER THE KIDS LEAVE, THERE ISN'T a soul within a mile. We are lying on our backs, holding hands. There is a magnificent cloud formation passing overhead. We open our eyes when the cloud is blocking the sun, and close them when the sun shines through again. It's a good time to talk.

"Flower, a few weeks ago, you told me you were a dancer. Sharing the story seemed scary to you, but it is important to me. Can you tell me about dancing in a club?"

"It's a thing you do to music. Kind of wiggle around a little bit."

"Here we go again. Ladies and gentlemen, let me introduce Little Miss Secrets."

She shakes her head and looks away.

"I don't like the part about secrets," I say. I get up from the blanket. "Need to go. See ya around."

"Wait, Jesse. What is it you want to know?"

"Please tell me about your dancing career," I ask again.

"You don't want to know."

"I want to know."

"Not important."

I get up again.

"See ya."

She grabs me by the foot. I stop and wait.

"Sit back down and be a good little boy. I'll tell you a very painful story. I've only told this story to one other person. Her name was Danny Gee."

I lay back down on the blanket, and she rolls toward me. She rests her head on my arm. I am on my back, looking at the clouds.

She places her arm across my chest. I like to be close to her. I am interested in this story, but I am petrified of this story. We now have a one-way relationship. She can tell me anything, but there is no way that I can ever verify if her story is the real deal or just a fantasy. I may not believe her story, but I can't challenge it.

"Why is it so hard to tell the truth?" she asks.

"Everyone asks for the truth, but no one wants to hear the truth," I reply.

For a long time, we listen to the waves breaking on the beach. Sometimes the waves are quiet, but every ten minutes or so the sound is like a shotgun. Loud as an explosion. The waves are breaking, and my heart is ready to break, too.

Flower's eyes are now closed, and she is motionless for a very long time. I don't know if she is thinking about her answer, or sleeping, or dead.

"Remember I told you the story about my father chasing me around the house? So drunk? Swearing? Swinging his belt? I thought he would kill me."

"I remember."

"He was out of control. He slipped on newspapers, and after he fell down I tried to punish him. I lit a match and threw it. The papers instantly went up in flames. Our house went up in flames.

"Jesse, you have to realize that I have never been so scared. I was petrified. I didn't know what happened to my father. Was he dead? If he was dead, I thought I would be arrested for murder. I had no place to go. I had no money. I had no clothes. I have never been so scared. My father beat me constantly, and he was responsible for my mother's death. I wanted to get as far away as I could. I ran and ran and ran.

"When I couldn't run anymore, I crumbled to a curb. I sat with my head between my knees and sobbed. Two young girls in a rusty old pickup slowed down. As I looked up through my tears, they pulled to the side of the road and stopped. They watched me for a minute, and then they both got out of the truck. They sat next to me. One on each side.

"I looked at them. I turned my head from left to right. They looked like hell. No makeup, filthy, messy hair, ripped jeans, dirty sweatshirts. Scuffed, ripped sneakers. Although they looked terrible, they didn't seem mean. They were young girls. Just like me. They both smiled. One of them patted me on the knee.

"'Do you need a ride?' one of them asked. I smiled through my tears. I nodded my head, yes. I climbed in the truck and sat between them. The floor-mounted stick shift was between my legs. One of them asked where I was going. I didn't have an answer. The girl who was driving looked at me and asked the hard question.

"'Are you running?'

"I broke down and cried again. They both seemed to understand.

"'We're going to work,' the girl who was driving said. 'Why don't you come with us?'

"They looked so bad that I couldn't imagine what kind of job they had, but it didn't matter; I was no longer sitting on a street corner.

"The girls introduced themselves. The small brunette in the passenger seat said, 'I'm Peanut.'

"The blonde who was driving said, 'They call me Harley.'

"They were both cute and spunky. They were talking so much they interrupted each other. They were dressed in hand-me-down, yard-sale rags, but they had the potential to be very attractive young ladies. *Maybe someday they will find the energy to clean up,* I thought.

"We parked behind a building with a huge, neon sign that said: 'Mardi Gras Gentlemen's Club.' I had heard about strip clubs, but I had never been in one.

76.

"The Mardi Gras was cavernous. A gigantic, circular bar took up most of the room, and there was a stage in the middle. The floor was spotless, the tables were clean, the mirrors were glistening, and the staff looked professional. I was surprised that the bartenders were women.

"The Mardi Gras was dark. This was a good place to hide. If police were looking for me, they wouldn't find me here. I didn't care what kind of business this was, because, for the moment, I was safe. My new best friends, Harley and Peanut, were taking care of me. In that instant, I didn't even think about my father.

"I felt comfortable in this dark place. I felt inconspicuous, and I started to calm down. The music made me relax. My mood changed.

"I was tired of running, exhausted from crying, and I was starving. I hadn't eaten in two days. The girls took me into the dressing room, and I sat on a bench. I stared into space. Other girls were in various stages of undress, but no one seemed to notice me. A beautiful girl with dark brown skin was rolling a joint. Several of the girls were eating some kind of stew that had been served on paper plates. No one paid attention to me. No one cared.

"Harley brought the manager into the dressing room.

"'Dante,' Harley said. 'This is my friend Flower, and she loves to dance. She needs a job. I think she needs a meal, too.'

"'Flower? That's a good name!'

"Dante was short and heavy. He tried to look tough. He had bowed legs, and his greasy, black hair was parted in the center. His eyes were squinting. His work boots had extra-thick soles.

"Dante asked, 'How old are you?'

"Before I could answer, Harley piped in. 'She's eighteen, just like me. We were in the same class in high school.'

"'Oh, that's good,' Dante said. 'You don't look old enough, but our customers really like the young stuff. If you get up on stage and dance a set, we will pay cash and you can keep the tips. We'll call it an audition. And we'll feed you. Is that okay?' he asked. Before I could answer, he walked away. He turned back and spoke again.

"'I have some paperwork for you to fill out.'

"'Don't worry about the paperwork,' Harley said with a smile. 'Dante can't read.'

"'Don't you like him?' I asked.

"'I wouldn't trust him with a tuna sandwich.'

"'So, how old are you, anyway?' she asked with a playful smile.

"'I hate to tell you. I'm only fourteen.'

"'Ha,' she said. 'Me too. Peanut is an old lady; she's sixteen.'

"Minutes later, Dante came back.

"'I can't find the application now. We'll do it later.'

"'I never asked you. Do you like to dance?' Peanut smiled.

"'I love to dance,' I answered.

"'My set is coming up,' Peanut said. 'Sit at the bar while I get dressed and then watch me dance. It's really fun, if you like music.'

"They walked me out, hand in hand, and sat me at the bar. I was alone again. At this time of day, there were very few customers. Some quiet background music was playing. I sat on the barstool, turning a napkin over and over. I was uncomfortable. *Maybe I should go*, I thought. Where would I go?

"Two young girls came out of the dressing room and sat on either side of me. They were gorgeous. They looked kind of familiar, but I didn't know who they were.

"The girl on my left jumped up from the bar stool and held her arms out, as if in a talent contest.

"'Ta-da!' she said. 'What do you think?'

"It was Peanut. I didn't even recognize her. She had changed one thousand percent. Eyeliner, rouge, mascara, lip gloss, hair that had been teased up high. Glitter all around. And she was three inches taller in her platform high heels.

"'Oh my God,' is all I said.

"Harley jumped up, too. She bowed, and I applauded. They had transformed from trailer trash to lovely ladies. I couldn't believe my eyes.

"'I think we should get Flower a pick-me-up. A little bit of courage.' Peanut flagged the bartender.

"'Hey Reggie,' she yelled.

"Peanut introduced us. 'Reggie, this is my friend Flower. She is a virgin dancer, but today she is going to break her cherry.'

"Reggie laughed. She was a middle-aged woman who looked like she had been dragged through a tough life. Her bottle-bleached-blonde hair was stiff and had been slicked back in a duck's ass. She had no makeup. She wore baggy, denim carpenter's jeans that were a size too long and scuffed men's work boots. She had at least ten silver bracelets on her left wrist and many tattoos of bracelets on her right wrist. She had two rings on every finger of each hand. When she looked at me, her toughness melted away. She smiled with a twinkle in her eye, reached across the bar, and patted my hand.

"'You will do fine, honey,' she said.

"She bent down and made a drink. She placed it in front of me.

"'Have a Captain,' Reggie said. 'It's on me.'

"The Captain looked like Coke but tasted like coconut. It had a wedge of lime on top of the glass and two long straws. The drink, whatever it was, calmed me down and fired me up at the same time. There must have been a hole in the bottom of the glass. It disappeared quickly. I don't know why I was so thirsty, but within a heartbeat, there was a refill.

"Out of nowhere, the loudest voice I ever heard came booming from a speaker over center stage. It scared the hell out of me.

"'Ladies and gentlemen. Welcome to the Mardi Gras. Please direct your attention to our center celebrity dance floor. Now, straight from a sold-out performance in Los Angeles, we are proud to introduce the lovely, the talented, the bubbly little doll of dance. Welcome today's first shining star at the Mardi Gras. Let's put our hands together for Peanut!'

"One customer quietly clapped. The music stopped for a second. A rotating spotlight started pulsing out of a ceiling fixture. A siren wailed for a full minute. I thought we were being raided. The sound came from a single source over the dance floor. All eyes were on the empty stage. Peanut hopped off the barstool, ran over to a tiny set of stairs, and climbed up to the middle of the large, center stage. Her skirt was tight, and her shoes were thick, but she did a good job of navigating the stairs.

"All of a sudden, music started blaring from ten different directions. The noise just about lifted me off the stool.

"Peanut was beautiful. She looked so different from the raggedy teenager in the gas guzzler. Her vivid, bright, ruby-red lipstick matched her incredibly short skirt. She also wore a minuscule, white tank top and dainty, white cotton socks inside platform high heels. She scrunched down in front of me and yelled, 'You'll think I'm crazy, but I really do have fun!'

"And she did act crazy, and she did have fun. As each new song came on, she smiled and flashed an animated thumbs-up, as if each track was a gift to her.

I could read her lips. 'I love this song!'

"She danced her little ass off. She smiled at every single man in the club. I think she really enjoyed being in the spotlight. If a man passed a dollar bill to her, she would scrunch down and thank him.

"Seeing her dance and have fun with the music was comforting. No one bothered her. The bouncer, who was as big as Oklahoma, was right there. He kept his eyes on his girls and on the customers.

"Of course, Peanut ended up naked except for her lacy white socks and her platform high heels. I should have been shocked, but this was, after all, a strip joint. I was getting the picture.

"Customers slowly started walking into the club. They usually came in alone and sat by themselves. They made no eye contact with other patrons, and I got the feeling they were embarrassed to be at a strip joint.

"Reggie got me another drink, and that built up my courage.

"'Let's dance together!' Harley said. 'Dante won't mind.'

"She grabbed my hand and took me into the dressing room. We raided the lost and found.

"It was easy for me to make a decision. I loved music, and I loved dancing. And for the moment, I was safe.

"Harley took me by the hand again, and we both got up on stage. The DJ introduced us.

"'Ladies and Gentlemen, now, for the first time at the Mardi Gras, direct from an extended engagement in Miami, we are proud to introduce the two sisters of seduction. Let's hear it for Harley and Flower. Let's give them a huge Mardi Gras round of applause!'

"Two old men mildly clapped their hands.

"'Most of the men here are so sad,' Harley said, as we waited for the music to queue up. 'They seem like they're stuck in lonely marriages. Some of them look like they've never been laid. Our job is to make them feel like they are alive for a few minutes.

"'My goal, when I am on the stage is to see how many men I can get to smile.'

"'Great goal.'

"And that's what we did.

"We danced together, and I was imitating her moves. When she took off her top, I took off my top. When she shimmied out of her skirt, I slipped my skirt off, too. Peanut and a few of the other girls at the bar cheered us on. They were yelling my name 'Flower! Flower!' For the first time in my life, I felt like a star.

"At the end of the first set, we still had our G-strings on. We got a standing ovation from the dancers at the bar, and a few smiles from the customers.

"'These guys usually don't applaud,' Harley said. 'They just throw one-dollar bills.'

"'I can live with that,' I said with a smile.

"The music started again, and it was time to get down to business. The business of getting naked. I followed Harley. When we finished that song, we were bare-assed, but we had done our job. I looked down at the dance floor, and there were bills all over the place.

"'This set is yours!' Harley said. 'This batch of money is yours.' We danced one more time. After three songs, we were totally naked. From beginning to end. After the next dance, there was even more money. Mostly ones but some fives, too.

"I walked around, picked up the bills, and smiled at each man. Even though I was in the spotlight, I was safe. My makeup was over-the-top, my hair was teased and sprayed with glitter, and my platform shoes lifted me up three inches. I didn't expect any policemen to be looking for me in this club, but if they did come in, I no longer looked like a scared fourteen-year-old girl.

"Dante smiled at me. 'Where did you learn to dance like that?' He patted my ass. He let me order from the menu. Two burgers and an order of fries filled me up. I danced three more sets. He paid me in cash, and with the tips I had more money than I had ever seen in my life. A huge wad of dirty, filthy, disgusting, crinkled-up bills. I was so excited.

"When Dante asked me to come back the next day, I was thrilled, but then horrified. I hadn't thought about the night, and I had no place to go. I didn't want to go out on the street. I thought the police might be looking for me.

"Harley and Peanut took me home to their second-floor apartment. It was a disaster. The few pictures that were on the wall were lopsided. There were rock posters that were fastened to doors with yellowing scotch tape. Ash trays were overflowing. Dresser drawers were open. There were dirty clothes on the floor. There were shoes in every corner of the room. The kitchen was the worst. I don't think there was a clean glass in a cabinet, and the sink was jam-packed with dirty dishes.

"The couch was covered in magazines and clothes, but they just pushed that stuff to the floor. They found me a pillow and a ratty old blanket.

"That night, I slept better than I had in years. The girls said I could chip in on the rent.

"The next morning, I woke up early. I had experienced the most peaceful sleep I'd had in years, and I wasn't worried about my father. I looked around at the mess and decided to give them a treat. Maybe I could give back. I quietly washed and dried the dishes. I picked up the magazines and sorted clothes in two piles for the laundry. I emptied the ashtrays. I mopped the bathroom and cleaned the sink.

"The girls were thrilled at the new look of their apartment, and they assured me I was a welcome addition. They went through their closets and put together a new outfit for me. This time, everything matched.

"That day, we had fun on the way to the club and talked about the music, the dance moves, and the regular customers.

"On my second day in the club, Dante walked up behind me and started to massage my neck. Than he moved his hands to my backside. I froze. If I looked up the word 'creep' in the dictionary, I would see a picture of Dante.

"Peanut tapped him on the shoulder.

"'Hey Dante,' she said. 'You might want to think twice; Flower's boyfriend is huge. And he is very jealous.'

"Dante walked away.

"She winked, and I gave her a hug.

"One night, after a few weeks of dancing, old issues came back to me. I started thinking about the horrible house fire. I wondered what happened to my father. It was a low point. That night, I just stared at the wall. Harley and Peanut had long since gone to sleep or passed out. For the first time since I left home, I felt alone.

"I felt like a china doll. My head felt ready to crack, but I didn't want anyone to look inside me. I didn't want anyone to see who I really was.

"In the morning, as we were getting ready for work, I asked them a favor.

"'Before we go to work today, can you drive a little out of the way?'

"'Sure,' they said.

"As we drove by my old house, all I saw were ashes. The house was completely gone, and yellow plastic tape surrounded the property.

"I didn't know if my father was dead, in a burn unit, or on the street looking for me. At that point in my life, I wasn't interested in the news, but a local paper was left in the dressing room. The headline said that a man was burned to death in an accidental house fire. It gave the address of our little house. I had a feeling of guilt but also of satisfaction.

"My father would never hurt anyone again."

It's a wonderful beach day. Huge, cotton-candy puffs of mist slowly pass overhead and, since it is warm, each brief shadow is refreshing. Flower is sharing. I like to hear her story. She takes a big breath, rolls over on her back, and looks up at the sky. Flower is a great narrator. It is unrehearsed and coming from way down in the bottom of her heart.

"Do you want more?"

"More, please."

"After I read the newspaper article about the fire, I was overwhelmed. It was all hitting me. What had I done? What would happen to me in the future? I had no plan. I was living day to day.

"As most strippers age, they either end in the big house, the bug house, or the box. The girls I worked with joked about their future, but it wasn't funny.

"I became lonely and privately cried a lot. Some nights I would sob myself to sleep. The girls told me to try smoking a joint. 'Just to calm down,' they said. I choked and gagged, and they laughed. Soon, I got the hang of it. I relaxed.

"After six months of dancing at the Mardi Gras, the club was shut down for an expired license. All of us underage dancers were taken to a detention center.

"It was probably the best thing that ever happened to me."

77.

"WHILE I WAS IN DETENTION, I met a social worker who changed my life. Her name was Danielle Giovanni, but everyone called her Danny Gee. The inmates would scream, 'Yo, Danny Gee,' every time she walked by. They all loved her.

"Danny Gee was as conservative as a judge, hard-hitting as a nail gun, and as dependable as a slinky walking down the stairs. She was about five-five, and probably weighed less than a hundred pounds. She wore huge, black-rimmed glasses. Her hair was styled in a flat-top. I never saw her with makeup. She looked like someone's younger sister. Or someone's younger brother. She always wore cowboy boots. She must have had twelve pair. She wore tight jeans. She wore a dark hoodie sweatshirt, and her hands were always in the pockets. She looked tough. I can't remember her smiling much, but when I walked into her room she always made me feel special.

"Danny Gee somehow helped me discover an aptitude I never knew I had: She challenged me to read.

"She also understood my family situation. Danny Gee had been there, too. Her personality was as big as the outdoors, but she was gentle. She was calming. She never let emotions get in the way.

"For some reason, we bonded. I liked her instantly, and I knew that she liked me. When we talked, she was totally tuned into my story. She shared the most genuine expression of love I had ever experienced.

"Danny Gee had grown up in the projects, and she was the sixth child in her family. Her mother had several different husbands.

"She told me that, by the time she came into the world, her mother had given up. She never knew her real father, but it just didn't matter. She had many different stepdads. She was basically raised by her siblings. Alcohol and drugs were more important than food. She was always hungry. She remembers being given booze at a young age to quiet her down. She found out later that all the kids were given eyedroppers of booze in their baby formula. She was always tired, and she missed a lot of school. She was not able to keep up with other kids. She couldn't perform routine tasks, was less physically active, and very lethargic. She was always sick. When she was growing up, her house was always full of fleas. Her mother's solution was to wear cowboy boots in the house.

"She knew first-hand about welfare, food stamps, reimbursements, and benefits. She knew about the systems and the scams. And she knew about abusive family relationships.

"Danny Gee told me that her first job, at thirteen, was selling loose joints on a street corner. She started drinking in bars at fifteen, and was prescribed Valium at seventeen.

"When she was nineteen, she was housebound. Her daily routine was to move from the couch to the bathroom. She existed on beer, pills, and Twinkies. She thought she would die in a tenement.

"After a state-sponsored detox and a long-term recovery experience, she got sober. She was twenty when everything changed. She started to eat right. Walks turned to working out. She slept on a schedule and took care of herself. Her health improved. She went to school and liked it. She eventually got a college degree at night school. Now she is a powerhouse.

"Danny Gee understood my life, and she always took my call. She would meet me any time, any place. She always told me the truth. Sometimes the truth hurt. She was the friend I never had.

"When I got out of jail, I tried to find another job. No one wants to hire a convict. I went back to strobe lights and screaming DJs. Dancing was the only thing I knew how to do.

"Danny Gee told me I had just made the biggest mistake of my life. She said my job at a club would take me right back to drinking and drugs. She was stern. She was right!

"Most of the girls in the circuit were young, like me. Most had been abused, raped, or neglected. Many were kicked out of their homes by jealous stepmothers. In order to numb our feelings, we all took Percs, or Oxy, or whatever we could get our hands on. The public wants to put exotic dancers down, but most of the girls were just trying to get by. This life wasn't my choice, but I had very few choices. I just wanted to survive.

"Most of us wanted to pretend we were someone else. I made enough money to pay for my pills. When I was sixteen, one of the dancers introduced me to heroin. She taught me to shoot up. This is what she did every day, so it almost seemed natural. It was cheap and available.

"Track marks in my arm started to show, so I stuck a needle in my elbow, or between my toes, or in my groin every day. My habit was so bad it took me to a lower place than I had ever been before. I never turned tricks, but that was just a *yet*. It would have happened sooner or later. If I did, it would just be a So what? moment.

"The tips were incredible, and I made a lot of money. But guess where the money went? If I wasn't using drugs, I would have made a fortune. But if I wasn't using drugs, I would have killed myself.

"I finally got busted and went back to jail.

"The good news is that, while I was away, I got to work with Danny Gee again. She encouraged me to sign up for classes. My favorite was English. I had constant tutoring. Most girls in lock-up don't care about books, so the teacher bent over backward to help me. I read everything she suggested."

Flower stops talking. She rolls over on her stomach and looks at the waves.

"What a great beach day," she says. "Thank you for letting me rant. This is really good therapy."

I stretch out and put my arm under her head. She turns over on her side and faces me. She snuggles in and puts her arm across my chest. She sighs. After a minute she continues her story.

"I guess getting busted was the break I was looking for. I was forced to kick my habit in jail. It was not a detox by any means. I was put into a cell where I puked my guts out for a week. I had to clean it up myself. I was sicker than I have ever been in my life. But as I slowly began to sober up, I decided to change my life. I decided to start a new chapter.

"Danny Gee gave me direction. I went to AA meetings in jail. I took books out of the library and signed up for any class that was offered.

78.

"THE OTHER SAVIOR IN MY LIFE, of course, was Aunt Carrie. As you know, my aunt owns Jaspers. While I was locked up, we became pen pals. I wrote to her every day, and she wrote to me every day. She sent postcards from SeaWorld, The San Diego Zoo, and the Mission Beach boardwalk. One time, she sent me a Padres hat, and another time I got a Chargers t-shirt.

"She sent me an article in the newspaper about Jaspers, and she sent me the new menu. In her letters, she talked about labor costs and food portions. It was all new to me, but I was flattered that she treated me like an adult. She told me about the best-selling items on her menu. She wrote about the challenges of running the restaurant for ten hours a day. She said she wished she had someone she could trust to work with her.

"When I was about to be released, Aunt Carrie made an offer I couldn't refuse: She suggested I move to San Diego, live with her, and work in her restaurant. It was the best offer I ever had. Aunt Carrie sent me a bus ticket and said I could pay her back out of my salary.

"I was so excited. A real job with someone who trusted me! Aunt Carrie helped me focus on the positives. I owe everything to Aunt Carrie. We made endless trips to the mall, and she helped me pick out respectable outfits. A regular restaurant customer was a dentist. She bartered with him to get my teeth straightened.

"Aunt Carrie helped me change my hair style and my smile. She helped me become a lady. She taught me the ropes of the restaurant business, and now I manage the lunch shift. I go to school one night a week. On the rest of the nights, I go to AA meetings or NA meetings all over town.

"I am so happy to be free of drugs and booze."

There is a long silence.

"Jesse, I am such an addict! Sometimes when things get bad, I think I could go back to using drugs in a heartbeat. That's why I stay so close to recovery meetings."

Flower doesn't move for a long time. I finally realize she has fallen asleep with her head on my chest. I feel her rhythmic breathing.

As far as I am concerned, we could stay in this position forever.

79.

AFTER WE LEAVE THE BEACH, WE go back to my place and I make toast. We finish a full loaf of sourdough bread with strawberry jelly and cream cheese. Flower eats like she hasn't had a meal in weeks. She keeps finding conversation to extend our time together. She tells me everything I have tried to find out before. I love this side of her.

She gets reflective again. "I was in a dark place," she says. "I drank against my will. When I was using drugs, I gave everything away. I lost my self-esteem, my pride, and my hope. I felt like I was mentally ill, emotionally abused, and physically broken."

"I like listening to you, Flower," I say. "Because you just described the way that I feel."

80.

BLOSSOM'S EARLY-MORNING FLIGHT FROM SPRINGFIELD, MAS-SACHUSETTS, to Seattle, Washington, arrived on time. She stood in the pick-up area waiting for Jeb to meet her. When she finally got him on the phone, there was a long silence.

"Oh no!" he said. "Today? I thought it was tomorrow!"

When her cab arrived at Bad Boy Burgers, Jeb was nowhere in sight. She lugged one bag through the pouring rain. The cabbie was happy to sit in his car and wait while she made a second trip.

As she shuffled through the parking lot, she was appalled by the mess. The lot was full of butts, wrappers, and cups. No one had policed the lot in months. *Absolutely unacceptable,* she thought.

The inside of the restaurant was worse. It hadn't been cleaned in weeks. As she lugged her bags in the door, Blossom saw Jeb mopping the pick-up area. There was a full inch puddle of water every customer had to wade through. He looked at her, scrunched, and shook his head.

The overall appearance of the restaurant was disgusting. It reminded her of the day she applied for the job at Bad Boy Burgers in Massachusetts. Mustard residue was crusted on counters. Empty containers and coffee cups were left on tables. Napkins and straws were on the floor.

The temperature was annoyingly hot, and there was no music. Both items should have been on the manager's daily checklist.

Lastly, the single employee on the service line, a large, disheveled black woman, was sitting with her fat ass on the pick-up counter. Her back was to the restaurant while she looked at her phone.

Blossom wanted to scream, but, since no one even knew who she was, it would have been a waste of time.

This was not the welcome Blossom had expected. The reunion with Jeb was painful and stressful. His hug was short. There was almost no eye contact and only one short sentence was muttered.

"Most of the staff quit," he said.

Jeb was overwhelmed with the murders, the investigations, and the drastic decrease in business. He looked physically exhausted and emotionally shattered. His shirt was two sizes too large, or he was two sizes too small. He was so different from the man who hired her. He was so different from the man she had fallen in love with in Springfield.

Jeb looked like he had lost twenty pounds. His face was gaunt, and his shirt was filthy. There were big bags under his bloodshot eyes. He had been crying. He was watching his business go down the tubes. Police were walking a beat on the perimeter of each store, and reporters were inside. A photographer in a soaking wet raincoat was taking endless pictures of the building, the parking lot, and the staff. This was a game to the news media. They were happy to have a personal interest story. People were buying papers.

A young college-aged customer stood in the pick-up line with a t-shirt that read: "I survived Bad Boy Burgers!"

Jeb was summoned by a policeman.

"Not again," he said to her as he shook his head.

He asked Blossom to wait in his tiny office. The officer seemed to be asking about the security camera. She could see Jeb's mouth, and it looked like he was saying, "I already explained it!"

He started pointing to the cameras located around the store.

Before the officer left, Jeb gave him a cup of coffee and a box of fries.

At least he hasn't lost his sense of community, she thought to herself.

Jeb waved to Blossom. He was using hand motions, as you would if you were directing traffic. He was asking her to come out of the office.

They stood in the middle of the dining room. He spoke as if he had just realized how bad things looked. It was almost like he had awoken from a nightmare. He looked at Blossom and started to shake his head.

"Oh, Blossom. We have a problem." The three employees who were standing nearby stared at him. The policeman who was finishing his fries looked, too.

Jeb spoke loud enough that everyone could hear him talk.

"You flew out here to live with me, but this isn't going to work."

"What?"

"We can't just live together."

"What? What are you talking about?" Her voice got shaky.

"I have to take you to the airport."

"What? Leave? I haven't even unpacked! Are you sending me back to Massachusetts?" Her laugh was nervous. "What are you talking about?"

"Blossom, I am sorry I couldn't pick you up, but this won't work. We have to go to the airport."

"Jeb. What are you doing? What are you saying?"

Jeb got on one knee and looked up at her.

"Let's get married."

"What?"

"I want to close our chain for three days. I want to take you to Las Vegas, and get married. I want you to be my wife. Will you please marry me?"

Blossom had an instant flashback of her life. She was abused by her father. She missed time in school and lived on the street. As a young girl, she fought her way through a lonely life. She didn't have companionship. She didn't have tutoring, counseling, or guidance. Finally, here was a man who encouraged her. A man who mentored her. A man who loved her.

"Yes, yes, yes." She bent over and helped him up, and the few employees applauded. The policeman applauded, too.

"We will go tomorrow?"

"Oh my God. Yes, yes, yes! I have nothing to wear."

"You will! Thank you so much for coming to my rescue." He was still talking loudly. He was almost in tears.

She was definitely in tears.

"Yes, yes, yes," she said again.

"And, when we return, the employees will give you a belated bridal shower.

"And lastly, when we get back on our feet, I want to host a wedding party. We will have a huge, colorful celebration, right here in our restaurant.

"I promised to marry you, Blossom, and that's what I want to do."

She blew a huge bubble and let it burst. She took the gum out of her mouth, put it in a coke cup, and kissed him for a long time.

81.

JEB WAS PREPARED TO SPEND SEVENTY-SEVEN dollars on a marriage license. He was also prepared to spend an extra dollar for the credit card transaction. Best of all, there was no waiting period, no blood test, and no hoops. In and out! Single guy to married guy. Boom.

On the short plane trip to Vegas, Jeb's mind was on recent tragedies, and his emotions were on future challenges, but Blossom was here, now. He had to force himself into the moment.

Jeb wanted to get married because it's what he promised.

Jeb also wanted to get married for a bigger reason. He wanted to remove any suspicion of his inappropriate relationship with a female hitchhiker. Jeb had so many negative feelings from his affair. He wanted to bury his feelings alive until they stopped kicking.

Jeb had already booked a venue for their wedding. It included a little flair and a lot of extravagance. He was not thinking of the cost or the logistics. He wanted their wedding day to be special and elegant. He would also have the details of their day captured by a professional photographer. He would post pictures of their wedding in every newspaper in town. When you are getting married in the make-believe, kaleidoscope world of Las Vegas, every little bit helps.

When they got to Vegas, a limo took them directly to the Stratosphere Hotel. It was the tallest freestanding observation tower in the United States. Jeb had chosen a suite with a private balcony on the top floor.

Blossom's only challenge was to shop for a new wedding outfit. There were at least a hundred bridal shops in Las Vegas. She was armed with Jeb's credit card. He planned to escort her around town but to stay out of the decision-making process.

They met with the hotel concierge. After a brief review of the details, they relaxed in their suite with a floor-to-ceiling view of the city. Blossom was overwhelmed with the spectacle.

Blossom got frisky and insisted they sign up for a roof-top thrill ride called "Insanity." It was a giant mechanical arm that would hold them out, one thousand feet over the ground, as they spun in circles.

"This is crazy," said Jeb. "We may not make it to the altar!"

"I don't care!" she screamed at the top of her lungs. "If we die today, it will be fine. I am the happiest girl in the world!"

"I love you!"

They spun in gigantic claws that were perched over the edge of the tower. They had become daredevils on this ride, and they had become daredevils in their life as they planned their new journey together.

At the wedding, Jeb's new wife was dazzling in her two-piece, butterscotch outfit. She wore matching shoes and a starched, white, lacy blouse. Jeb had a professional photographer take dozens of pictures. These wedding photos would hang in their Seattle office for everyone to see.

After an early-morning ceremony, they did the town. Blossom wore her new outfit and her birdcage wedding headpiece for the day. Jeb wore his slacks and sport jacket with a boutonnière in the lapel. Every single person they met commented on their wedding attire and wished them well. It was a splendid day.

A circus show, a gondola journey, and a roller-coaster ride filled their day. Making love filled their night.

82.

IT'S A LAZY MORNING, AND FLOWER'S neighborhood is quiet. The weather is a perfect seventy degrees. This is the kind of day that Californians get used to, but that people from other parts of the country can't even imagine. We sit on her newly painted thrift-shop rocking chairs, and enjoy french toast and bacon for breakfast.

Flower is wearing a dainty, pink sun dress and colorful sandals. Her hair has been pulled back into pigtails, and red ribbons keep everything in place.

I am wearing cutoff jeans and a ten-year-old Harley Davidson t-shirt. My flip-flops are falling apart. My hair has not been combed.

We spend so much time together that we are now comfortable with sharing. Sometimes our questions are lighthearted. Other times our questions cause pain. We like being together, we like to share, and we are both good listeners.

"Have you ever been in love?" I ask Flower. Just making conversation.

She puts her coffee down and looks at me. Her face becomes serious.

"You don't want to know."

"I want to know."

"You mean like, the truth?"

"Why is it so hard to tell the truth?"

"The truth hurts."

"Have you ever been in love?" I ask again.

"Unfortunately!"

I am suddenly sorry I asked.

"I was hoping you would never ask that question."

"One day, when I was dancing at the Mardi Gras," she says, "a tall, well-dressed, handsome young man came in. He was on crutches. He was with some friends who seemed to be taking care of him.

"He walked very slowly and looked like he was in incredible pain. He climbed up on a bar stool and just sat there while his friends went off to play pool. He had eyes that pierced right through me. I kept trying to look away, but his smile was mesmerizing. When I finished my set, he gave me a ten-dollar bill. Most guys tipped a dollar. Some didn't tip at all. When his friends got ready to leave, they called him Topper. As he stood up, he turned to me and waved.

"The next day, Topper came in again. He smiled as if we were old friends. He called me by name.

"'Hi, Flower!' he shouted from across the floor.

"After that, Topper came in almost every day. He was conservative and didn't shout obscenities or catcalls. He was clean-shaven, no visible tattoos, tall, well-dressed, and respectful. His name was David Topingham.

"Topper told me he was a car salesman. I found out later, from one of his friends, that he was gifted. Topper was the number one Chevy sales rep in the country.

"'He can make any man open his wallet or make any girl open her legs,' his friend said, and then he looked at me. 'Oh, sorry,' he said.

"Topper told me that while he was delivering a new Chevy, he was hit broadside by an out-of-control tractor trailer.

"'Brakes failed,' he said.

"His leg was crushed, and after six months in a hospital bed he was now driven around by his friends. He had a medical disability. His buddies played pool, and Topper watched me dance. He wasn't a big drinker, he was gentle, and he was easy to talk with. I spent hours with him between sets. He asked me to join him for dinner one night, and I said *yes*. We had a wonderful evening. I told him about my horrible past, and he told me about his wonderful childhood.

"Even back then, I realized that Topper had a mesmerizing power over me. I began to think he could convince me to do anything.

"A month after we met, he had another surgery. I moved in with him to help him during recovery. He became hooked right before my eyes. His pain meds were taking over, and he couldn't get enough. The doctors started him on semi-synthetic opioids. Oxycodone and hydrocodone. After the surgery, he would wake up in the night screaming in pain. He started having nightmares. The doctors discussed reducing his dose, but instead, over time, they ramped it up.

"One of his friends helped him score substitutes on the street. He found the cheapest and most readily-available fix. Topper became a heroin addict.

"The heroin calmed him down, but I knew it was only a matter of time before he became a slave. I begged him to stop before it was too late, but he couldn't put the needle down. He wanted me to join him. Misery loves company. After a while I said *yes*.

"I stopped fighting and let him shoot me up, too. We had high points and low points, but our life was never the same. His supply was endless. I just stopped going to the club. The time we were together was like a vibrant, violent, scary movie. It was so, so sad. He lived in a nice place. We had music, and movies, and went out to the best restaurants. He bought me outrageous outfits, and I felt like a star. We had all the drugs we wanted. I will never forget the time I spent with Topper.

"During a high point, the two of us took a trip here to San Diego. He liked my Aunt Carrie. She liked him. Topper loved San Diego. He couldn't get over the warm weather, the beaches, and the boardwalk. He wanted to move here. He could easily get a job at any dealership in San Diego.

"As his drugs started to spiral out of control, he never had the energy to pack up and move.

"In the beginning, I thought we would live together forever. He was the only man I ever loved. But I really didn't know if I loved him or his free drugs.

"I went to see my social worker, Danny Gee. I respected her more than anyone I ever met. I told her about my relationship with Topper. She listened and then told me what I already knew.

"Danny Gee said, 'You are prostituting yourself by accepting his free drugs.'

"I never called Danny Gee again. I never answered her calls. I didn't even read the letter she sent me.

"After that, as Topper became totally hooked, everything changed. He lost weight. He stopped showering. He only cared for his needle. I tried to stay away from him. His free drugs were a magnet.

"We finally drifted apart, and I went back to dancing. One night the club was raided, again. I got busted, again. I went to jail, again.

"I have not seen Topper since.

"But, here's the bad part, Jesse. It's the sad part of the story. The scary part. You will hate this part, and I am sorry to even talk about this."

"I want to know what keeps you awake at night," I say.

"You want the truth?"

"Nothing but."

"If Topper walked into my life today, I think I would run to him. I know I wouldn't be able to resist. I wouldn't be able to help myself. He had a power over me. His eyes would penetrate my soul. He would smile, and I would crumble. I don't think I could say no to Topper. I couldn't say no to his drugs. If he offered me a needle, I think I would take it. I would give up everything I have with you for five minutes of blackness with him.

"I'm sure this thought scares you. It sure as hell scares me. But I believe that I am powerless over Topper. I am so sorry to burden you with this, Jesse. I do love you. You and I are best friends, but he was my master. I was his slave. You wanted the truth, but sometimes the truth hurts.

"But," she says, "I don't think that Topper will ever make it to San Diego. He is probably dead now.

"I am so sorry, Jesse, but you wanted the truth."

83.

THE SIGN IN THE AIRPORT SAID, "It's Vegas, Baby!" Because of the laid-back marriage laws, Blossom was now married to the man of her dreams.

After a three-day honeymoon, Jeb and Blossom jumped into their business. Blossom led the way and dove in head first. She had a motivational meeting with the staff. Everyone who stayed with the company got a small raise. She talked about the need for improved product, presentation, and personality. Parking lots would be policed, floors would be vacuumed, and counters would be wiped. And no one would ever sit on a serving counter. Ever.

Blossom had the energy that Jeb lost. She called an electrical contractor and ordered motion-sensitive lighting to be installed all around the buildings. She increased visibility, music, and staff in all locations. She developed an advertising promotion.

"You can't keep us down!" was her new message. She implied that someone was targeting them. They were the underdogs. Everyone loves an underdog.

Blossom met with a graphic designer. The ads they produced pointed out that the restaurants had the same great food but new energy.

"Come on in and become a customer again."

She called a local news station and scheduled a series of press conferences.

Jeb was astonished, but, all of a sudden, with her energy, he could see the light. They both could see the end of the tunnel.

84.

DEAR DIARY_____:

I miss Jeb so much, but he dumped me! Just like every other man I have ever been with. I am beginning to punish him. Slow and steady. Just like he punished me. I could have just killed him. That would be easy. I have done it before, but he deserves more. I have to be more creative. I want to hurt him, slowly. I will hurt him in a place where it really makes a dent in his life.

Instead of killing him, I am killing his business!

85.

FIG SETS UP ANOTHER CONFERENCE CALL for me with Chief Charles Upton.

Upchuck is well aware of the killings and the lack of progress. He says he is optimistic for a fast solution, but his voice is shaky. Since I haven't met him, I just listen. My friend, Fig, is a good cop and digs in.

"Upchuck you don't sound too confident. What's on your mind?" he asks.

"I'll tell you what, mister! I have to confess something: This girl, or guy, whoever, that does these dirty deeds is a mystery person. The killings are done right in the front of security cameras. This person is one rotten tomato. We have all watched the videotape a hundred times, but guess what? Facial recognition software is absolutely dead in the water."

"What do you mean?"

"We can't figure this one out, mister. We can't identify a thing. Never seen anything like it. I'm sure it's just a fluke, but there is always something in the way."

"Like?"

"The software is supposed to measure distance between the eyes, width of the nose, and the shape of the cheekbones. All that crap.

There was facial hair that doesn't match anything we have on record. Also, we can't match any of the images of the killer or killers to any social media, licensing bureau, or housing databases."

"You can't even match the photo to Facebook? What's up with that?"

"Check this out, Mister," he says. "We are scratching our heads up here!"

86.

As time goes on, Flower continues to share concerns about her sister. She and I spend even more time together. I think we are like lost souls trying to be found. We are going through a dark tunnel looking for the light. Making small motions but no waves. Not knowing what to do. Doing nothing. Doing everything. We have a lot in common.

We go to meetings. We grill hamburgers on my deck. We take Mia to Dog Beach and watch her chase the waves.

We hold hands all the time, but that's all we hold.

There is a lot of chatter in the recovery halls about the next AA "Round Up." It's a massive get-together. A sober weekend in San Francisco. Many of our friends plan to make the trip. Since we are two lost souls who are trying to be found, we plan to go, too. Over a thousand people will be at the final dinner.

I reserve a poolside room at the Handlery Hotel in Union Square. I specifically request two beds. Flower and I never talk about the rooming issue. We are adults. We can share a room.

After an early-morning flight from San Diego, we check into our room. I am a little concerned. There is only one bed. Neither of us makes a comment. Instead, we walk out on our little balcony and stare at this amazing in-town marvel. All rooms along the outside perimeter of the property face into a small pool that has been squeezed into a central courtyard.

There is so much to see in San Francisco, and we do it all. The weather is refreshing, and there is a delightful breeze. We take a trolley ride, and we see the Golden Gate Bridge. We grab lunch at Fisherman's Wharf, and we watch the sea lions.

I keep thinking about the double bed we will share tonight. I decide to order a rollaway from housekeeping, but I put it off. Back at the room, we shower and play dress-up in our evening outfits.

Flower looks amazing in her skimpy, low-cut, short, backless gown. I have never seen her in high heels, and I am amazed at how picture-perfect her long legs are. One simple string of white pearls and plain white earrings make her skin glow. She is more effervescent and gorgeous than I have ever noticed. She is confident and flashes a huge smile.

In her past life, Flower worked on a stage wearing platform high heels, a micro-short skirt, and a scandalous tank top. Tonight, she could grace the cover of *Vogue* magazine as a radiant, refined debutante.

I am in a dark-blue blazer, tan slacks, and polished dress shoes. I look very plain and totally unspectacular next to this beauty.

The main event is an impressive, magical experience. With over a thousand people in attendance, we truly believe we are not alone in our addiction. We sit with our friends from San Diego and are overwhelmed by the energy of the crowd. The guest speakers are real people who tell their story about a heartbreaking disease and a miraculous recovery. They share their pain, their decision to change the direction of their downward spiral, and the constant diligence it takes to continue on this path. They talk with love, encouragement, and humor.

It's a subdued, soft-pink evening in San Francisco, but we each have a bright, Madras attitude. We can feel the excitement in the air. Taxis, trolleys, and tourists all move in different directions at the same time.

Instead of taking a cab, we meander back to our hotel. She takes my hand.

"We only have one bed," I say.

"Gee, I didn't know you could count that high." She giggles.

"I need to order a rollaway."

"Are you expecting someone to stay with us?"

"I can't sleep in that bed with you."

"And why is that?"

"Too small."

"We have the largest king-size bed in the world."

"I will probably just fall asleep."

"Like hell you will. What else you got?"

"When we met, you told me you couldn't sleep with me."

"I lied."

"You're too young for me."

"You're not too old for me."

"I'm too small."

"Good things come in small packages."

"I'm a one-woman man."

"You don't have a woman. Your wife left you."

"We're from different walks of life."

"It's okay. At least we can walk."

"After my accident, I don't think I can . . ."

"Oh, yes you can. Don't you think we can be lovers?"

"Oh no! We can't fall in love."

"Why is that?"

"If we fell in love, it would be nice for about two weeks, but then you would find out I am a jerk. You would kick me out. I would start drinking. Then I would lose my job. I would live under a bridge. I would starve to death."

"I already know you're a jerk, and you don't have a job. We should be lovers."

"Like kissing and stuff?"

She sings, "I wanna kiss you all over. And over again. I wanna kiss you all over. Till the night closes in."

She stops and looks at me.

"But if you don't think we should be lovers, would you at least give me a trial kiss?"

"What's a trial kiss?"

"A test to evaluate our suitability."

"Our what?"

"Just want to see if our lips fit together. You know, like when you buy a pair of shoes. You try them on first, right? I want a trial kiss to see if it's really worth the effort of getting all involved with you. I want to see if our lips fit."

She reaches up and gently puts her lips on mine. It is a very quick kiss, but there is an explosion. An electrical connection. Fireworks.

"They fit! Our lips fit!" she shouts. She jumps up and down. "Oh boy, this will be great!"

I am shocked and pull back.

She reaches up, kisses me again, and her tongue slides in.

She smiles.

"Just a little more of a formal examination." She smiles at me.

"See. Now that wasn't too painful. Was it? Let's go to our room. We should be lovers. Or if you don't want to be lovers, then would you at least just do one little favor for me?"

"What's that?"

"When we get to our room, please undress me, tuck me in, and give me another trial kiss."

Our first real kiss happens in the lobby of the hotel. The desk clerk just stares. Flower lets me take a breath, and I gasp for air. She then grabs my tie and leads me like a pony. The next real kiss is on the elevator. It continues in the hall as we walk to our room. As I unlock the door, our kiss becomes more of a commitment. Before the door even slams behind us, our lips lock together.

Her kiss is warm. Like marshmallows from a campfire. It's cool, like cream-cheese frosting right from the beater. It's slippery like Jell-O shots.

I hear quiet background music playing in the room, but pyrotechnics are exploding in my brain. We start slowly, each pulling back. Teasing. Then our tongues go to work. Darting back and forth. In and out. Then finally we almost choke each other. The real kiss lasts forever without a breath. It is soft and slow. It is hard and fast. It is heavy and needy. We are playing a game. We both win.

Our hands are holding each other's heads. I am afraid to be too pushy. I am afraid to be too pliable. The temperature in the room is chilly, but we are both sweating.

We undress each other at the same time. I gently undo zippers, clasps, and snaps. She ferociously tugs, rips, and jerks. My zipper is wrenched down. Shoes and socks are yanked off. My shirt buttons are popped.

"Maybe we should look at the pool first," I say. I start to walk out on our little deck. She pulls me back into the room.

"The pool will be there in the morning!"

We fall on the bed but then slide onto the floor. A table is pushed out of the way, and a hassock is kicked over.

I get greedy, needy, and pushy.

We make love on the hotel room floor for what seems like forever.

"I have no idea who you are," she says.

"I am the same Jack in the Box I have always been. This is the first time I have been wound up."

We crawl to the bathroom and fill the gigantic Jacuzzi tub. She dives in first and pulls me after. She holds my head under water. If I drown with her tonight, it would be fine. I am ready for whatever happens. We make love in the tub. Energizing bubbles magically rise up under me. The massaging action keeps me strong.

Then she races me back to the bed. We are both soaking wet, but it doesn't matter.

At 4am, I get up, use the bathroom, and brush my teeth.

She gets up and uses the bathroom, too.

Back in bed I whisper, "I am so sore."

"Too sore for more?"

"Well, not that sore."

Her head goes down, and she kisses me for a long time. When I explode, my back arches up and my hands squeeze her shoulders. Every muscle in my body is hot, white, and strong. Then every muscle goes limp. She curls up in my arms, and we go back to sleep.

When we finally come back to life, it is daylight. We gasp in horror. Our hotel room is a catastrophe. Clothes are strewn all over the room. Underwear is hanging from a pole lamp. Pillows are on the floor, furniture has been moved. A small end table is on its side.

"Flower. I really like you!"

"I'm crazy about you, Jesse!" she says.

87.

AFTER OUR SAN FRANCISCO TRIP, FLOWER, Mia, and I are inseparable. For the next three months, everything in our world is right.

"You were talking in your sleep last night," she says.

"What did I say?"

"You kept saying I love you. Over and over."

"Really?"

"For a while I thought you were saying my name. You know, like,
'I love you, Flower.'"

"But . . ."

"You were saying, 'I love you, Fig.'"

I try to hit her. She catches my hand, and we hug. Then we fall
on the couch. Then we are practicing our kiss again.

I've ordered in-home delivery from our favorite Italian restaurant.
Spaghetti with meat sauce. We will decide on a movie and just stay
in for the night.

After we pay for our delivery, she looks at me with her big eyes.
She asks a question.

"Would you mind if I slip into something more comfortable?"

"Of course not."

She comes out of my bedroom totally naked.

"I have another secret I should share." She is president of the Secret Keepers Club. "I love to be naked. Some people might call me a nudist. Some would say I prefer the commando lifestyle. I simply say I love to be bare-ass."

I look at this free spirit. Just when I think I know everything about her, there is always another surprise. Last week, I saw her naked in our San Francisco hotel room, but it was dark and I was busy.

Now, this full-frontal display is different. She is not being sexual or sensual. She is being natural. Comfortable in her own skin. She is beautiful with her clothes on, but this is almost a spiritual experience. Her nudity is a matter-of-fact thing. She places napkins on the coffee table, opens the take-out packages, and spoons our pasta into big bowls.

"Want some parm cheese?" she asks.

She sits in the rocking chair in front of me and says, "Dig in."

Nothing is strange. Nothing is unusual. Aren't most people naked when they eat spaghetti?

"How long have you been going around naked?"

"Actually, I was naked when I was born. You can ask Aunt Carrie. She was there."

"I mean how often are you naked these days?"

"I am always naked under my clothes."

I am not making progress. I can't get answers to my questions. I don't even know what my questions are.

She is so normal, and I am the jerk. Again.

"Mia will love to lick these plates." She places them on the floor.

We watch a movie, but I cannot concentrate. We are on the couch, and she is undressed. Her hand is resting on my lap. I look at her more than at the movie.

"I just noticed something," I say. "You don't have any tan lines."

"My favorite beach is Blacks," she says. "Have you ever been there?"

"I know where it is. I have viewed it from the top of the cliff, but I have never made the trip down to the beach."

"Let's go tomorrow!"

"A nude beach? Really?"

"Not nude, silly. It's C/O"

"What's C/O?"

"Clothing Optional."

"So I can leave my hat on?"

She smiles.

I can do this, I think to myself. *I am cool. I am a cosmopolitan man. I can fit in.*

We head to La Jolla. There is a Glider Port at the top of a huge cliff that leads to the second largest nude beach in the country. It's called Blacks Beach.

"The walk down the cliff is really steep for a normal man," she says. "Since you are challenged, it may take all day." It is a joke, but I have trouble laughing.

"How long is the walk?"

"Only five hundred-fifty steps down. About two hundred are actually wooden stairs, and the rest are rocks."

When we get to the beach, she strips. I am so self-conscious that I keep my shorts on. She doesn't care or even notice.

We pass a very obese man. His belly is down to his mid thighs.

"That man has no penis," she quietly comments. We laugh.

It seems that most people here are real. We see the guys who probably order extra fries with their burger. We see the women who probably have candy wrappers stuffed under their car seat.

But, we also see men and women who are beautiful. Trim, tan, active, and natural. We watch a volleyball game with near-professional players. Everything is normal except the outfits. There are none.

"There is only one perfect ten on this whole beach."

"Who?"

"You." I smile at Flower as I take my shorts off.

"I love you, Flower."

"I love you, too, Jesse."

88.

WE GO THROUGH A COLORFUL, CALM, satisfying period in our lives. We are on the same wavelength. The same page. We seem to know what each other's needs are, and we instinctively know how to satisfy those needs. My very existence, for the first time in my life, is easy. I am happy, and I think Flower is happy, too.

I will remember these days as the most peaceful time in my life.

89.

I walk into Jaspers.

"She's gone!" Jamie says.

"Who's gone?"

"Flower's gone!"

"Did she go to the bank?"

"No, she's gone!"

Jamie, the waitress, starts crying.

"Gone? Where? What are you talking about, Jamie?"

"Just walked out with some guy!"

"What? Who? What are you talking about?" I ask again. "Slow down, Jamie. What's wrong?"

There is a long silence. "Jamie?"

She cries.

"She walked out with some tall, shitty, shifty, slippery city-slicker. An asshole jerk. A real no-count. Never saw him before. Definitely not from California. Flashy, fidgety, edgy, jittery. He kept looking into her eyes. She was surprised to see him. She definitely knew him, though. When he walked in, she ran to him and gave him a big hug. Like her best friend in the world. Or lover. Oh, I'm sorry. I shouldn't have said that. But a big, big hug. And then the kiss. Went on forever. She was holding on tight. One foot up in the air, bending her knee. Like in the movies. Whispering, laughing, looking into each other's eyes. Made me sick!

"They sat in the window seat." Jamie cries. "Your favorite seat. He talked and talked. I couldn't hear what he was saying, but he never shut up. Just kept talking. Fucking motor mouth, if you ask me. Oh, I'm sorry for swearing. He was offering something, and she was onboard, hook, line, and sinker. Holding his hand. She was staring into his eyes. I have never seen her look at anyone so intently. She was mesmerized.

"He kept trying to give her something, and she kept pushing it away. Kept shaking her head. Like, saying, 'No, no, no,' but smiling at him the whole time.

"Jesse, I kept hoping you would come in," Jamie said. "You know, like Superman. Here to save the day. Flower kept looking at the door. Maybe she wanted you to come in, too.

"The whole time, he was trying to give her something. She kept shaking her head. Then he reached out and held her hand, and she didn't pull it away. He definitely put something in her hand. A pill, maybe. She tipped her head back, put it in her mouth, and downed a glass of water.

"Ten minutes later, they walked out holding hands. He was leading. She was following. She said she would be gone for awhile."

Jamie starts crying again. "What's happening?" she asks.

I go to Aunt Carrie's house, and she is in tears. Broken-hearted. Crying. "It's my fault," she says. "He just came in. Out of the blue. We had met before, years ago, and I liked him then, but this time he was different. Not the same person. He asked where Flower was. I made a mistake: I told him."

"What was the guy's name?"

"Something stupid. Maybe a nickname. Top Hat, I think. That's all I remember."

I go to Flower's little house, and it's totally locked up. I see one little night light in a hallway. A radio is softly playing. I bang on the door. I kick at a storm window. I yell at the top of my lungs.

I call Fig. "I think she is in there, and I'm worried that something bad has happened," I say.

Fig orders a "Wellness Check."

Within minutes, there are three police cars and an EMT vehicle blocking the street. Seven uniforms have shown up. Fig shows up, too.

The police break in. Forcefully. The door and lock are smashed. Flower staggers out of her bedroom wearing a very small v-neck t-shirt. She is tugging on the front of the shirt to cover her crotch, but it's not working. She is dizzy. Walking unevenly. Leaning against the wall. Smiling as if nothing is wrong. Inquisitive as to why all these people are in her living room.

There is no eye contact. She doesn't seem to recognize Fig, and she doesn't acknowledge me. She is very confused and has trouble standing up. She holds on to the back of a chair to help with balance.

"Hi guys," she says. "Come on in." As if this is a cocktail party.

"Put some pants on, Flower."

She looks at me as if I am a stranger. Then she looks down.

"Oh. Okay." She stares at me with a quizzical look.

As she walks away, she is tugging the front of her t-shirt down to her knees, but the back rides up to her waist. Three policeman go in to watch her get dressed.

"Hey guys," I shout. "I appreciate that you are here to help, but can you please give the lady some privacy?" Even at this terrible time, I realize how much I care for her.

The EMTs ask lots of questions, but since she refuses treatment they have no authority; they pack up and leave.

Fig and I know the story. Topper gave her an Oxy, or a Perc in the restaurant. She went with him for something else. My guess is he gave her a roofie. A Flunitrazepam. They are not approved in the United States but are available in fifty other countries. It's like a Benzo on drugs. It's used as a pre-anesthetic.

We take Flower to Aunt Carrie's and leave her there. She passes out on the couch. I head back to Jaspers.

Jamie, the waitress, is in the middle of the kitchen. She is not working. She is sitting on a black-plastic milk crate, and she is crying. She tells me she is sorry, but she knows were Topper works.

"Where is he, Jamie?"

"He gave me a business card. In all the confusion, I forgot."

She reaches in her apron pocket. He works at a Chevrolet Dealership in town.

"He told me to call him the next time I need wheels."

I call Fig. "He moved out here, got a job, and then went to find Flower."

90.

WHEN I SEE FLOWER THE NEXT morning, she is sick. Retching, dizzy, sweating, and full of remorse. She tries to gives me a hug, but it is very awkward.

Aunt Carrie leaves us alone. Flower sits and stares for a long time.

"Topper walked into Jaspers out of nowhere. He sat right there in the big booth and told me how much he missed me. He told me he loved me. Then he talked about this new designer experience. A drug called Flakka or something. He said I had to try it just once. 'It's not addictive,' he lied. He said this would change my life. It would calm me down, build me up, give me strength and a new feeling of peace."

"Remember what I told you about Topper?" she says. "I told you he could sell me anything. He has an unnatural power over me.

"He begged me to take a Perc, right there in Jaspers. After an hour of talking, I finally said *okay*. I kept hoping you would walk in, but you didn't walk in. You didn't come to save me, Jesse. Damn you! God damn you." She pounds on my chest with both hands, then drops to the floor, sobbing.

After crying for a long time, she continues her story. Almost whispering.

"Back in my house, he gave me this Flakka thing. I became paranoid and delusional. I had no frame of reference. It was the strongest dose of anything I have ever had. It hit me instantly. I felt so happy. I felt so sad. I felt so strong. I thought I could lift a car, but I could barely stand on my own two feet. I was flying high and baseline calm. I was blissful, and I was groggy. I was standing on the ground, but I wanted to leave the planet. I was standing still, but my mind was moving in five different directions at once.

"Jesse." She starts to cry. "I love you so much. More than anyone in the world. But this guy has a perverted, transcendent, scary power over me. He always has. He is the devil. He makes me dizzy. Maybe it was a flashback of our time together. Or of our drugs. The ups and downs.

"Now, my recovery is gone. All the time I spent in meetings. All the time I worked on my program. All gone," she says. "All the long talks with my sponsor. Gone! All the steps. All my friends. Gone. All out the window.

"Most of all, I will probably lose you. The only person who matters. You will probably go. How could you possibly stay with me after all this?

"That bastard! I hate him. I hate him. I hate him," she says. Her fists pound down on the kitchen table over and over. "Don't let me be with him again. Please. Don't let me see him. I beg you; please don't let him touch me."

I feel like we are in a scene from Porgy and Bess.

After a long silence, she stares, trancelike, and mumbles.

"There's more," she says. I can barely hear her. She looks past me, and she breaks down again. Choking, sobbing, gasping for breath.

"I was blacked out, Jesse. You gotta understand. I was out of it. Totally gone. Please don't hate me. I don't remember a thing.

"When it was over, Topper said, 'You are a star.'"

"What are you talking about?" I ask.

"He pointed to a tripod. He was so proud of himself. He took videos of us having sex. He showed me part of it. I was so sick. I ran to the bathroom and puked my guts out. I pushed him and beat on his chest, but I was too weak. He told me he has the whole video on his cell phone.

"He is going to blackmail me, Jesse. He wants me to steal money from Jaspers! He wants me to steal money from my aunt. He wants five hundred dollars a week, or he will show the videos to her. He will show his phone videos to my Aunt Carrie."

There is a long silence.

"Aunt Carrie knows about my past, and she has helped me change. She worked hard and watched me transform into a new person. She loves me! Now this will just break her heart. I can't do this to her."

She cries. "Topper is just crazy enough to tell her. He is slimy enough to show her his phone video. He is sick. He is despicable.

"He is like a skunk in an elevator. Everyone knows that he stinks, but he can't smell his own shit.

"I want to kill him.

"If I can't do that, I will kill myself."

91.

FIG GIVES ME THE NEWS. "FLAKKA is a newer generation of bath salts. Who the hell would ever think of taking bath salts? He scrunches his eyes. "They are synthetic, psychoactive drugs made in foreign labs. Related to something called cathinones, whatever that is."

He picks up a tattered piece of lined, yellow notepaper and starts reading. "'Flakka causes bizarre, dreamlike behavior, and then jolting, disturbing paranoia and delusions.' Word in the lab is that Flakka is a combination of heroin and methamphetamine. Oh yeah, it also includes a healthy dose of Rohypnol. That's the date-rape drug. It's odorless and colorless. You don't even know you've had it till after you've had it. Then it's too late. You are fucked. Literally.

"'Withdrawal will kick in in a day or two after the last dose,'" he reads. "'It will include extreme agitation, jerking muscles, involuntary movements, and paranoia.' And she will be sicker than has ever been in her life. For weeks.

"And here's the bad part. This stuff is so addictive that she will do everything in her power to get more. She will give up her health. She will give up her job. She will give up her relationships. She will give up you!"

He puts the notebook page back on his desk. Then he picks it up and crumples it into a ball. He tosses it toward the trash. Two points.

Flower is faint. She is nodding out, and her head is bobbing. Her chin is on her chest. Then she lifts her head and smiles.

"I'm okay." She looks up and says, "Everything is cool."

Then she stands up and runs to the bathroom. There are five minutes of retching and dry heaving.

When she comes back, she is dizzy. She fades out. She falls onto the couch, and her eyes roll back in her head. Her eyes are glassy. Her nose is running. Every two minutes, her gaze seems to glide in and out of consciousness.

"We better get her into a detox before the shit hits."

Fig makes a call, and we drop her off at the same detox I went to, years ago.

92.

FIG HAS A LUKEWARM BEER. I have a lukewarm coffee.

When I am pissed, my face scrunches up. I don't notice a change, but everyone else does.

"Don't blame yourself," Fig says.

I hyperventilate. "That fucking bastard! He took advantage of her," I say. "But guess what? He gave her drugs, but that's not a crime we can prove. There is nothing to hold him on. He is free. If he keeps going back to her, she will OD or kill herself! Or kill him."

"Yup."

"I really like her, Fig," I say, "but I am helpless!"

I look at my friend, a career cop who has seen it all.

"Fig. I have made a life-changing decision. This may be my worst decision, or it may be my best decision. You are my friend, so I will tell you.

"I have decided to commit murder!"

My friend's eyes open wide, and he stares at me.

"I still have my service revolver," I continue. "I am going to find this guy, Topper, and I am going to kill him. Then, you, Fig, my best friend, will have to arrest me. I will spend the rest of my life in jail, but it will be the best gift I can give to Flower. There is no other option."

Fig stares at me and takes a sip of his beer. "Maybe there is another option," he says. "I need to make a phone call. Might take a day or two to connect. Don't do anything stupid.

"In the meantime, I want you to talk to this psychotherapist. She has a good reputation and can help you with your issue."

"What's my issue?"

"She will think of something!"

He flips a business card to me. The name on the card is Becka Black.

93.

BECKA BLACK IS ABOUT FIFTY. SHE is average height and weight. Her hair, however, is not average. She has had one side of her head shaved down to her scalp, and the other side is long and hangs down to her shoulder. On a model, it would be a fashion statement. On a psychotherapist, it eliminates all hope for respect and confidence.

"So," she smiles. "Why are you here?"

"My girlfriend was taken advantage of by a guy from her past," I say.

"How do you feel about that?" the psychotherapist asks.

"I hate that question," I say. "If I knew how I felt about this, I wouldn't be paying you a hundred bucks an hour."

"Oh, sir. Please control your irritation. Let me ask another question. How long do you think she has been seeing this other gentleman?"

"Forever. And he is not a gentleman! He is the scum of the earth."

"Well, at least we know how you feel." She laughs. I don't laugh with her.

"And how long has this issue been challenging your peace of mind?"

"Two weeks."

"How do you feel about that?"

"I'm sorry. I can't sit here for an hour." I start to get up.

"Same price."

"You are jeopardizing my serenity."

"Do I detect hostility?"

"Does the word hostility mean the same thing as pissed off?"

"Tell me about the last time you saw her. The weather, what she was wearing, what music was playing in the background. The time of day."

"You want me to go through that shit again? I'm trying to bury it."

"When you bury your feelings, they are still alive, and they continue to kick."

"Let them kick."

"If you think your girlfriend is obsessed with another man, then why is she still with you?"

"Because I have a puppy."

"Sir?"

"That's my feeling."

"Is that your feeling, or is that a fact?"

"Feeling."

"Feelings are not facts."

"I have a right to my feelings."

"You have a right to your feelings, but you shouldn't use your feelings to attack someone else. Until they are facts."

"Here's a fact: This whole visit is a waste of my time."

I start to get up again.

"I can help you, but you have to help yourself."

"I can't help myself. That's why I came to see you. I am trying to stuff my feelings."

"How often do you have these feelings?"

"Every waking hour. And sometimes when I am not awake."

"Let's start with this premise. You have been through trauma. You are tortured. But I don't think you're crazy," she says.

"Why?"

"Because you are seeking counsel."

"I can't stop thinking about what she did," I say. "The things she did with this old boyfriend are drowning me. I keep going over and over the story. The picture in my head is bigger than life."

"Try this," she says. "Try to reduce the size of the picture in your head from the size of a billboard to the size of a postage stamp."

"Oh, yeah. Like that's going to work!" I get up again and start to walk out.

"Sir, would you like to make another appointment?"

"Don't call us. We'll call you."

I leave the therapist's office, but I am worse than I was before. Shrapnel has exploded in my temporal lobe.

I focus on the crime. Was this a misdemeanor or a felony? Can there be a pardon?

It doesn't matter.

I have to find peace the old-fashioned way.

94.

THE STAR BAR IN SAN DIEGO'S Gas Lamp Quarter opened in 1972. The founder vowed that everyone would receive an honest drink for an honest price. This morning's honest drink is a shot of Jim Beam. The honest price is three dollars and twenty five cents

When the door is unlocked, I enter. I bark my order as I walk across the empty room. My shot of "Gentleman Jim" is on the bar before my ass hits the stool.

The short, tapered glass is heavy. The thick bottom gives the illusion that the drink may contain more liquid than it really does. It's all brilliance and bullshit. The sides of the glass are wet, either from the atmosphere, the dishwasher, or the bartender's fat, dirty fingers. There is a thin, round, paper coaster under my glass.

I put a five-dollar bill on the bar.

I notice the name "Anthony" sewn on the bartender's work shirt. There is no recognition, no eye contact, and no comment. He doesn't touch my five. He walks away.

At this early hour, I am the only customer in the Star Bar, but I am not a stranger here. There were times when I was asked to leave. Another time, I was carried out and dumped on the sidewalk. I have blacked out, passed out, and been punched out at the Star Bar.

The jukebox is quiet, and the TV is in closed-caption mode. The silence in this big room is bloodcurdling.

I hold on to my drink tightly. I squeeze the tiny glass with two fingers of my left hand. My right hand is useless. It was bandaged last night in the ER.

The love of my life went back to a guy from her past. More than that, the guy from her past gave her drugs. Again.

I am heartbroken. I like her so much. I love her. I want to take care of her, but it's out of my hands. I can't stop the gerbil wheel. Round and round. My mind is an asshole. What did I do wrong? I experience a level of powerlessness like never before. I am feeble. I am exploding with rage. I am petrified. My self-worth is non-existent. When you love someone who has an addiction, your emotions volley between honeymoon and hurricane.

I would like to find the guy from her past named Topper. I would like to tie him to a tree trunk with barbed wire and shoot his knee caps out. I would like to hang him by his fingers six inches over an alligator pit. I would like to stake him down on top of a fire-ant colony and pour honey on his balls.

The bartender walks by every few minutes, but he never stops at my station. He has not said one word to me, although I hear him talking with other customers. They chat about the weather, the special of the day, or the Padres game.

Three hours later, my shot glass is still full. Two fingers of my left hand are still holding on for dear life. I want to drink. I am afraid to drink. I need to give it up, but I'm afraid to let it go. My arm is sore, my back aches, and my fingers twitch. My mind is in the *off* position.

I am marinating my thoughts out loud to myself.

"Here's the deal," I say.

Anthony sees me talking to myself, turns around, and walks away.

"I am fucked," I say to no one.

"I am an alcoholic. I cannot have one drink without wanting the second drink. After that, there is no reason to count.

"One sip from this glass and I will be graveyard dead. Or I will wish that I was dead."

I get Anthony's attention and slide a twenty-dollar bill in his direction.

"Will you please do me two favors?"

He stares.

"Please pour this drink out, and please get rid of this shot glass."

Without comment, he pries the tiny glass from my fingers and pours the powerful, brown liquid down the drain. Then he slides the shot glass into a to-go box and drops it to the floor. He reaches under the bar and finds a hammer. He bends down and smashes the little glass over and over and over and over and over again.

"Hold on," Anthony says as he stands up. These are the first two words he has spoken to me all day. I don't know if this is a literal request, or a symbolic reference.

"Hold on," he says again.

He takes my five-dollar bill and my twenty-dollar bill off the bar and walks to the cash register. He throws my bills on the top shelf and comes back with a handful of ones. He slowly counts out twenty-five one-dollar bills.

"There is an afternoon meeting right around the corner," he says.

"It's at the big church." He points in the direction of the church.

"A lot of business people go. Truck drivers, secretaries, cops. Hookers, too. It's called the Coffee Break Group. Starts in fifteen minutes."

I run to the big church. I am sweating, and there is a dull screaming between my ears. I can't think. I don't want to think.

Tears are rolling down my cheeks.

"I got out alive," I say to myself.

People who don't drink can't understand this. People who are addicted just nod.

I am now sitting in an AA meeting waiting for my mood to change. I need to formulate my thoughts. I need to clear my head.

Someone comes in from the back door and sits next to me. It's the bartender from the Star Bar.

"Hi," he says. "My name is Anthony, and I'm an alcoholic."

I give him my left hand to shake.

He looks at the cast. "What happened to your right hand?"

"Wall."

The meeting starts, and today's topic is gratitude. I have none.

A guy in the front row starts the sharing.

"I started stealing booze from my father when I was thirteen. I never used drugs because they interfered with my drinking.

"I am grateful my wife has invited me to move back home. She told me that after I had six months under my belt, I could come home. Saturday was my six-month anniversary. Six months without a drop."

Everyone applauds.

"Congratulations!" someone shouts.

"Back in the big bed," someone else shouts. Everyone laughs.

A man in a grey suit speaks in a monotone. He stares forward. "I just got an update from the hospital," he says. "I am so grateful. It looks like everyone will be okay. The mom is still in ICU, but the kids are on the mend." He chokes.

"I don't even know what happened." He hangs his head. "I was having lunch with my buddy. Nothing unusual. Hell, we've had lunch at that place a thousand times. Maybe I had a few drinks, but no more than any other day. You can ask the bartender.

"The police will be asking the bartender.

"The mom was picking her kids up from school. The arresting officer said I must have blacked out just before I t-boned her car.

"I've already lost my job, and I will lose my license. My wrists are black-and-blue from cuffs. They've added resisting arrest to the charges. My attorney says there will be jail time. I will be living in the Graybar Hotel.

"But, thank God, the family will be okay. I am so happy that everyone survived."

He breaks down and cries. "I am so grateful!" he says.

A woman who is about thirty slowly raises her hand and speaks in a very low voice. Almost whispering. She is wearing a conservative black dress with a tan sweater draped over her shoulders. Her light-brown hair is short and neat. Her makeup is minimalistic. She is composed and well-spoken.

"I am so grateful that my daughter is back in my life."

She starts to cry. "She really didn't speak to me for almost two years.

"There was an upscale cocktail lounge in the lobby of my office building. As we left work every night, someone would invite us all to have one quick drink on the way home.

"I would call my daughter.

"'I'll be home about fifteen minutes late,' I would start to say, but she usually hung up. When I got home, hours later, the house was dark, and my daughter had locked herself in her room.

"In the morning, she would get herself off to school. I was either still in bed or vomiting into the toilet.

"I never knew if she had anything to eat. I would run to the kitchen and look in the sink for dishes. I would sort through the garbage looking for an empty frozen-dinner box.

"I just couldn't be there for my girl." She is fighting back the tears.

"Then, I got here. Then I got sober. You guys showed me how to go one day at a time without a drink. Everything in my life has changed.

"Last night, my daughter asked if we could talk. She climbed in bed with me. As she lay next to me, she just stared at my face and stroked my hair.

"My fourteen-year-old baby girl fell asleep in my arms.

"You have no idea how grateful I am."

95.

"Where the hell have you been?" Fig shouts. "I've been trying to find you for two days. What happened to your hand?"

He doesn't wait for an answer.

"You don't have to kill Topper."

"Why not?"

"I made a call. There is an option. I have an acquaintance," he says. "I've never told you about my acquaintance because I didn't think you would approve. But now, you might! Approve, that is."

"His name is Anatoli," he continues. "Think of your worst nightmare. Think of a two-hundred-pound gorilla with a shaved head, scars on his face, and a gold tooth. Think of a guy with half an ear missing. That's Anatoli."

"Why do I need to know this?"

"He fixes things."

"What kind of things?"

"Your kind of things!"

"He kills people?"

"Anatoli never kills anyone."

"So, what?"

"He fixes things."

"Fig. I am in pain here. You are playing word games. What the fuck are you talking about? Who is this guy? What does he do? Why do I care?"

"Anatoli fixes things. He is on a first-name basis with every drug dealer, Russian criminal, and club owner in the city. He knows the police, the judges, and people in the penal system. Anatoli usually charges an up-front fee for his services."

"What are his services?"

"He fixes things."

"Jesus Kee-riste!" I say.

"Here's the deal," he says. "Anatoli does the things that we, in the police business, can't do. He goes after the real sick bastards. The bastards the law can't touch. And he fixes things."

"Okay. I approve. But I don't know what you are talking about. Or who. Or why."

"Employees in our court system are overworked, underpaid, and crippled with bullshit laws," he says.

"Tell me about it!" I say.

"I will. I will tell you about it!

"Last year, we arrested a phony minister from a church that he called Heavenly Rewards. The pastor convinced thousands of God-fearing retirees to invest in his fellowship. He claimed that, since this was a religious organization, all transactions were safe and beyond reproach. He promised that stockholders would double their investment.

"The church floundered, but the good Reverend ended up with mansions, a jet, and a collection of rare, vintage automobiles.

"His Ponzi scheme bilked thousands of elderly families out of their entire life savings. Many of his victims filed for bankruptcy. A few committed suicide. Because of his religious stature, the minister couldn't be prosecuted. He walked.

"After the trial, we helped Anatoli find the preacher. We believe that the Reverend was hung upside-down for hours at a time. The skin around his ankles was ripped and shredded. His toes were all broken. His scalp was full of scabs. While the Reverend was with Anatoli, his properties were transferred to an international investment corporation. His classic, antique automobile collection disappeared. Cash was returned to investors, and no one complained about the ten-percent finder's fee. The minister lost everything, including his homes, his auto collection, and his family. He is now living in a state-run ward for the destitute. He has a constant tick and keeps jerking his head from left to right. When anyone new walks into his room, he starts cringing and shuddering. He can't sleep more than a few minutes at a time."

"I like it," I say.

"We recently tried to prosecute a pedophile who owned a private school for at-risk girls. After charging thousands of dollars a month for a high-school education, the pedophile befriended the most vulnerable. They got special privileges. Many of the girls went crazy, and some had to be sent to an institution. This case will be in the court for years. In the meantime, due to a minor technicality, the judge let the pedophile walk. He was back on the streets.

"We helped Anatoli find him.

"After three weeks in Anatoli's care, the pedophile was emotionally and physically broken. Every single bone in his right hand was crushed. He will never jerk off again. All of his bank accounts have been emptied. Anatoli's special team took ten percent. The pedophile is living under a bridge."

"I love it."

"Anatoli has broken many laws, but the reason I won't bust him is that sometimes there is a higher calling. He can do things outside the system that I can't do through proper channels. There are hundreds of cases where people who were guilty laughed their way out of court. Now they are not laughing. Anatoli owes me a favor," Fig said. "So, if you are interested, there will be no startup fee for you. Just the spoils of war."

"The spoils of what?"

"But only if you are interested."

"I am interested! I am interested! What am I interested in?"

"He has a team. A beautiful, young, Russian girl who is the best pickpocket in the world. A few lawyers, some accountants, and a very, very gifted computer technician. They have all been in Russian prisons and they have an unusual point of reference. They can incapacitate a car, empty a bank account, and hack a computer. And that's just for openers."

"All of this is legal?"

"Of course not!"

96.

TOPPER WAS A HERO. EVERYONE LOVES their drug dealer. Car sales were great, but Topper's real passion was building his drug empire. He had a predictable route, and his customers could count on him.

One of his weekly stops was an upscale gentleman's club. The dancers had become reliable, regular customers.

As he finished his business, a beautiful young dancer asked if she could buy him a drink. She had an inviting smile and a Russian accent.

"Of course," he said.

As the dancer started the small talk, she glided her hands along his shoulders. She looked up at him and smiled. They were almost within kissing distance. She rubbed his neck.

"Oh, that feels nice," he said.

"There's more where that came from."

She glided her left hand from his back down to his thighs and then his buttocks. She leaned in and rested her right hand an inch from his private parts. She teased him as her fingers gently clawed at his inner thigh.

"We are such a beautiful couple," she whispered. "Where's your phone? Let's take a selfie!"

After the picture, there was a tap on Topper's shoulder. He looked up to see a giant of a man with a shaved head, a gold tooth, and a scar.

"You take pictures of dancers?" The big guy yelled.

"No! No!"

"Cell phones not allowed! Pictures of dancers not allowed!" The giant grabbed Topper's cell phone and dropped it into his beer.

"Oops, sorry," the gorilla said.

Topper stood up to complain, but the Russian landed a powerful blow to his kidney. Topper doubled over. As he tried to stands up again, the Russian punched him in the face. He instantly lost two front teeth.

Topper was pushed backward. His head smashed on the cement floor. The Russian towered over him.

"I give you phone back, now," the big guy said.

The Russian raised the beer glass as high as he could, and poured the amber liquid onto Topper's face. The beer splashed into his eyes and, as the phone slid out of the glass, it landed on Topper's cheek bone, right under his eye.

"Oops. Sorry," the Russian said again. He kicked the phone a few inches away and crushed it under his gigantic boot.

The enormous man with the bald head dragged Topper to a side door and dumped him in an alley. When Topper tried to stand, he cried out in pain. His pants were bloody. His lip felt like it had been hit with an axe. His tongue found the space where two front teeth had been. He hurt so badly that death would be a blessing.

Topper was dizzy and could barely stand. He cried out in agony and had to literally crawl to his car. As he backed out of his parking space, he heard soft popping sounds. All four of his tires had been slashed. Topper reached for his wallet, but his pockets were empty.

When Topper finally got home, he reported his stolen credit card. He was told that his card had maxed out within the last hour. Not a penny was left. His checking account had been closed.

Topper heard pounding on his door. Uniformed men forced their way in.

"You selling drugs?"

One of them instantly reached into a kitchen cabinet and removed a small bag.

"They are not my drugs!" He was handcuffed and quickly booked on a federal drug-trafficking charge. As he was pushed from the house, he fell down the front steps. Since his hands were behind him, he landed on his face, breaking his nose.

After spending two nights in lockup, Topper was found in the prison shower. *Slipped on soap and cracked his skull* was the final ruling.

97.

MY GIRLFRIEND, FLOWER, SPENDS A WEEK in the same detox that saved my life. She also goes to The Last House on the Road for a month. When I pick her up, I get to see the director, Big Jim, again.

He remembers me.

"I'm glad you're still sober, Jesse," he says.

Before I can thank him, he offers a comment.

"You look like shit! Are you eating? Are you sleeping? Do you have any friends?"

"It's hard," I start to explain.

"Who the hell ever said it would be easy?" he asks. "Before you can pick up your girlfriend, I want you to sit in on a meeting. There is one starting in ten minutes."

Big Jim is right. I do look like shit. I feel like shit too. The meeting is good for me, and it helps me calm down.

I get Flower's suitcase, and we walk out to my car. She is still in a daze.

There is no need to tell her about Topper's strange disappearance. She doesn't need to know about Anatoli. She doesn't need to know what she doesn't need to know. My new favorite line.

I drop her off at her little house, and she wants to sleep. We make plans to go to an AA meeting later that evening.

A few hours later, when I get to her house, there is a note on her kitchen table. It's addressed to me.

My Dear Jesse.

I am so sorry for my disappointing activity with a man from my past. I am sorry this happened. I wish it didn't happen. But it did.

I am sorry I took his drugs. I am so sorry that I have let you down. But now, after a month of being clean, I want to go back to him.

No. That's not true.

I want to go back to his drug. I want to lose myself again. I cannot think of anything else.

I know where he works, and I will find him. If you can wait for me, I will be back. If not, I understand. This obsession is bigger than any feeling I have ever had.

I am going to find Topper and experience that drug one more time.

I do love you.

Flower

98.

I CALL MY AA SPONSOR. "JIGGER, I don't understand. Can you explain it?"

"Easy," he says. "When an alcoholic goes back to drinking, it's like making love to a gorilla. You're not finished until the gorilla says you are finished."

That was not the answer I wanted.

I call Libby.

"She left me!" I say. "I don't understand."

"Of course you don't understand."

"What?"

"You are a selfish, self-seeking, self-centered man. You can't think past your dick!"

"Libby?"

Libby is Fig's wife, but she is also my friend. She is the one who monitors my prescription refills. She's the one who gets me to the doctor for appointments.

"I don't understand how she could do this to me," I say again.

"You don't understand because you are only thinking about yourself. You have been hurt, you're full of fear, you're wondering what's going to happen to you. You! You! You! Don't you ever think about Flower?"

"What about Flower?"

"Have you ever put yourself in her shoes? What did those shoes feel like when her father beat her? What did they feel like on the day she ran away from home? How did those shoes feel when she danced on stage the first time? Just for a dollar bill? Just to survive?"

"Libby, I have never heard you talk like this."

"Well, maybe you should get your head out of your ass."

"Libby!"

"Jesse. She wasn't looking for a drug. She was looking for relief. Drugs were just the vehicle. Flower is a beautiful, classy, refined young woman, but she is also a scared, runny-nosed little brat. She is waiting for her father to come back and rescue her."

She looks at me and says, "The fifth habit in the book is 'Seek first to understand!' Go read it!"

99.

THREE DAYS LATER, FLOWER LEAVES A message, apologizing for her disappearing act. She says she has decided not to see her old boyfriend.

I am pissed. I am resentful. Resentments are the biggest cause of relapse. I am so full of resentments that I am going nuts. I think of a solution. I think of escape. I think of picking up.

100.

FIG TELLS ME TO CALL FLOWER. Libby wants me to call Flower. Aunt Carrie begs me to call Flower.

I feel like a fucking school kid. Everyone is telling me what to do. I am doing just fine without that girl in my life, thank you! Why would I ever want to open up those cuts and bruises? Am I stubborn? You bet! Am I pig-headed? Am I a pussy? Am I a jerk? Damn right!

I keep rationalizing her story. The part about Topper taking advantage of her? I understand that part. He walked into her life. Out of nowhere. She was a helpless victim. I get it.

But the other part is different. The part about her wanting to go back to him, to take his drugs, and to fuck him again. That's another story. I wake up ten times a night. The story goes around and around in my head. I think of the two of them together. Did he really take advantage of her, or did she love every single minute of it?

If she comes back to me, will it be because she wants me or because she can't find him? Will she think of him when we make love? Will she shout his name when she masturbates?

If I don't come to terms with this, I will be very, very dead.

I want to talk with her, but I shouldn't go into a negative conversation when I am already negative.

I call Jigger. Sometimes he makes me feel good. Other times he makes me realize that I am reckless, irritable, and discontent.

"I need to tell you a story," I say.

"Okay, let's take a ride."

We meet at a commuter parking lot. I jump in and start.

"I think I'm crazy."

He pulls to the side of the road and shuts the car off.

"We don't have to take a ride, Jesse. I already know that part."

"You know?"

"Since the day we met."

"What should I do?" I ask.

"You're fucked," he says.

"I think I want to drink!"

"Then you're really fucked."

"Can't you help me?"

"Doesn't work that way, buddy. But if you do drink, I'll come to your funeral. You know. Say a few words."

"Jigger!"

"But you will be stone-cold dead. So it won't matter what I say. I might just tell jokes."

I ignore him. "Something happened."

"Tell me a story. Tell me a long, long story."

I laugh at my sponsor. Jigger is a great guy. He has been sober for twenty years. When he was drinking, he went through the same stuff I am going through. He always has time to listen. He never tells me what to do. He never gives me advice. He only tells me his side of the story. If I can get something out of it, that's my gain. If not, it's my loss.

I am quiet for a long time.

"Jesse," he says. "I don't need to ride around with you if you're going to sit there and be quiet and stuff."

I punch him on the shoulder.

"This is so hard," I say.

"Hard as getting sober?" he asks.

I change the subject and ask him a question. "Was getting sober hard for you?"

"Getting sober was the second hardest thing I've ever done."

"What's the first?"

"Staying sober. Staying sober is the hardest thing I have ever done."

"Why?"

"Think about it. Getting sober is a short-term project. A few days or a few weeks. You get rid of the shakes, the pukes, and the shits. You keep a few meals under your belt and have a good night's sleep. All of a sudden, *boom*. You're sober.

"Staying sober is the hardest thing I have ever done," he says. "There's always a reason to reevaluate your decision. Your favorite team won the Super Bowl or didn't win the Super Bowl. There's a wedding celebration. Everyone else is drinking! A year later, the same couple has a divorce celebration. There is a birthday, a holiday, or a cookout. There's a funeral. Your next-door neighbor offers you a beer while you're cutting the lawn. The guy at work offers to buy you a cold one on the way home.

"Jesse, I can't help you get sober," he says. "I can't help you stay sober."

Instead, today, he gives me a priceless gift. He gives me his time.

"So what's the issue?" he asks.

"My girlfriend doesn't have a pure past."

"Did you have a pure past?"

"That doesn't matter."

"Oh. I get it. Different strokes. "

"I keep going over this stuff. My mind goes round and round," I say. "Like a gyroscope. She drives me crazy!"

"I don't think she wakes up in the morning and says, 'I am going to drive Jesse crazy today.' She does what she needs to do! You drive yourself crazy.

"Jesse," he says. "Take your finger out of the light socket! Stop encouraging the pain. Stop looking for chaos in your life. Instead of going over and over this thing she did a long time ago, make a list of the good things she does every day. Remember why you fell in love with her in the first place."

"I will try that, but I really think I'm going crazy."

"You may be going crazy, but you are not there yet."

"How close do you think I am?"

"I think you are one thought away from being crazy. Instead of blaming your mother, or your school, or the government, blame your ego."

"That's too simple."

"For me," he says, "It was my ego that caused me to be jealous of my wife. It is your ego that forces you to prove yourself, again. It's someone's ego that starts a war."

"Okay. Maybe I need to make some positive changes."

"Have you made any changes, yet?" he asks.

"I went to see a therapist."

"How did that go?"

"She asked me how I felt and charged me a hundred dollars."

"Will you go back?"

"Hell, no."

"See, you are already making positive changes."

101.

I IGNORE FLOWER'S CALL BUT LISTEN to her message.

"Jesse, I'd like to talk with you. Would you please call me?"

The next day, I ignore her call again, but I listen to her message again.

"Hi, Jesse. I called yesterday, but maybe you didn't get the message. Would you please give me a buzz? I miss you. I would like to talk. Thanks a lot."

Now who is begging? Ha. I feel like I am finally in control.

The next day, her message is a little different.

"Jesse. I want to take you to lunch. We will pick you up at eleven o'clock sharp. Not going to a fancy place, so you don't have to get all gussied up. But the place we are going to has your three favorite things. They all start with the letter *S*."

We? Who is we? I wonder.

S? What starts with S? I wonder.

She has my attention.

The next day, at 11am sharp, Flower is at my door. She looks amazing. A white micro-miniskirt with fringe, a white, embroidered blouse with snaps instead of buttons. A white cowboy hat and white, snip-toe western boots.

I am hooked. Again.

She bends over and pets Mia. It breaks the ice.

"Mia is happy to see you," I say.

"I am so happy to see Mia. And you! Well, are you ready, cowboy? We're here to get you."

"Who's we?"

She points out the window of my condo, and I see a limo driver standing at attention. He is next to a Chrysler 300 white stretch. He is holding the door open, and he waves.

"Where are we going?"

"For me to know," she says.

The trip to the Mountain View Beach Club only takes a few minutes. This is the trashiest joint in town. Right on the boardwalk. It's noisy, rowdy, filthy, and smelly. The food is overpriced, the beer is warm, the glasses are dirty, and the waitstaff is rude. When I was drinking, it was my favorite place. I love it.

As we approach the beach-side patio, I see Fig, Libby, Aunt Carrie, and a bunch of friends from the force. There are AA friends, too. There are pitchers of soda. There are hot dogs and nachos all spread out on a long wooden table.

Even though this is a weekday, there are plenty of scantily clad young ladies enjoying the weather.

"So what are my three favorite things that start with the letter S?" I ask.

"Sand, sun, and skin." She laughs.

I get warm welcome pats on the back from my friends. I get a very warm hug from Flower. Right in front of everyone. It starts as a therapeutic hug. It is kind, caring, and loving. It's an all-hands-on-deck, knock-your-socks-off, hold-on-tight, and don't-let-go kind of hug. It is a squeeze-the-air-out-of-each-other kind of hug. It's a keep-your-arms-tangled-around-me-forever kind of hug. We are alternately giggling and crying. She stops hugging long enough to back away, look at me, and then hug again.

Then we have a long trial kiss.

Our relationship is strained, but we have no claim on each other. We are just friends. Neither of us wants to change our status. It's amazing how well things work when we get our egos out of the way.

"Do you love me or hate me?" she asks later.

"The opposite of love is not hate," I reply. "The opposite of love is indifference. I will never be indifferent to you!"

She hugs me again.

I take her to an AA meeting, and she shares.

"It's not all lollipops and unicorns out there," she says. "The last month has been so bad. I couldn't even get up. I stared at the TV all day long. The TV wasn't even on."

Although her recovery friends are saddened by her relapse, no one even raises an eyebrow. They are glad she made it back from hell. They are glad she made it back alive. She resets her sobriety date. She now has one month of clean time. Progress, not perfection.

Flower and I hug hello. We kiss goodbye on the cheek. We have a different relationship than most couples have. We have recovery. We understand a huge life-concept: one day at a time. It's all we have. We are grateful for today, but understand we may never have a tomorrow.

Our recovery friends all understand this concept, and, because of their constant work to stay sober, they are the most touchy-feely people in the world.

102.

AFTER THE MEETING, WE SIT IN the car, and she starts crying.

"Jesse, I am so alone right now. I have you, but I have no one to talk with about deep stuff, life stuff, girl stuff. In my past there was a very special person who understood me more than I understood myself. Do you remember when I told you about my social worker in Massachusetts? She was a professional, but she was also my friend. My only real friend. She helped me so much."

"You told me about someone named Danny."

"You remembered! Her name was Danielle Giovanni, but everyone called her Danny Gee."

"That's what I said."

"You remembered!"

"I remembered because she seemed important to you."

She reaches out and squeezes my hand.

"Danny Gee was the only sober friend I had at that time. She always told me the truth. Sometimes I loved her. Sometimes I hated her. But she was always there for me. Now, here I am, so many years later. I am in AA, but something is missing. Obviously missing. I fucked up again. It's resentments! All about resentments. Resentments toward my father. Resentments toward my sister. Resentments toward my old boyfriend. All about resentments. I've become a resentment junky. I am a resentment monster. I'm walking around holding onto a red-hot coal, expecting someone else to get burned."

She turns and looks directly in my eyes.

"Did you ever cross paths with someone in your life you wish you could bring back for one day? One conversation? One hug? Danny Gee explained that we both suffered from childhood abandonment issues. I didn't even know what she was talking about.

"I wrote that term, *abandonment issues,* on the back of a Burger King receipt. I kept it on my dresser for a year. I looked it up a thousand times, but I still don't understand it. I would love to talk with her one more time, but I don't even know if she still works at that jail. I don't even know if she is still alive."

103.

NEW TECHNOLOGY WAS DESIGNED TO CUT costs and increase service. The part about increasing service is crap. Nobody is buying it. Service has decreased in all sectors of business by at least a thousand present.

I wade through endless voicemail messages, never-ending telephone prompts and choices. A recorded voice says, "Please listen carefully to all of the menu selections, blah, blah, blah."

I'm transferred from one department to another and talk with at least twenty rude, uninterested public servants who just want to get me off the phone. Get me out of their face.

I'm finally transferred to a friendly voice.

"Hello. This is Danny Gee," she says "How may I help you?" She is receptive, gracious, and warm. She sounds excited when I mention Flower.

"Where is she? What is she doing? Where does she work? Is she okay?"

Four questions at once.

When I say we live in California, Danny Gee remembers a family connection.

"Aunt Carrie?" she says. "A restaurant? Right?"

"You have a great memory," I say.

"Is she okay?" She might be waiting for bad news.

"She has changed so much since you knew her."

"Is she okay?"

"Good news and bad news," I say.

"Is she okay?" Danny Gee's voice sounds exasperated.

I tell Danny Gee about Flower's long sobriety and about the devastating relapse. I tell her about a guy named Topper.

"I remember that name. I told her to stop seeing him."

Then I change the subject and tell Danny Gee about Flower's wish.

"She is aching to see you again," I say.

There is a long silence.

"I would love to see her again, too! Of all the girls I ever worked with, I had the most meaningful relationship with Flower. I have thought about her so many times. She is a very special person. But how could I possibly see her? We live three thousand miles apart. I am here, and she is there."

"I would like to surprise Flower," I continue. "She needs some encouragement. She needs a bombshell. She needs a kick in the ass. Flower is so down on herself after her relapse. She needs a reaffirmation that she is a good person. She needs a friend. She needs your support.

"Danny Gee, will you please come to San Diego?"

"I would love to, but I just can't afford it. I simply cannot justify that kind of a trip."

"I have unused credit-card miles," I say. "Enough for a ticket. A round-trip ticket to San Diego. I would like to send you a ticket."

I can hear the wheels churning in her head from three thousand miles away.

"I have vacation time scheduled in two weeks and absolutely nothing to do."

"I would love to orchestrate a surprise," I say.

"I would love to be part of the surprise."

We talk for a while and plan a trip. I agree to FedEx the tickets.

We are almost finished, but she has a question.

"Does Flower ever talk about Sassy?"

"Who?"

After a pause, she retracts the question.

"Oh, never mind. It's nothing."

"Who is Sassy?" I ask again.

"Oh, no one. Never mind. Please ignore the question. I really look forward to meeting you."

"Okay, Danny Gee. I'll meet you at the gate."

As I hang up, this new name explodes inside me.

Who is Sassy? I wonder. Is this another one of Flower's secrets? Flower is the queen of secrets.

Maybe Sassy was a girl she danced with in a club, or maybe someone she met in jail.

Will this new name rent space in my head for twenty-four hours a day? I fight to let it go. I decide that I will not beat myself up with an invisible whip.

104.

I MEET DANNY GEE AT THE gate, and I instantly like her. As Flower had described, she is all of five-five. She is all of a hundred pounds. She is dressed in basic black. She is wearing a long-sleeved, black t-shirt, Her black jeans are tucked into her black, square-toe, buckaroo cowboy boots. She has a wide, black-leather belt with a huge brass buckle.

We arrive at Jaspers just as the lunch crowd is thinning out.

Flower sees Danny Gee and stops in her tracks. She stares. She looks at me and then at Danny Gee. She is confused. Her head rotates back and forth. She screams at the top of her lungs. Danny Gee screams, too. They run across the room and collide. They hug. They jump up and down. They act like best friends. They act like soul sisters. They act like little girls.

Restaurant patrons smile at this display of affection.

Flower can't figure out how this all worked, but for the moment, it doesn't matter.

We sit in the big booth in front of the picture window. Both girls are giddy. They talk about nothing. They talk about everything.

Danny Gee moves in with Flower for a week, and they become roommates. They visit Seaport Village. They have coffee in Old

Town. They sit on a bench at Mission Beach. They walk through the Gaslight Quarter.

They have lunch at a little café in Rancho Santa Fe.

We all get together for dinner each night.

After a week of one-on-one time with her mentor, Flower seems calmer, more confident, and more comfortable. On Danny's last night in town, we are all back at Jaspers, sitting at the big red booth.

Danny Gee reaches out and holds her friend's hand.

"Flower. There's something I've wanted to talk with you about since I got here. There is someone we should discuss. I have been waiting for the right time. I've been waiting for you to bring it up. But here we are now, on our last night together. I can't leave San Diego without asking.

"Do you ever think about Sassy?"

Flower looks like she was hit in the face. She shrieks as if she stepped on cut glass. She looks up to the ceiling. Maybe she is praying. Her head drops down to the table. She is quiet, but I think she's crying.

I don't know what's happening, so I force myself to be quiet, too. I thought Sassy might have been her cellmate in jail. Now I am really confused. And scared.

I stare at the two of them. Flower chokes and gags. She drops her head down again. She cries. I stay quiet.

Danny Gee is quiet, too. She reaches over and taps my hand.

When Flower finally speaks, she is trying to be strong. Her voice is scattered and shattered. Familiar emotions.

"I think of Sassy every day." She talks quietly. "I want to send her letters. I want to send Christmas gifts. I don't know where she is. I don't even know what state she is in. Do you know where she is?"

There is no answer.

"I can't even write to my daughter."

I sit up straight. I suddenly become wide-awake crazy. Aunt Carrie is shaken, too, but her eyes are wide open. She might be excited about the news. Her head is going back and forth between the two girls.

"I can't even send a birthday card," Flower continues. "I would love to find her, scoop her up in my arms, and bring her here to live with me, but I can't even take care of myself. How can I possibly take care of a little girl?"

"Where is she? Is she okay? Is her adoptive mother good to her? I have wanted to ask you about my baby, more than anything. I was afraid of your answer. Since my relapse, I just expect bad news. Better to not even ask."

I am blindsided.

Flower slows down and becomes composed. Strong again.

"I can't see my daughter, but I do what I can. I buy gifts for little girls at a homeless shelter. Sassy would be thirteen now, so I buy gifts for little girls who are about that age. I buy arts and crafts and books. The cards I include are always signed, 'From your friend, Sassy.'"

Now we are all crying.

"Flower," Danny Gee says. "Now that you are kicking the demons out of your life, I will share a story. Your daughter is adorable. She is healthy. She is a well-mannered, happy, young lady. She is tall for her age and trim. She has your eyes. Sassy takes ballet lessons and is on the soccer team. She plays the clarinet in a school band. She is also very smart. She gets great grades in school. When she was adopted, her new mom decided to let her keep the name you gave her. Her mom calls her Sassafras. Everyone else calls her Sassy."

Flower looks up again, and then starts sobbing again.

"Flower, Sassy is asking about her birth mother. She is too young to see you now, but her adoptive mother said that, when she turns eighteen, she can meet you. In the meantime, you can send gifts and notes to me, and I will forward them to her family. And I don't need to say this, but I will: I cannot tell you her last name, what school she goes to, or even what state she lives in. So please respect my position and don't ask.

"Here's the good news. If you stay sober, I will bring you all together. You can see Sassy in five short years. Save your pennies for a ticket."

People in the restaurant try not to stare at four adults who are holding hands and crying at the same time.

We take Danny Gee to the airport, and the goodbyes are beautiful and tearful.

In the car, Flower talks in a monotone.

"Jesse, I want to read this note to you.

"Not receiving psychological support equals abandonment. Abandonment creates toxic shame. Shame lingers from the messages I heard when I was a kid. The messages were: 'You are not important. You are not of value. You will never be good enough.'

"When my father beat me, he let me know that I was worthless. Danny Gee asked me to focus on positive things in my life. One positive thought a day.

"Wanna know my positive thought for today? It is that I know my daughter is in good hands, that she is safe, and that, someday, we will meet.

"Again."

105.

LATE ONE NIGHT, MIA SITS BETWEEN us and looks back and forth. She licks my fingers one at a time. Then she licks Flower's fingers one at a time.

Flower is dressed for comfort. She wears sweat pants, a hoodie, and oversized, fluffy sweat socks. Her hair is up in curlers. She looks terrific.

"I am so embarrassed," she cries. "I have had many relationships in my life. My relationship with you, Jesse, whatever it is, is the only relationship I ever cared about. I want us to be best friends. I want us to be more than that! But I've been screwed over by men. I can't believe guys. Every man I have ever known has been beautiful, but a lying sack of shit!"

"Well, I am ugly but honest."

She laughs, hits me, and gives me a hug.

Even though my mind is in race mode, this is a good time in our lives.

Flower and I spend our afternoons with Mia. Long walks are therapeutic. The weather on the beach is magnificent. Our life together is one-day-at-a-time, or one-minute-at-a-time, or one-decision-at-a-time. No agenda, no forced questions, no phony answers.

Folks in recovery have lots of friends and lots of fun. It seems there is at least one celebration every week. There are potlucks in someone's back yard, or cookouts on a deck. Sometimes there is a garage band playing songs we all know. We always take our King Charles. Mia is the hit of every party.

We gather with our friends after morning meetings. We squeeze together in front of the 101 Diner in Encinitas. Mia sits under the tiny table and enjoys pets from seven people at the same time.

After evening meetings, we meet for dinner. Twenty or thirty people invade a Chinese restaurant or an Italian pizza buffet. We laugh, shout, and act like fools, but no one ever orders a drink. Mia is happy to nap in the car while we socialize. Between the main course and the dessert, Flower and I walk hand-in-hand to the car. We put Mia on a leash, and we let her relieve herself. This new addition to our quasi-family brings us together. It is a spark that is igniting our damp fire.

Flower continues to work at Jasper's restaurant, and I continue to go as a customer.

She spends nights at my apartment, and I spend nights at her little house. Mia is usually in the middle. The three of us lie in a bed and hug for hours. None of us want this to end.

But I am not happy. I am not content. I can't stop my mind. My mind is an asshole. It is focused on the past.

I laugh at myself when I think how many hours I have spent going over something she said, or something she didn't say. I agonize over the amount of time I have wasted, wondering what really happened, or what didn't happen. I try to rephrase a response that I made, or a response that I should have made.

I raid my bookshelf and read everything I can find on resentments.

I realize that, when I can accept the past, I am in control.

106.

"Jesse, you are in such a slump," Flower says. "No smiles, no smirks, no sneers. No jokes! No joy! No fun. No fantasy. What is your goal in life?"

"To make you happy."

"Now, that's an impossible goal," she says. "Real happiness comes from within."

"Have you been reading your self-help books again?"

She smiles and punches me.

"What should my goal be?" I ask.

"Your goal should be to make yourself happy."

"Now *that* is an impossible goal!"

"Why?"

"I don't know what makes me happy. I have been trying to figure that out my whole life. When I was drinking, I could be happy for a while, but then there was usually vomit involved."

"Well, let's talk about what makes you happy now," she says. "Do you like quiet or noise?"

"I like noise. I like racket. I need background distraction. I always want the radio on. Or two radios on at the same time, tuned to two different stations."

"Who is your all-time favorite rock group?"

"Pink Floyd."

"Do you like to be around people, or do you like solitude?"

"I would like someone to call me, but I don't want to answer the phone. I would like to be invited to the party, but I don't want to go. I want someone to fuss over me, but I want to be left alone. I want to be held while I am isolating."

"What's your favorite type of food?"

"Ice cream."

Two days later, she calls. Her voice is in urgent mode.

"Jesse, I'm taking you out tonight. I want you to wear your disgusting ripped jeans, your Dark Side of the Moon t-shirt, and those ratty old sneakers with the holes in the toes."

"What's up?"

"I want to show you what it's like to be happy." She is animated. "I just scored two tickets to a Pink Floyd tribute band called The Machine. We will be front-row center. The music will be so loud it will hit from all sides. You may want to bring earplugs, but I won't let you wear them.

"You will be in a crowd, but you won't have to talk to anyone.

"It will be too loud to think, but you will be thinking about how good your life is. Your visual senses will be on psychedelics. Your mind will be shattered. Your eardrums will ring for weeks. You will love it. And I am treating to dinner."

"What?"

"Ice cream."

During the show, the group poses the question we all ask ourselves when we look in the mirror.

"Hello? Is there anybody in there?"

The concert is psychedelic. The strobe lights are haphazard but organized. The music is exciting, extravagant, and energizing.

When the last song comes up, every single person is on their feet. Everyone is shouting. Everyone is pointing to the ceiling.

Pulse. Pulse. Pulse.

107.

DEAR DIARY_____

*Time to reinvent myself. Right in the middle of my project.
Today, I ended up in a high-traffic, low-cost strip mall. The
hairdresser looked surprised when I picked shades that included
black, brown, dark-grey, and white. The colors added ten years
to my life. I explained that I was trying to hide from an abusive
boyfriend. She calmed down and helped me in my transformation. We used extensions that were all different lengths. I
started to look like any middle-aged woman who has given up
on herself.*

*At a thrift shop, I became more conservative than ever before. I
found an out-of-date, dark-green sport jacket that my mother would have thrown away. I found a tan, plaid blouse that
almost makes me sick. I found a pair of tan hushpuppy boots. I
added a pair of tortoise-shell glasses and hanged them from my
neck on a long, brown peeper-keeper.*

*At home, I gently washed my new hairdo and just let it hang. I
removed all previous makeup and replaced it with a flat, gray*

foundation. I looked like someone who has spent their entire life living in a subway station.

I almost barfed when I saw myself in the mirror, and then I laughed out loud.

I started the apartment search again. Time to find a new home.

108.

DEAR DIARY_____

My new landlord is a dream. She is a delightful, sophisticated, elderly woman who lives in a beautifully maintained Victorian mansion. Her home is right on the outskirts of town.

Her name is Mrs. Carol Peacock. She is eighty-six, and according to her daughter she is perfectly capable of self-care. Mrs. Peacock and her daughter would like an extra person in the big old house, just for companionship. She has short, gray hair that is professionally permed every Wednesday at 11am. Mrs. Peacock has a large suite of rooms on the second floor. There is an automatic stair-lift to help her gracefully ascend the levels.

I have my own bedroom and bathroom on the first floor. So far, no one has complained about toothpaste on the mirror. I have unlimited use of the kitchen and a living room that looks like it came from Better Homes and Gardens. *They call it the study. There is a maintenance man and a cleaning lady. The TV has a closed-caption option. I am within walking distance of the bus route.*

Mrs. Peacock has been helping me feel comfortable. "When you need to fetch medications or supplies, or even groceries, dear," she said. "Just take the Park Avenue. She is a beautiful car but elderly, just like me." We laugh. "My husband bought her new in nineteen-ninety, but she's still in good shape. We keep her well maintained." Mrs. Peacock pointed to the keys on a hook near the front door. I looked out at the magnificent, twenty-seven-year-old, dark-green Buick.

The TV is always on, and closed-caption details glide across the bottom of the screen.

The networks are still covering the string of unsolved murders at Bad Boy Burgers. Aerial photos, interior shots of the building, and interviews with employees all continue around the clock.

It seems to be a loop, and the images never change. The same pictures have been shown for days.

Suddenly, the rotation changed, and a new image flashed on the screen. A new announcer was talking. She was more show biz than news biz. She had a beautiful smile, a perfect hairdo, a killer body, and a dress that would look better at a cocktail party than on a TV screen. Her hot-pink sheath flashed a glimpse of a black strap. Her name ran across the bottom of the screen: Dixon Jackson.

This beautiful reporter looked like a hooker, or a stripper, but there she was, on TV talking about Detective Collins. She was talking about a murder, but her smile was a mile wide. For Christ's sake, girl, *I want to shout at her.* Stop the sweetness. This is death you're talking about!

"We have news now," she said. "That a Detective Jesse Collins will consult on the case."

I was shocked.

"He has been tracking the suspected killer for years," she continued. "Unfortunately, Detective Collins has been hospitalized since an almost-fatal shooting over a year ago. He says he is on the mend and has been invited to consult with the Police Chief, Charles Upton, on this case."

The closed-caption message changed too. It said: A former FBI detective is being called out of retirement to consult on the Bad Boy Burger murders. It is thought that the detective may have insight into the suspect.

She throws her diary down. It lands on the floor. She screams.

"Oh no! Jesse Collins is coming back into my life? Jesse Collins is coming here to Seattle? Oh sweet Jesus! Oh God.

After some quiet time, she picks up her diary and writes again.

Jesse Collins is the biggest pain in my ass. What the hell? I know I didn't finished him off the last time we were together, but I thought he would be in a wheelchair for the rest of his life.

He is starting to stink like raw sewage.

I don't know how he found me way back then in New Jersey, but he just crashed into my apartment. I shot him. Later he found me at a cookout in Boulder, Colorado. I shot him again. Now I need to find him and blast him out of his time zone for good.

I know how to find him. I have spent my life working with computers. This is what I do best. Right now, nothing is more important than finding Jesse Collins!

109.

EVERY MORNING, I MAKE A DECISION to be honest. Then someone says, "How are you doing?'"

"I am great," I say. There I go, lying again. Maybe tomorrow I can be honest.

"I am going crazy," I say to my AA group. I live in excess and have no boundaries. I build walls instead of relationships. I isolate. I deny my own needs. I am afraid to share anything of myself.

"But, my problem is not the problem. My problem is the incredible amount of time I spend thinking about the problem.

"Sometimes I go to a meeting because I am afraid I am going to drink. Other times, I go to a meeting because I am afraid I am going to think."

Flower and I meet for dinner, and she says,

"How was your day?"

"Oh, it was great," I lie.

Maybe tomorrow I will be honest.

110.

FIG IS HAVING A TOUGH YEAR. His wife, Libby, has changed her diet.

"It happened so slowly," he said. "I almost didn't notice. First, she gave up meat. She just stopped serving hamburgers, steak, hot dogs, and Taylor Pork Roll, and it was just fish, fish, and more fish." He frowns. "Called herself a pescatarian. Whatever that is. I like fish as much as the next guy, but seven nights a week? Geez! I got to the point that I hated fish.

"Six months later, she became a vegetarian. Eggs and cheese, okay, but now, no fish. I miss fish so much.

"Then it got bad."

"Bad?"

"After watching a documentary on animal abuse, she went vegan!

"Vegan!" he shouts.

"I had to give up my eight favorite things! Mayonnaise, cheese, butter, gravy, beef, bacon, Ben, and Jerry's."

"She forced you to give up that stuff, too?"

"No. I can eat anything I want. I just feel guilty eating a rare rib-eye steak, while she's eating kidney beans and quinoa."

"Quinoa? Didn't he play for the Red Sox?"

Out of pity, I invite Fig over for dinner.

As we settle in, I produce an extra-large, meat-lovers pizza. To enhance our dining experience, we add meatballs, sausage, bacon, shaved steak, pulled buffalo chicken, and thinly sliced pastrami. It is topped with Sriracha and mayonnaise. We drizzle melted butter over the top. Just because.

Without Libby present, we can eat like real men. Or real pigs. We have taken over the entire kitchen.

Fig is watching a Padres game. I make believe that I am watching a Padres game. Since my apartment is dark, I settle into a corner chair and become comatose. Every time the Padres catch a ball, Fig screams, and I jump. Every time the Padres miss a ball, Fig screams, and I jump.

Fig was my better half for years. He has taken care of me, covered for me, and gotten me out of many jams. I like being with him. I am not good with personal attachments, or foo-foo relationships, but if I had to confess, Fig is my best friend. There, I've said it!

It has become a chilly, sweat-shirt evening in Southern California, and there's a light breeze fluttering in through the open window. A neighbor's wind chime is jangling, but I can't identify the song. I walk into the living room to close the window.

Suddenly there are earsplitting explosions. I feel sharp pieces of something fly into the room and smash into my face. I drop and cover my head. Then there is an eruption of earthquake magnitude. It sounds like metal smashing against metal. My large picture window has been shattered into a thousand pieces. The floor is covered in glass. I grab my pistol, but I am slower than I used to be.

Fig, however, is on his feet in a heartbeat. Pistol drawn. Doing his job. A great cop. Out in the yard, looking for something. Anything.

When we put on the ceiling light, I see bullet holes in the wall opposite the busted window. Pictures have fallen to the floor.

When the police get here, they scour the neighborhood but find no one.

The next day, Fig gives me the news. The bullets found in my apartment wall were hollow points. Maybe a small hand gun.

"I think Kiki has found you," he says. "We never even thought to hide your name and address. She has you in her sights, again.

"Let's do a magic trick," Fig says. "It's time to make you disappear. Poof. You will now become invisible. We need to find you a new address."

111.

MY NEW DIGS ARE A FURNISHED condo in an upscale high-rise a few blocks from the ocean. I now live on Island Court.

This private condo was owned by a drug dealer who was put away for a long time. Since he paid in advance, the unit has become seized government property. Fig says I can use it for the remaining seventeen months of the lease.

The condo was professionally decorated. The main room is a gigantic combination living room, dining room, and kitchen. An oversized couch and two matching love seats face a propane fireplace. A wall-to-wall picture window has a southerly exposure toward the Giant Dipper. I am still in Mission Beach, but now even closer to the ocean.

Life is good.

Fig pulled some other strings. I now have a new Social Security number, a new, unlisted phone number, and an invisible address.

112.

FLOWER'S TEXT MESSAGE TELLS ME SHE will be an hour late.

"I am getting my hair done, but I'd like to stop by for a visit after that."

I find my camera and ride the elevator down to the lobby. I settle into a bench near the front entrance. The space is peaceful and well-decorated. There is soft music playing.

When I see Flower pull into the lot, I walk out and open her car door.

"I love your new hairstyle!" I say, as I snap endless pics. "I love the color, the trim, the style. What a difference. What a great job."

She pushes past me.

"My hairdresser was sick today," she says. "We have rescheduled for tomorrow."

113.

FIG AND I TALK ABOUT THE killings. "I can't figure it out from way down here," I tell him. "Upchuck invited us to come up there and look around. I want to take him up on his offer. I have to go the scene of the crime and see the whole Magillah."

"Magillah?"

"Yeah. A long involved story with great detail."

"Where do you come up with this stuff?"

"I have to be at the actual locations and survey the parking lot. I have to physically walk the streets. I am not a psychic, but my perception of the crimes will only work if I am there."

"The map doesn't work?" asks Fig.

"The map is only two-dimensional, but I have to live the map in 3D. I need to be at the location. I don't know how it works, but I want to walk those spots that are on the map. I need to see the neighborhood. I need to see the exact location of where each body was left. I want to saunter around the block."

"Saunter?"

"I want to draw my own map in my head. The roads, the parking lots, the alleys, the bus route, the local highway. Right now, we know nothing! No name, no description, no prints.

"If I could get to Seattle, I would check all public transportation, including Amtrak, The Link Light Rail, the SLU Streetcar, and the Seattle First Hill Car. The transit website has a listing for a 'Rider Community.' Over 50,000 people chat, and we can post an outreach request asking if anyone has seen these two unusual characters."

"You are working overtime, my friend."

"I am not working at all. I want to go up to Seattle.

I want to talk with the taxi companies," I continue. "What about Uber? How did the killer get to and from the locations of the killings? Is there a ball field, a rail line, a forest, or a ravine to hide in?" I have to find what the local cops have missed.

"I can read reports and watch parking-lot videos all day, but that is not the same as pinpoint accuracy. I need to find some intel on my own. Sometimes I have a sixth sense. I need to use it."

The next day, Fig says, "I touched base with Upchuck. He has confirmed our invitation: 'Come up and look around.' On our own dime of course."

"Let's go. It's the least I can do for Flower. "

114.

"WANNA TAKE A ROAD TRIP?" I ask Flower.

"Where we going?"

"Seattle."

She just stares.

"It's time for me to talk with the owner of the Bad Boy Burgers chain, and maybe it's time for you to be in the same town as your sister. Who knows? You might even say hello."

"You think I am cruel for not reaching out to her, don't you? Well, I did reach out to her. I sent her a letter telling her how much I hate her. I told her she was a piece of shit and I never want to see her again. So there! Why do I have to reach out to her? She could reach out to me. After all, she is older. She is the adult in this relationship. She should call me."

"After your letter?"

"It was only a letter."

"It's like using a pen to stab someone."

She gives me a dirty look.

"Are you drinking poison, hoping someone else will die?"

"Screw you."

"In the meantime, you are the one being hurt."

"I am not being hurt."

"Really?

"I can handle this. I'm okay. I can do this. I've got it covered."

"Flower, in recovery, we have this process. We are encouraged to look at our resentments. We make lists of people who have hurt us. We make lists of people who have been hurt by us. On each list, we try to see what our part was. Is your sister on any of those lists?"

"She is on all of those lists."

"The next step in recovery is to make amends for our part. Our part only. Then we move on. I'm not telling you what to do, but I ask: Have you been carrying this grudge long enough? You are mad at your sister for walking out thirty years ago. I get it!

"But Flower, you don't know why she left. What was her part? Maybe there is more to the story than you even know. Maybe if the two of you sat together, you might see things differently. It doesn't matter if the glass is half empty or half full. The longer you carry the glass, the heavier it gets. Maybe it's time to put the glass down! There are only three options in every situation. You can accept it, you can change it, or you can leave it!

On the flight from San Diego to Seattle, Flower is hyperventilating. She makes three trips to the rest room in the two and a half-hour flight. Instead of her usual smile, she exhibits a short, horizontal line, like something out of a horror movie. Her eyes are in fixed-focus mode, straight ahead. Her jaw is clamped shut. Her neck muscles are tight. Fig and I enjoy the silence.

Flower and her sister meet at baggage claim. The tension lasts for a half second as they look at each other. Then the two sisters scream. They race into an embrace. They hug and cry and giggle and make a public spectacle. They laugh and then they cry. Then a tight hug. They jump up and down and laugh. Then they cry again.

"Why do girls cry?" I ask Fig.

"Happy. Sad. Overworked. Underpaid. Over-stressed, under-loved. Oh yeah. And penis envy."

After a long sister-sister reunion, we all sit together and wait for bags. The girls hold hands and say almost nothing. Very cautious, very reserved. Then they say goodbye to us and walk toward the parking lot. They are going to Blossom's apartment. We are going to work.

115.

"I AM SO SORRY," SAID BLOSSOM, as they walked to the parking lot.

"I am so sorry, too," said Flower.

"I love you, Blossom."

"I love you, Flower."

"I want to start," Blossom said, before the car door even closed. "I want to talk first. Please let me talk."

They sat in the car in the underground parking lot. The key wasn't even in the ignition. The parking lot was cold, dreary, and creepy. Blossom started the engine to turn on the heater.

"I know you are furious at me for leaving, but I had no choice.

"I have a secret that is killing me. I don't want to have a secret. I have to tell you something. I want to tell you everything. I need to tell you now. Maybe it will help you understand. I can't keep it inside any longer. It can't wait. I can't wait.

"He fucked me!"

"What?"

"He fucked me. Our father fucked me."

"What?"

"He fucked me!"

"What are you talking about?"

"That bastard. He fucked me!" She screamed. She pounded the steering wheel with her fists.

"Over and over. Night after night. Nightmare after living nightmare."

Blossom started sobbing. Almost like a convulsion.

Flower grabbed her sister's wrists.

A family that was getting into the car next to them stared. After turning on their headlights, the family drove away.

"Our father staggered into my room, night after night. Drunk!" Blossom continued. "He fell on top of me. He fucked me! It was unbearable, but I couldn't move. He pinned me down. On the first night I said no, and he choked me. I thought I would die in bed with him on top of me. He ripped my nightgown off. He was fat, sweating, and incoherent. He had disgusting breath. And his cock was inside me. He hurt me so much. I was afraid to pee for days. Mother didn't believe me. She was afraid of him, too. All she could say was, 'Don't talk that way.'

"Night after night, I prayed he wouldn't come into my room. I pushed my dresser against the door, but he just muscled in past it. Mother didn't hear the noise, or she just ignored it. He just came in again, and again, and again. I was going crazy.

"I was so ashamed! I felt like trash. Maybe it was my fault. Maybe I gave him the wrong signals. Surely, if I was a good girl, he wouldn't have come into my room. But he did. I blamed myself. I felt lower than dog shit. I wanted to stop him, but I couldn't. He was too big. He was too strong. He was too drunk!

"I started to scream, and he punched me out. No one even mentioned the bruise on my face. Hell, we have both gone to school with black-and-blue marks. When I came to, he was inside me. I had never had sex, so I didn't even know what it was all about. He was pounding away. He hurt me so much!

"Flower, I didn't want to leave you in that hell-hole with him. I wanted to stay and take care of you, but I couldn't even take care of myself. I had to run. He fucked me. He fucked me. He fucked me."

They sat in the underground parking lot for a long time, holding hands, staring into each other's eyes. Crying. Like best friends. Like family. Like sisters.

Blossom continued talking in a daze.

"There were many times, after I left, that I reconsidered my decision, but I just couldn't go back. It was hard living on the street, but as bad as it was on the street, it was never as bad as it was at home with that bastard.

"I left with nothing. No clothes, no money. Not even a toothbrush. Talk about bailing out. I should have taken his wallet after he passed out. I should have taken money out of his pants pockets. I just couldn't think that far ahead.

"I literally ran away in the middle of the night. I ran as far as I could. The first night, I was so cold. I went to a park and crawled up next to a wall. The next day I was cold, hungry, and thoroughly depressed. I was scared shitless.

"I walked and walked, but when I saw some street kids in town, I asked them where I could find food. They welcomed me into their community. A girl stood up and hugged me. I told them a little of my story. They told me about their trauma. We had a lot in common. Then they taught me the ropes. One girl took me to a soup kitchen. Another girl explained the process of getting into a shelter. Another girl walked me to the Salvation Army, and I got a sweat shirt, some long pants, and a rain coat.

"'It will keep you a little warmer during the night,' she said.

"I was offered booze, but I knew what that did to our father. I almost got sick just thinking about drinking. Some of the kids were hooked on drugs. I didn't want that, either. Most of the kids were good but just ended up in bad situations. Parents like ours. Family trauma. We weren't the only kids who were beaten! They all came from families with alcohol, drugs, sexual stuff. Lifetime scars. They had all come from broken homes. They had broken bones, broken families, and broken hearts.

"Many of the kids talked about changing their lives. Booze, drugs, and resentment got in the way. Many of them found terrible part-time jobs. Some of the boys had sugar daddies. They would jump in a strange car and come back a few hours later with cash. Girls would just walk away but never talk about where they had been. When they came back, they would treat the rest of us to french fries and donuts. We took care of each other. I fit right in.

"But, I did want to get a job. I only had one skill. I learned my trade as our father was standing behind me swinging his belt. I learned how to clean toilets. I found out there was a need for that line of work That's what I did. At that point in my life, I had no money, I had no home, I had no pride."

Blossom started the car. As she drove out of the parking lot, she drove into a downpour. The rain blocked everything. She slowly merged into traffic. The wipers were clearing the window, but there was nothing that could clear their tears.

Two blocks later, Blossom started breathing heavily. It was almost scary. Was she having a panic attack? She slowed down to a crawl. Cars behind them were beeping.

"What?" Flower asked.

Blossom nervously shook her head and tried to see through the tears. She wiped her eyes with her free hand. She slowed down even more, and pulled the car into a rest area. She stopped and shut the car off. She turned in her seat and looked into her younger sister's eyes again. Her face became ashen, and she trembled. She reached across the car and took both of Flower's hands.

"My story. My story is so bad. My story keeps me awake at night. My story haunts me during the day. My story is driving me crazy."

After some painful quietness, Blossom stopped crying. She talked again, as if in a trance. She spoke in a very low voice.

"I have something else to tell you. Something terrible. I have a blueprint for revenge. It's like an old video in my mind. Skipping over and over. Repeating. Constantly replaying. It is despicable. I have to tell someone. If I don't get it out, I will explode. It is an every-day thought. It is an every-night obsession. I can't get rid of it. I can't rest. Please don't judge me.

"I don't believe in God," Blossom continued, "but I have prayed to a God I don't know. I prayed for revenge. I prayed for justice. I prayed for some kind of horrible punishment.

"Flower, I am so full of guilt for my prayers. When most people pray, I think they usually pray for something good. I have prayed for something bad. Something very bad."

"What is it?"

"Flower, I have prayed that our father would be tortured. I have asked God to let him burn to death. I have prayed that our father would die in a horrific fire.

"I have prayed that our father would burn in Hell."

116.

"BLOSSOM, YOUR PRAYERS WERE ANSWERED!"

117.

ON THE FIRST DAY AT THE station, we check in, and I finally meet Upchuck, aka Charles Upton. He is about five feet, eight inches tall and in very good shape. He is prematurely gray, with a deep, husky voice. His eyes seem to be burning. Maybe the stress is getting to him. He seems to be in the middle of five things, and people are lined up with questions to ask and papers to sign. He offers his services but says we are on our own.

Fig and I spend three days walking the town. We visit the locations and sit in the parking lots. We sneak through back yards and comb through side streets. We visit all the neighboring businesses.

We watch the videos, and we talk with Jeb. We review the notes the Seattle PD has compiled.

"I can't understand it," Upchuck says. "She is in and out in a flash. She must be the most organized person in the world. She struts in, or shuffles in, or waddles into a parking lot, conducts her business, and walks out."

"How long does it take?" I ask.

"Five minutes," he says. "Each time. Every time."

"You mean, from the time she enters the video surveillance area till the time she walks off-screen is only five minutes?"

"Five minutes," he says. "Five minutes at a time!"

We all sit in silence but continue to think about our strategy. We plan to go to every coffee shop and convenience store in those areas. We can ask people if they have seen an incredibly rotund bag lady.

The next morning, Upchuck calls us in. He has a concerned look on his face.

"Fig," he says, "You are my old buddy, and I appreciate the help you can give us in this investigation. But, right now, my boss is threatening my job. He wants me to do this through the proper channels. He says there is no reason for you and Jesse to be way up here. From a different state. Doing my job.

"'If you can't do your job' he said 'We will find someone who can.'

"Fig, we are all under so much stress. So much inspection. I am under scrutiny.

"I understand the part about Jesse's girlfriend and her sister, and all that stuff, but I need to take care of this investigation. I need to do my job.

"So, I'm telling you what, mister." He looks at Fig. "By the end of this week, I need to respectfully kick you guys out of my town.

"You have to go, but come back to Seattle as a tourist some time. I'll buy you a burger."

Later that day, Upchuck calls us back into his office. Fig and I walk in together. There is a stranger sitting in the corner.

Upchuck continues his previous conversation. "This serial crime is getting out of hand, and I have let it go too far. The media is in my face, the mayor is kicking my butt, and the governor is up my ass.

"The scope of this series of crimes is beyond anything we are capable of dealing with on our own. At least, that's what they say.

"Starting today, this is now a federal issue. I have been encouraged to bring in the FBI, and I would like to introduce Walter Woodbury."

People in the agency affectionately have nicknames for each other.

"Hey, Woody," I say.

"It's Agent Walter Woodbury." He glares at me sternly.

His quick reply and negative attitude pisses me off. Instead of congratulating him for being admitted to the FBI, I start thinking that he is a loser.

I look at this young kid. Special Agent whoever. A newcomer to the agency. Still wet behind the ears. He is five-ten and big. His black suit is a size too small, and the jacket and slacks don't match. They might have come from two different thrift shops. His mother probably ironed his wrinkled shirt. His buzz cut is sticking up at odd angles from his head. He missed a few whiskers when he shaved. He has dandruff. He has an overbite, and there is a slight separation between two upper front teeth. The gap is the thing you would remember if you tried to describe him later. He is sweating. His hand is clammy.

"So Woody," I say. "How long have you been with the agency?"

"It's Agent Woodbury." He emphasizes the pronunciation. "Since I will be taking over this case, we no longer need your help, Mr. Collins. Your government thanks you for your service. You may leave now."

I am shocked. This young kid talks like a ventriloquist, with his mouth mostly closed. Maybe he is trying to hide the gap in his teeth. Maybe he is self-conscious because he is new at his job. Maybe he is scared shitless.

His dismissal of me is so abrupt it activates my Personality Disorder Meter. My meter is going off the charts. The gauge wavers and works its way up the scale. At an eight, Woodbury would be a loser. At a nine, he would be a jerk. Now, at a ten, he is definitely an asshole.

"Hey, Woody," I say. "I was with the FBI while you were chasing cheerleaders."

"It's Woodbury . And yes, I am relatively new to the agency, but it's official. I am an agent."

"But, since I was with the FBI before," I say. "Why do you need to be here? Kind of redundant. Like *déjà vu* all over again. Get my drift?"

"It is my understanding, Mr. Collins, that you were let go from the bureau. Or asked to leave. Or discharged. Substance abuse, I think." His remark stabs me to the core. I feel like a rusty, serrated steak knife has been jabbed into my heart.

"We will no longer need your services. I have been authorized to reimburse you for your expenses so far, but we will only pay through the end of tomorrow. That will give you time to pack your toiletries and check out of your hotel. Thank you."

I ignore him and sit back down. I am in a daze as I listen to Special Agent Walter Woodbury mumble orders to the staff. He is talking, but his teeth are grinding together.

"Document everything in a murder book. I want witness statements, observations, photos, forensic reports. And I want two copies of every report."

"Two copies?" I say

He ignores me. "Don't let up. Look at the elapsed time between the killings. Map all locations on a board right here in this office. Pinpoint all possible escape routes.

"I want to know about potential friendships, relationships, and loyalties. If you looked before, look again. Things change. Continue to interview witnesses. Have everyone back for a second interview.

"Check all video surveillance against facial recognition.

"One last thing: Let's check what we know about DSM-5 personality traits.

"Here's what we are looking for: Someone who regularly breaks or flouts the law. Someone who constantly lies and deceives others.

Someone who is impulsive and doesn't plan ahead. Someone who doesn't feel remorse or guilt."

"Hey Woody," Fig says.

"It's Special Agent Walter . . ."

"Geez, I know your name. Have you ever heard of a thing called narcissistic personality disorder? You know, like an ego problem. We had a guy like that once. He disappeared and no one missed him for three weeks. Not even his wife."

Woodbury's face turns crimson.

"Anyways, Woody," Fig continues, "You just got here, and you couldn't possibly know this. Jesse has detailed, directed, and followed up on every single item you just mentioned. Been there, done that. The maps you asked for are hanging in our staff room. The bus schedules are in a folder. Guess what the folder is named. Wanna guess?

"Bus schedules."

Woodbury looks at Fig and coughs. He says, "I knew that, but we have to be thorough." All of a sudden, his demeanor changes. He acts like he stepped on his tail, or his dick. He looks nervous.

"In the agency, we are coached to investigate from a new perspective. Never rely on another person's work. We are going to start from scratch."

"That should speed up the search," Fig says.

"Yeah. Go get 'em, tiger!" I couldn't resist.

The next morning, Fig, Flower, and I head to the airport. On our way to San Diego, Fig says, "We were asked to leave. Were we discharged, or have we been kicked out?"

"I've been thrown out of better barrooms than this!" I say.

118.

AFTER THE CONFRONTATION WITH SPECIAL AGENT Walter Woodbury, I become despondent.

I binge-watch movies all night, sleep all day, and walk around in a daze. I give up on my healthy lifestyle and revert back to my coronary-artery favorites. It's rare steak, crisp bacon, and melted Velveeta for me. Three times a day.

I stare at the big, fluorescent numbers on my bedside clock. One something. Two something. Three something.

Being kicked out of the Federal Bureau of Investigation for drunk and disorderly conduct was understandable; I deserved it. Being let go from a case because some snot-nosed, wanna-be agent is showing his make-believe muscle is another thing. I am helpless. My self-esteem is shot. I was not good enough to find a killer. I am not good enough to do the job. I was relieved of my duty.

Why does this rejection hurt so much? I get the message loud and clear. It is the same message I have been hearing my whole life:

"You are not good enough!"

Now, so many years later, I realize the story I heard growing up has never changed. It was like an old cassette. Over and over. I am still hearing those old tapes. I am still getting subliminal directions from my father. It's all his old comments, critiques, and disapproval.

"No one has been killed in a long time." Fig frowns. "I think it's over."

"No one has been killed in a long time." Kiki smiles. "I bet they think it's over."

119.

DEAR DIARY_____

Today, instead of killing someone, I decide to kill some time, I went to my favorite coffee shop. It's called Momma's. It's a small, family affair. It's cozy, comfortable, and colorful. The overweight matron who sits at the cash register is probably Momma. There are two good-looking young men who do all the work. Probably Momma's boys. One son, Toby, the oldest, is the most attentive to me. He is very gentle, and he speaks slowly. He keeps his face still and straight so I can read his lips. Perhaps he knew someone who was deaf.

Toby is thin. His most prominent feature is his nose. If he were a woman, he might resemble Barbara Streisand. I can't tell if the eyelashes are naturally thick or if he uses mascara. He might use some eye shadow, and sometimes I think he might have used lip liner.

When he gives me his hand, it is barely a touch and is always clammy. He wears the same pair of tight, acid-washed jeans every day. I suspect he washes them every night. They are ripped at the knees and frayed at the bottom. He wears scuffed cowboy boots. There is always a lacy shirt under his jean jacket. The back of the jacket is embroidered with flowers and small birds. He tells me he did the embroidery himself. The sleeves of the jacket and shirt are always pushed up to his elbows.

Toby makes a big production of cleaning my table and wiping down the wooden chair I will sit in. He always calls me by name and takes my elbow as I sit down. Sometimes he sits right at the table with me.

Toby tells me about his family.

"My mother worked very hard to build her business.

"My brother thinks he is a stud muffin. Those are his words, not mine. All he cares about is pussy." He scrunches a disapproving grin. "We are so different. He is with a new girl every night. Most of them are customers. Or they were customers at one time. They seem to disappear after he takes them to bed. He raises his eyes.

Today, Toby is flirting with me. Maybe because I am deaf. Maybe because he wants to be in competition with his brother. Maybe because he thinks I am safe.

He tells me he has never been married, and I wonder if he has ever gotten laid.

"My mother is out sick today," he says. "I have been to check on her twice. After you leave, I will bring her some chicken noodle soup."

The lunch crowd has thinned out, and Toby joins me at my table. He sits like a friend, not like the owner. He crosses his legs tightly.

Our conversation can go in many directions, but today I am bored. Why not have some fun? I think. I feel guilty, but who cares?

"Can you keep a secret?" I ask.

"Oh my goodness. Yes. Of course!" he smiles. "I am the best secret keeper in the world. Actually, I have a secret I never told anyone. I know what it's like to keep a secret.

"I went to a nude beach."

"What?"

"Nude. Naked. Bare-ass."

I watch him blush. His face turns pink.

"You went to . . . ?"

"Yes. I hope you don't think less of me, but I had to tell someone. I couldn't carry this secret forever. I am not good at keeping secrets."

His whole demeanor changes. He goes from a confused young man to a nervous little boy.

"I have to admit, it was pretty scary," I continue. "You know that moment when you actually unhook your bra and let it slide down your arms, and you are standing there, topless? It feels good. I have never been topless in my life," I lie.

He glances at my blouse. Then he quickly looks back up. He blushes. I smile to myself.

"But, you know what's even scarier than that?" I ask.

He just stares, afraid of what will come next.

"I squeeze his hand and lean into him. I make a gesture to whisper in his ear, and he turns his head slightly. He leans in, too. Before I talk, I give him a little kiss. Right in the ear. A tiny wet willy.

He jumps, as if this is a mistake. He is so shocked. I don't know if he will have a heart attack or an orgasm. He sits back down.

"So do you know what's scarier than taking your bra off?"

He slowly shakes his head.

"The scariest thing is when you take your panties off. You slide them all the way down. Right to the blanket."

He gawks at me as if I was discussing a murder.

"And you don't want to bend over to let the world see your naked fanny, so you just try to kick them off, but they get caught. And there you are, kicking one foot with your undies stuck around the ankle. Trying to keep your balance and your dignity. And you are trying not to have any eye contact, but you accidentally look up and see fifty people staring at your asshole.

He gulps.

"I went to the beach alone that day, but I wish I had a man with me. The next time I go, I want you to come with me. We could take naked pictures of each other. Maybe your brother would like to see the pictures."

Toby abruptly gets up. "I have to go to the restroom facility." I wait for thirty minutes, but he never comes back.

120.

Today, the newspaper suggested that customer counts at Bad
Boy Burgers were almost back to normal. No one has been
killed in any of Jeb's parking lots for a while. Sales may actually
be better than before. His customers have a short attention span.
The pickup windows always have a line, the insides and outsides
have been re-tooled with new light fixtures. There are now staff
members walking the perimeters several times a night. The
building is immaculate, the food is great, and the prices are fair.
They host fund-raisers, they offer free food to social causes. They
provide uniforms to a kid's baseball team.

Mostly, Jeb and Blossom are visible and involved. When she is
on-camera, she always blows a bubble. Jeb probably thinks she
looks cute. I think she looks like a slut.

Jeb's life is wonderful. My life sucks.

He is in heaven, and I am in Seattle.

Time for me to go back to work.

121.

ACCORDING TO HIS NEIGHBORS, PAUL PEARLMAN was the nicest guy in the world. That's what his wife, Paula, said, too. He was a great family man, a devoted husband, and he never had more than two items on his "honey-do" list at any time.

Since their youngest son had a mild form of autism, Paul and his wife focused their energy on their kids. The boys, now six and eight, were close enough in age to have the same interests. Every night, Paul and the boys took turns reading to each other.

When his teaching year ended, Paul dedicated his summer to having fun with his boys. Last year it was a beach trip, but the boys didn't do well in the sun. This year they planned a road trip. Nothing fancy. Just time in their new car. The kids were thrilled. Different motels each night. Unusual scenery. And the kids got to pick out the food. The kids always wanted burgers.

On their second day in Seattle, they took a trip to the tallest point in the city. The Space Needle opened for tours during the 1962 World's Fair. The observation deck, at five-hundred-twenty feet, offers a panoramic view of Mount Rainier and the Cascades. The ride to the top of the Needle only takes forty-one seconds. The guide book said that, on windy days, the elevators has to slow down. The boys had lots of questions about that.

Later in the day, they went back to their motel. The pool was fun. While the boys took turns jumping off the diving board, Paula grabbed restaurant menus from the office. The boys would get to pick a place for dinner.

The name "Bad Boy Burgers" had them giggling.

"They won't serve you," Paul said. "They only serve Bad Boys."

"Maybe we can find a place called Good Boy Burgers," said Paula.

The burgers and fries at the Upper Rainier Beach location of Bad Boy Burgers were great. The kids loved the dessert called "Worms and Dirt." It was chocolate pudding with gummy worms mixed in and crushed chocolate cookies on top. After their meal, the family headed to their car. As usual, a fine mist covered everything in Seattle. Visibility was a challenge.

As Paul and Paula buckled the boys into their car seats, they noticed an elderly man shuffling toward them. He was bent over with a huge disfiguration on his back. His top coat was covering the deformity, and his fedora was too large. It was obstructing his view.

"Looks like Quasimodo," Paul said.

"Quasi-who?" said one of the boys.

"Not even funny!" Paula said to him, sternly.

"Sorry," Paul said.

The old man had glasses and a scraggly, gray goatee. He walked slowly and relied on his cane to get through the lot. Every step forward seemed to be painful. He was bending over, and his head was tilted to one side. As he approached the car, Paul put his window down. Perhaps the old man would be looking for a few bucks, and Paul would gladly oblige.

The single gunshot was aimed straight at Paul's head and exploded on impact. Paula and the kids were caught in the blood bath. They all screamed. Paula passed out. Paul was dead. The old man shuffled out of view.

122.

"The killer is back," Jeb screams. "Still here. Here again. Another dead guy."

123.

DEAR DIARY_____:

I love counting my cash. I am happy there is still over one hundred thousand dollars. The money from my mother's estate was a surprise, of course.

All my relatives had their eyes on my prize. They offered self-serving, ingenious schemes to help me handle my newfound fortune.

"Let me invest it for you," said my uncle.

"I'll put it in a safe place for you," said my cousin.

When I wanted to take the money out of the bank, I had to explain the reason to a banker in a baggy suit. I hated him.

Finally, I walked up to a teller and asked for cash.

She called the manager.

I thought the banker would have a heart attack.

I stored my cash in my backpack and stopped going to family reunions.

My cash was the gateway. It gave me the freedom to remove the thorns from my previous life. My cash gave me control. It's all about control.

Seattle is clean and green; that's what the locals say. I think it's dreary and depressing. And dumpy. And what about these stupid coffee shops? Google says there are at least sixteen hundred of them.

I don't know how I feel, but if revenge is a feeling, then I feel wonderful. I just wish I could see the look on Jeb's face every time the police come calling. They believe each killer is a different person. If they only knew.

Since the killings started, I have changed so much. Some changes were by choice, some by chance. Most were a life-or-death challenge.

In the old days, I wanted to fit in. Be part of. Even though I was born with a disability, I wanted to belong, to look like everyone else. I was obsessive about following fashion trends. I wanted to be popular.

While all my old flames were being extinguished, I had to hide in plain sight and act as if nothing was happening.

Now it's different. Because of my new goal, I have to be out in the open. Now I have learned how to jump from one identity to another. I am getting good at it.

I love the research, the planning, the detail, the role-playing, the observations, and the fantasies. I want to fit in for a few minutes and then fade out. I want to disappear forever. I want people to forget me as soon as I walk away.

Whatever the case, I have adapted. Sometimes I have become a reflection, but other times I have blended into the woodwork. Shaken, not stirred.

124.

Jeb sat in a daze. He stared ahead. He half-looked at Blossom and half-looked into space. He blamed himself.

He was aloof, distant, remote. He couldn't sleep. He was exhausted during the day. Eating was a foreign concept. Sex was out of the question. Even his favorite hobby, building his business, was a chore.

"Maybe we should just shut down!" Jeb said to Blossom.

"Go out of business?" she said.

"Declare bankruptcy. Go back to Massachusetts."

"What would you do?"

"I could get a job in any burger joint in town. I would be okay with that. I don't need to own this stupid hamburger chain."

"You cannot give up!" she said.

125.

DEAR DIARY_____

I love thrift shops! With a little cash and a lot of ingenuity, I can be anyone. No one cares how often I go into a shop. No one even notices how much time I spend browsing, trying on clothes, or looking in the mirror. I have found out how to be a new person. I can transform myself. I can be a young girl, a technician, a fat lady, or a hunchbacked old man. This is so much fun!

Who will I be next?

I am prepared to hurt Jeb more than he has ever been hurt in his life. It will be a long, slow, wonderful process. I will drag it out and enjoy every minute of it. He won't even know what hit him, but it will hurt him. I will break him in half.

It should only take a few more unfortunate tragedies. A few more months. I will only have to eliminate a few more of his stupid customers, until he is forced to close up his stupid restaurant chain for good! He will become a sick, desperate old man. No other women will ever want him. When his stupid Bad Boy

Burger restaurants are boarded up, then I can move away from Seattle. I hate it here.

It would have been easier to just kill Jeb outright. Wham, bam, thank you, man. That would have been efficient, but that would be too quick for him. After hurting me as much as he did, he deserves to suffer. He is such a sick prick.

126.

AT FIRST THE POLICE WERE VERY tactful when they questioned Paul's wife. Paul was dead, and her boys were traumatized. But now they were forceful. "Who is the killer? Was your husband in some kind of trouble? Did he have a problem at work. Did he gamble?"

Paula talked through her tears. "I'm sorry. I don't know who he was or what he wanted. The bump that was under his coat was scary. It was up by his shoulders. He was bent over and leaning on a cane. He was wearing a crumpled-up black hat. There was a lot of long, greasy, gray hair hanging out from under it. In front of his eyes.

"It all happened so quickly. It was dark. It was raining. I was busy getting my boys settled in. That's all I remember." She cried again.

Jeb talked to the police for an hour, too, but he insisted he knew nothing about the killing, the motive, or the deceased man. They all reviewed the security tapes. Jeb was not a suspect, but there was a piece of the picture that was missing.

"Someone is targeting you!" Detective Charles Upton said. "We thought that different killers were sneaking onto your parking lot. Rifling tests show that all bullets came from the same small hand gun."

"What?"

"All of this mayhem has come from one gun. Maybe several killers, but definitely the same gun!"

127.

Back in San Diego, Fig brings me up to date.

"I talked with Upchuck, " he says. "They are at a loss.

"Police are still talking to Jeb.

"There are a few new twists Upchuck told me. They don't even know if they are targeting a man or a woman.

"Also, the first three killings were employees. Now a customer was tapped. No one else seems to have notice this yet, but newspapers and local TV reporters are everywhere. Even a national network has a human interest article on the killings.

"One paper sums up the story: 'Business at Bad Boy Is Bad.'"

128.

"My business is almost dead," Jeb said to Blossom. "I am almost dead. The media is making such a huge deal of this. The killings took place in different locations, but since then business is down at all units. Half my employees have quit, which is fine, because customers are just staying away. Take-out orders are slow, but in-store sales are down seventy-five percent. I am a suspect. They think I may have murdered my own customers."

"That's ridiculous!" she said.

129.

FIG AND I MEET AT AN upscale, waterfront shopping area near downtown San Diego. It's called Seaport Village. There is music playing from hidden speakers. We sit quietly at a coffee shop and wait for the June Gloom to burn off. There is gloom most mornings in Southern California, but as the sun cuts through the fog, it burns off. This mid-year weather phenomenon creates No-Sky July, or May Gray, but most locals just refer to June Gloom, regardless of the month. Some mornings the gloom is so thick you need headlights just to get to work.

Today, the fog burns off early. By 9am, everything warms up. The sun changes our attitude. We shift from exhausted to energized. It's good to be alive. The sailboats in the harbor offer a picture-perfect setting and help us focus on this issue. We are not ready to talk, but we are thinking of a killer.

We watch the joggers, the shoppers, and the bikini moms.

"It's not over," I say. "We should go back to Seattle. We've seen it all before. Same circus, different monkey. This is like playing Whack-a-Mole. It's like Rope-a-Dope. But we have more information now. We have stuff to go on. We have shoe sizes and shell casings. We just have to go deeper."

"We are not on the case," Fig says.

I ignore him. "We all know that random killings are the least solvable of all crimes. But, after time, investigations keep working, even if a killer stops or moves out of the area. The investigation might produce results. Maybe this isn't a random crime. What's the connection?"

"We are not on the case."

"But things change. Technology gets better. DNA recovery improves. Old friends change their minds. Maybe fall out of favor. Someone might be picked up on another charge and cooperate."

"We are not . . ."

I give him the finger.

"Someone might brag in prison. Someone might talk."

"I think the killer has an oversized ego. They are used to lying and exhibiting manipulative behavior."

"Ya think?"

"A complete lack of empathy. No remorse or shame. Staying eerily calm in dangerous situations. Carefully behaving irresponsibly."

"That's easy for you to say."

"We have to go back and look at all the surveillance tapes. We don't even know if we are looking for a man or a woman!"

"We are not . . ."

"I know." Fig's phone vibrates.

"It's Upchuck," Fig whispers as he answers it.

"Of course I have a minute. I have a lot of minutes.

"Actually, I'm with Jesse now," he says. "We are sitting on a bench by the harbor. You should be here. There is a girl in the shortest skirt I have ever seen, and she is bending over to pet her dog."

Figs eyes open wide as he listens to a question.

"Pink lace." He smiles at me.

He hits the speaker button.

We both lean into the phone.

"Boys," Upchuck says. "I just wanted to give you an update on your friend, Special Agent Walter Woodbury."

"Our friend? How's Woody doing?"

"I'll tell you what, mister! He is the biggest nothing-burger I've ever seen! He's like a cheap piñata. Once you break through the flimsy cover, there is nothing. Nada. Ix-nay. All brilliance and bullshit."

"Tell us how you really feel," I say, but no one laughs.

"Woodbury is full of diagrams. He is full of graphs. He is full of shit. He has a hundred notebooks and schedules. He is all about television interviews and radio talk shows. He is trying to impress a different reporter every day. He is reading up on murders from the past but not doing any work on the current epidemic. His office walls are covered with pictures of serial killers from years ago.

"Yesterday, while he was out, a visitor left a business card. It was an agent from a publishing company! Woodbury is writing a book! He is writing a goddamn novel! He is sitting in my office, on my time, on my dime, working on a best seller."

There is a long silence as Fig and I look at each other. Then we break out laughing.

"Guys! Please come back. Fig, Jesse. Please come back. You guys know more about this crime than Woodbury ever will. You have a personal interest. Come back to our city. I can't put you on the payroll, but we can get around that part. We have a few hotel rooms you can use. We can cover your air travel from an emergency account. We can pay for your meals out of one fund and process hours through another one. We will figure it out.

"There is a maniac on the loose. This killer is whacking our residents. Not a damn thing is being done to find this assassin. Please come back and put an end to this madness. Please come back to Seattle and catch this monster!"

Fig puts his hand over the speaker and raises his eyebrows.

I nod vigorously.

"First plane in the morning," he says.

We walk quickly toward the parking lot. Then we start to jog to the car. We are on a mission. We leave Seaport Village in the dust and make a beeline to the office. On the way, I call Erica.

"Do you have a few minutes?" I ask.

130.

ERICA RINGLINE IS THE BEST FORENSIC specialist in the business. She clears her schedule and is waiting for us.

"Can we go over everything you have learned so far?" I ask.

"I have learned nothing so far!" she answers.

"Is she a psychopath or a sociopath?"

"Does it matter?" she asks. "All killings were random. Now we know that the shooters were the same person, but the costumes were incredibly different. The killer in each surveillance clip actually appears to be a different person. Hats, hair, bandanas, and oversized glasses covered recognizable features. No electronic facial recognition. No fingerprints! This person is good. The killers appear to be different heights, but maybe that is from lifts. Probably oversized shoes, too. In every case, the killer went to a lot of trouble to stage these costumes.

"Psychopath or a sociopath?" I ask again.

"Does it matter?" she asks again.

"We need to have a press conference. The news dogs will want some scraps. I have to feed them something. So yes, it does matter."

"Tell them it doesn't matter. That will keep them quiet for two minutes. Then tell them that psychopaths and sociopaths aren't the same but they are close. That will keep them busy for another two minutes. Say they both have a poor sense of right and wrong and they both lack empathy."

"Good for another two minutes. We are on a roll. We need a half-hour meeting."

"A psychopath is caring. He will steal your wallet and then help you look for it.

"A sociopath, on the other hand, will steal your wallet, but he just doesn't give a fuck."

"Can I use that word during a news briefing?"

"What word?"

"Fuck."

"Fuck, yes.

"The psychopath has an incredible ability to blend in. He or she can come off as charming and intelligent. They're skilled actors whose sole mission is to manipulate people. They have a high estimation of themselves and a need for stimulation. They are pathological liars. They are cunning.

"And lastly, psychopaths aren't always violent, but they are all narcissists and manipulators. Did you know that many psychopaths are successful in the business world? They are ruthless."

"So you are saying that everything we know so far is an optical illusion."

"It's like a Salvador Dali painting," she says.

We take a break. I walk to an empty room and call my sponsor.

"Jigger, I think I'm going crazy," I say.

"Too late. You're already there."

"Thanks for your help, buddy," I say. "Last night, I had a brief image of a bottle of Jack Daniels. There was a big shot glass, and I was filling it up.

"Now I am really worried about you!" he says.

"Why?"

"You have never used a shot glass in your life."

"Thanks for your help, Jigger."

131.

"Fig," I say. "The owner of the Bad Boy franchise knows something. He knows more than he is fessing up to. He is hiding something. He is hiding the biggest secret in the world. We need to get into his psyche. We need to get into his face."

There is no way to prep for our meeting with Jeb. It is going to be a fly-by-the-seat-of-our-pants kind of day.

We settle in, and I look at Jeb's new wife.

"Blossom, will you please give us some private time?"

She looks at me quizzically and slowly leaves. Blossom and Flower wait in the lobby while we talk to Jeb.

I look at the troubled owner of this restaurant chain.

"Hey, Jeb," I say. "We are alone now. Your bride is gone from this conversation. Just us. Here. Now.

"Just you, me, Fig, Upchuck, and Woody."

"I prefer to be called Special Agent Walter . . ."

"Shut the fuck up!" we all yell in unison.

"Just a couple of guys. Hanging out. Shooting the breeze. Talking about guy stuff. Talking about the three Bs: booze, broads, and baseball."

Upchuck says, "Okay, mister. Time to talk."

Jeb looks at all of us. Scared of what's next.

"My perception of this story has changed," I say. "There is a new version rolling around in my head. In the beginning, we assumed some lunatic was on a killing streak. Or maybe a few lunatics were on a killing streak. Stupid stuff. We all thought your locations just happened to be the random scenes of the crimes."

"It doesn't make sense," I say. "The victims have nothing in common except that, in the beginning, the victims were all employees. Now, all that has changed. This time, a customer, a family man, was killed in your parking lot."

Jeb's eyes go blank, and his head tilts forward. He starts to squirm.

"You think I killed my own customers?"

"Worse than that!"

We morph into our good cop/bad cop routine. A dog and pony show. Maybe it's Abbot and Costello on steroids. Who's on first?

"Something is missing!" I start. "Some fact is missing. Some person is missing. You have information you are not sharing, Jeb. You are keeping a secret. What's your secret? This secret you are holding onto is killing you. Here's the bad part! Your secret is killing other people, too."

"There's a person, or a company, or a cause that is controlling you," Fig adds. "Who is holding you hostage?"

Jeb lifts his head, looks at Fig, looks at me, and then stares straight at the wall. His head bobs down again.

"My theory," I say out loud, "is that you know something you don't want us to know. What do you know? What do we need to know?"

"What is your secret?" Fig asks again, without a pause. We glance at each other. "Our next few hours are open. We are prepared to sit in this room all night long."

I say, "You are trying hard to make us believe these killings were random. Why? What are you hiding?"

Fig says, "We might have bought that bullshit story in the beginning. We ain't buying it no mo'."

Now it's my turn. "Jeb, every time I ask a hard question, you shut down. Every time I hint that you might know something, you change the subject. You are demonstrating every single nervous habit that I know.

"You are rubbing your face, constantly blinking, squeezing your lips together, and playing with your hair. And you are yawning. You are experiencing major stress. Textbook stuff!"

"And you can't make eye contact," Fig says.

"But now this isn't about you," I say. "We are conducting a murder investigation!"

"Jeb," Fig stands up, takes a big breath and screams, "Listen up, loud and clear!" Jeb jumps back in his seat. He looks like he was hit by a tire iron. He is ready to break.

Fig yells as loud as he can, "Jeb, What are you hiding?"

I whisper as soft as I can, "Jeb, what are you hiding?"

Good guy/bad guy at its best.

I slowly push a metal stack chair toward Jeb with my foot. It squeaks on the linoleum floor. I stop the chair right in front of him, and turn it around so I can straddle it with my arms on the back rest. Our faces are now a foot apart. I sit still and stare into his glassy eyes, waiting for a return glance, but he is focused on the floor. A full minute goes by. He looks very uncomfortable, and he is breathing heavily. I move my chair closer. Our faces almost touch. Now he can't look down, so he hangs his head back and glares at the ceiling.

"Jeb," I say slowly. "Look at me."

I drop my voice to a normal, conversational level. I talk very, very slowly to emphasize my point.

"If another person is killed, and it can be established that you knew the reason, or the person who was responsible, then you could be charged with murder. Do you understand what I am saying?"

There is a long silence.

"You could be charged with murder!"

Fig says, "This is called withholding information! Obstruction of justice!"

"It is called murder."

"Jeb, You will be as guilty as the person who is pulling the trigger!"

His head goes back again. Staring at the ceiling again. He looks so uncomfortable. Fig pushes a chair right behind Jeb.

I am two inches from his face. Like a dentist.

Fig is two inches from his ass. Like a proctologist.

He can't avoid us.

"Jeb, look at me," I say again, this time forcefully.

Our eyes lock. My eyes are focused. His eyes are revolving. Around and around. He appears to be dizzy.

"Jeb. You can be charged with murder," I say again. "You will lose your wife. You will lose your business, and you will lose your freedom. You will go to jail if you know who this killer is."

Jeb takes a big breath and chokes. His eyes well up, and he starts to sob again. He tries to push his chair back, but he can't. He stands up, looks around and starts to totter. He loses his balance. He slams down again. His hands go up to his head, and he covers his face. He starts to sob out loud. Very loud.

We let him cry for two full minutes. Then he shakes his head. Big turns. Left to right, as if to say, no, no, no.

"Okay, Jeb," I say. "Start talking! Now!"

"Okay. God damn it! God damn you! Fuck you! Fuck you all!"

We sit still. We barely breathe. We wait.

He starts looking down again and starts gasping for air.

Then he speaks, slowly. Almost in a whisper.

"Okay, I'll tell you. There was someone. There was a person who may be trying to get even with me. There was a person I was briefly involved with. Not for long. Just a few weeks. Nothing serious. Well, maybe serious to her. Just a fling to me. Well, a little more than a fling. Wait a minute. No! She was not a fling. Definitely not a fling. A fling would be something fun. She was not fun. She was a fucking disaster!"

Jeb stops talking. Maybe he is praying he will die before he has to confess.

He slowly starts shaking his head. Then the shaking becomes violent. We sit perfectly still. Barely breathing. There will be no distractions. Nothing will be in the way of his revelation. We will not move from this room for as long as it takes.

"She was just a hitchhiker."

"When did you meet her?" I ask.

"I met her about three months before all this killing stuff started."

He hangs his head and stares at his feet. There are now huge sweat stains under his armpits. His forehead is soaking wet.

"I don't even know her real name," Jeb says. "I think she changed her name when we met. She said the reason she was hitchhiking was to get away from an old boyfriend who was stalking her. She said he broke into her apartment. She said that, another time, he showed up at a picnic and caused a scene."

I sit up straight. I am at attention in my chair. I am suddenly more alert than I have been in years. I listen for the hammer to drop. Fig sits up straight, too. This admission is important for us. We know that the bullets came from Kiki's old pistol, but we don't know if she is the person still using it.

"She was so cute," he continues. "A foxy girl who was hitchhiking. I picked her up. I gave her a ride. Nothing wrong with that, right?"

We stare at him for a long time, and then, instinctively, we start to use the pry bar.

"Where did you meet this hitchhiker?"

"Route eighty, on my trip out here to Seattle."

"What part of the country?"

"Oh, some place in Colorado."

I stand up.

"What town?"

"No clue, but I had just stopped for gas. The receipt will show where I filled up."

"Think."

"Boulder, maybe?"

"Boulder, Colorado?" I shout.

"What did I say?"

"Everything! Tell us the rest of the story."

"I was bored from the long trip," he says. "I was falling asleep. I needed some company, and she needed a ride. Pretty harmless, right? She looked like she might be a source of entertainment. Just human, I guess." He smiles, but no one smiles with him.

"I just wanted to stay awake. She was so creative. In the beginning, she was really a lot of fun. If you know what I mean."

"I told her I had a girlfriend. I told her right up front that I was engaged to the love of my life. I even told her what my girlfriend's name was.

"She said that was no problem, because she only dated guys who had girlfriends or wives.

"She was a big tease. She had my undivided attention! Lots of T&A. We kind of fooled around in the car all the way here. It's amazing we didn't go off of the road.

"She was running away from something. When we got to Seattle, she had no place to stay. I was just trying to being a nice guy. Trying to help my fellow man. Or fellow girl." His laugh was nervous. He was looking for acceptance or understanding. He wasn't getting it.

"I had already booked a room, and it was an easy decision. I said she could stay with me for a day or two until she got a place of her own.

"We had a lot of one-on-one time together. One on one," he said again.

"But my girlfriend, Blossom, was on track to move here. To marry me.

"I love Blossom so much!" He sighed again.

"Tell us about the hitchhiker! Everything!"

"About five-five. Thin. Short, black hair. Incredibly energetic. Very attractive. Always moving. Jiggling. Constantly watching me. Never took her eyes off me. Smiling. Asking questions. She had so much energy. She wore me out."

"Why didn't you bring this up before?"

"Why? Isn't it obvious? I didn't want Blossom to know about this. This will break her heart. This will ruin our relationship. My time with that girl will destroy our marriage. It will destroy her. It has already destroyed me."

"What happened after you got to Seattle?"

"She stayed with me for a while. Every morning, I would ask her to leave. Every night, she would convince me she should stay.

"A see-through baby doll at the motel door convinced me. A pair of thigh highs and heels convinced me. Bare ass convinced me. I wasn't strong enough to say no. Instead, I would say, 'Okay, one more day. One more night.'

"She wouldn't leave. So finally I paid my motel bill for a month in advance. I grabbed my stuff and ran out of the room. She ran out of the room, too, but she was naked.

"I'm sorry," I told her.

"'You will be sorry!' she screamed. 'You will be very sorry.'

"She was a crazy woman. She was standing there naked, pounding on the car door. She picked up a lawn chair and heaved it at my windshield.

"She was shouting at the top of her lungs. Smashing the car with her fist.

"'Please don't leave me! Don't you dare leave me! You cannot leave me!'

"People came out of their motel rooms to stare."

"What else?" I say. "Tell us whatever you can think of, regardless of how insignificant it may seem."

"Well, there's one other little thing, but I'm sure it doesn't matter. Not important at all. Never mind."

"What is it?"

"Nothing."

"Something."

"Well, the girl had a disability. She couldn't hear. The girl could lip read from a mile away, but she was deaf."

"Holy shit." Fig and I jump up at the same time.

"What did I say?" Jeb asked.

"Everything!"

"That's it! That's her."

"Who?"

Agent Woodbury and Chief Upchuck stare at us.

Fig and I start pacing. Fig is punching the air like a heavy-weight fighter. He grunts in a very deep voice. "Hough!"

"Have you heard from her, after you broke up?" I yell.

Upchuck stands up.

"What's going on?" he asks.

Agent Woodbury's head is going back and forth, as if he is watching a tennis match.

We are standing over Jeb. He is lower than a dish rag.

"Have you heard from her again?" I shouted.

After a very long silence, he speaks quietly. "Email." He hangs his head.

"What?" I jump up again.

"Email?"

"That's her!"

"Who? What did I say?" Jeb asked.

"Everything!"

"What did the emails say?" I shout.

"She said she killed other men with a single shot. But she was going to kill me in a different way. Very, very, slowly. I didn't know what she was talking about."

"We know what she was talking about!"

"Where is that computer?" I scream.

"Get that computer!" Fig shouts to anyone. He shouts to everyone. "Send that computer to the Techs in San Diego, now!"

Agent Woodbury becomes dejected. He looks back and forth at the commotion. He has lost his edge. He has lost his case.

"Okay, everyone. Listen up!" I say forcefully.

Chief Upchuck stares. Jeb stares, too.

"This case has taken on a new twist. I am involved! Even if you don't want me involved, I am totally involved. If I have to live in my car and eat peanut-butter sandwiches, I am involved. I have a personal interest. I have personal knowledge. I have a vendetta."

"Tell them," says Fig.

"This girl, Kiki, has killed men in three different states. She shot me twice. She has tried to kill me twice. Two different times, in two different cities. She is a traveling shit show. She is moving around the country on a killing spree.

"Now we know how she gets around. Her mode of transportation is her finger." I make a gesture with my thumb. "She hitchhikes."

Jeb slouches even more.

"She is skillful, resourceful, determined, talented, angry, and crazy.

"It's all different now, somehow. Her act is different. Before, she was going after old lovers. Now she is targeting strangers. Why? Because she has a new mission! What is her mission?

"She is not going to stop on her own. We have to stop her.

"I know this girl!" I say. "I have to stop her."

The more animated we get, the more disillusioned Jeb gets. He slides down and is almost sitting on his back. He looks up and says, "I probably should have told you about this sooner."

"Ya think, Mister?" Upchuck says.

"I need to talk to my wife. I need to talk with Blossom."

He leaves the room, and the two of them enter an interview office.

The door closes quietly. There is no screaming. No yelling. No crying. After thirty minutes, she leaves the room. Stoic. Blossom is a strong woman. She looks straight ahead. There is no fight. There is no crying, but huge tears are streaming down her face. Dripping from her cheeks.

She walks toward Flower, and they hug. Flower doesn't know what just happened, but she senses it's bad.

Blossom takes Flower's hand and leads her to the exit. She stops and turns back to us. She makes a public announcement, but it is addressed to Jeb.

"Jeb and I will be getting a divorce!"

"Blossom, it was just . . ."

Blossom and Flower quickly exit the building.

Jeb cries again.

Flower and Blossom head to San Diego. I stay in Seattle and work on this killer jigsaw puzzle of a crime.

Back in San Diego, Blossom moves in with Flower. They work together at Jaspers Restaurant. They support each other. They sleep in the same bed. They whisper all night long. They hold hands. They finish each other's meals. They finish each other's sentences.

132.

DEAR DIARY_____.

I love my new landlord. Mrs. Peacock is the best thing that has ever happened to me. Even though I have been here for a few weeks, I am still impressed with the fabulous old mansion. I love my private first floor. Mrs. Peacock spends a lot of time on the second floor. I have access to a TV with a closed-caption option.

I can use the kitchen twenty-four hours a day. I can use the beautiful old Park Avenue anytime I want. I feel like I am queen of the castle.

Mostly, I think Mrs. Peacock likes me. Many nights we have dinner together. The housekeeper is a wonderful cook.

Last night, Mrs. Peacock reached out.

"I have my hair appointment later on this week," she said. "How would you like to come with me and have a new cut? A new color? A new do? It will be my treat."

I gave her a big hug. "Oh, Mrs. Peacock, thank you so much. I appreciate your friendship and your offer, but I am not ready for a change. I am just a plain Jane at heart."

The Seattle police department goes door-to-door throughout the city. They work one street at a time. When they visit Mrs. Peacock, they show her a picture of a girl with very short, black hair.

Mrs. Peacock graciously smiles.

"There is no one here who looks like that!"

133.

FIG, UPCHUCK, AND I TAKE A break for a few hours. Out of the office. Out of our mind. Looking for a spark. Looking for an answer. Upchuck gives us a tour of the city. We stroll through Pioneer Square and stare at the fifty-foot totem pole.

We drive down to Olympic Sculpture Park. We let our imaginations run riot as we walk this outdoor art museum. We enjoy the park's beauty and walk to Belltown. There is a great view of the Puget Sound and of downtown. We gawk at the "Giant Eyeball Benches." We also get a chance to check out the huge orange sculpture called "The Eagle."

Upchuck takes us to Elliott's Oyster House for some fresh local seafood.

"She is a bad-ass," says Fig. "She is angry, abandoned, and alone. I think she has an addiction. It's called revenge. She is getting even. In the process, she dehumanizes her victims."

"We know what she is doing. We know why she is doing it. We know how."

"She blends in. How does she fit in so well?"

"She is on a stage. She is playing dress up. She keeps changing her costume. She keeps changing her appearance. She changes her persona.

"This is not new. She has been changing her outfits since we first started following her. She was a classy girl in New York. Then she was a yuppie in Boulder. Now she is here. Somewhere in this town. Someone has to find her. I need to find her.

"She must have evolved again to fit in here. She has reinvented herself. Maybe she looks like a local. Maybe she is a grunge girl or a crew-cut punk. But now, with each new killing, she modifies everything again.

"She is in extreme-makeover mode. A young girl, a working man, a fat old lady. She is taking on new personalities. Acting the part. Dressing the part. Thinking the part. She transforms into each new person. She is so good at this!"

"In the meantime," the chief says, "the police department has had over five thousand tips. Phone calls, pics, and messages. We are working around the clock just trying to keep up. And we have viewed the surveillance tapes a hundred times. Frame by frame. There is no facial recognition. There is always hair, or a hat, or a mustache in the way. Whoever it is walks into view, confronts the victim, and calmly walks out of range. We have cruisers canvassing neighborhoods."

"Where do you think she lives?" I muse.

"Agent Woodbury thinks she might be in a low-rent apartment by herself."

"I disagree." Everyone looks at me. "An apartment house, even a low-rent joint, would require identification. She may still have a license from New Jersey, but it's probably expired. Her name would send up red flags. Even if that wasn't a problem, the picture would be different."

"You are right," says Fig. "And, just so you know, Woody, we have notified all registered rental agencies to flag anyone with her name."

"I'm sure she has changed her name."

"Where does she find her get-ups?"

Chief Upchuck speaks. "Woody here firmly believes she is shop-ping in theatrical supply companies. He has had our staff visiting every theater supply, costume rental, upscale wig firm, and stage makeup business in the North West. He also thinks the killer may have worked in show business."

134.

It is late at night, and Flower and I are having a quiet phone talk. It's her time, and I listen. She wants to consult on this case. I can't imagine she would have anything helpful to say, but I try to be polite.

"Her total persona changes," Flower says. "Not only on the outside, but on the inside, too. I think she becomes each killer. For a brief time, she *is* the young girl with a yoga mat. She transforms into the old man with the hump and greasy hair. First she becomes the person. Then she gets the outfit.

"This girl adapts her new costume to how she looks and feels. I believe she advances into a new state of mind and changes her looks. She changes her personality. She changes into a new person. Then she changes her outfits."

"Wait a minute," I pipe in. "What did you just say?"

"When?"

"Back there. Last paragraph."

"I don't know."

"You said she can change who she is. Who she becomes. Tell me more."

"She doesn't just change her clothes. She morphs into a different person. She becomes the killer. The clothes are secondary."

"Wait a minute. Wait just a damn minute." I talk too loud. "What's that animal that changes its color to blend in with the background?"

"Chameleon?"

"Please look it up for me."

Flower hits Google and reads.

"An animal that has the ability to change color, behavior, or movement to fit in."

"That's it. She is skilled at fitting in. She becomes a different person. She is using clothes, make-up, and willpower. She changes her personality. Then she gets the outfit to match. This girl is a chameleon.

"Flower," I say. "I will be staying in Seattle for awhile. I miss you. Why don't you and Blossom come up for a visit?"

"Special Agent Woodbury made it clear he doesn't want your help."

"I'm not here to help Woody. I am here to help Chief Upchuck. And I'm here to help myself."

"Why?"

"I can't sleep. I can't relax. I can't get comfortable with the fact that Kiki is out in this town. I let her escape. Twice."

"You didn't let her escape. You let her shoot you. Twice."

"Thanks for your support. Anyway, she has time on her hands, a pistol in her pocket, and wires crossed in her head."

135.

WHEN THE SISTERS GET TO THE Seattle airport, Jeb is there, too. He is holding the world's largest bouquet of flowers. It is so big it takes both hands. He can barely see over the top.

Women smile. Men laugh out loud.

Fig whispers, "When you see a guy with flowers, you know he really fucked up."

"The bigger the blunder, the bigger the bouquet," I say.

"I don't think his bouquet is big enough." We both laugh.

As we wait for baggage, Blossom sits as far away from Jeb as she can, but she clutches the bouquet.

"Blossom. Can we please talk alone?" he says.

"No! If you have something to say, you can say it in front of my sister and in front of my friends."

"I want to tell you I'm sorry. I am human. I am not perfect. I made a mistake."

"This is too personal for me," I say. "I need to take a leak."

Fig stands up. "Me, too."

Flower stands up. "Me, three."

We all laugh. Flower gets in-between us. The three of us hold hands as we walk away.

136.

"Blossom," Jeb continued. "I fell in love with you the day you interviewed at Bad Boy. We worked ten hours a day. We used the same tooth brush. You agreed to marry me.

"When I picked up that hitchhiker, I was just offering a ride. I told her about you. I told her about us.

"I am now a broken person in a broken world. I am asking you to make me whole again. I cannot live without you."

"I cannot live with you," she replied.

"You don't have to live with me. Pick your own apartment. You can rent any apartment you want.

"But I want you to work with me. In our company. On the day we got married, Bad Boy Burgers became your company, too. You own half this restaurant chain. The business needs you, the staff wants you. I love you."

She put the bouquet on a chair and ran to him. Their hug lasted a long time.

137.

ON MY SECOND WEEK BACK AT the Seattle police department, I bump into Special Agent Walter Woodbury. We see each other in the hall. He scrunches.

"Excuse me, Mr. Collins," he says, sternly. "I asked you to leave this city. I told you to leave this department. I said we would not pay for your time to work on this case. You were dismissed!"

"Hey, Woody! Nice to see you, too!" I smile. "I am in Seattle as a tourist. I am going to have a burger." I turn around and walk away.

Later that day, I listen to a message on my cell. Agent Woodbury says, "Mr. Collins I want you to leave this town at once!"

Since I am not overly impressed with bogus authority figures, I delete his message.

After dinner, we head up to our room. The girls put the TV on, and I am falling asleep.

Flower says, "Jeez. I forgot to bring a raincoat. I am in Seattle, where it rains every day of the year. What was I thinking?"

"No problem," Blossom says. "We can pick one up at a thrift shop. I get all my clothes at thrift shops."

My eyes rotate from half-closed to half-open. Like numbers on a Vegas slot machine. I become conscious.

I call Fig and wake him up.

"What?" he says.

"She doesn't shop at theater supply outlets."

"What? Hey, I'm trying to sleep over here."

"She buys her clothes in thrift shops."

"Thrift shops? Where did you come up with that stupid idea? Don't answer. I'm going back to sleep. You should go to sleep, too."

138.

"WHAT HAVE YOU LEARNED?" CHIEF UPCHUCK asks me.

We are all in his office. I look around. Blossom and Jeb are sitting on a couch holding hands. Flower is so close she is almost in my lap.

Agent Woodbury is all by himself in the farthest corner of the room, as if his invitation was an afterthought. His eyes are squinting, and he is glaring at me.

Fig is smiling. He already knows what I learned, because he was part of the process. The girls are smiling, too.

"Let's talk about what is not happening," I say. "This girl is not on stage. She is not trying to please an audience. She is not in a theater. She does not want to stand out. She doesn't want to fit in.

"She does not want you to remember a single thing about her.

"And she is not shopping in theater supply firms."

Agent Woodbury glares.

"So, gentlemen. You, too, ladies." I smile at Flower and at Blossom, who blows a huge bubble and lets it pop.

"She doesn't wear special professional outfits. She wears clothes that make her look commonplace, inconspicuous, and real. She wants to look unremarkable. She is so average that she becomes everyone. She becomes anyone. She becomes no one. She wears the most plain, run-of-the-mill, nondescript clothes in the world.

"Where does she get these run-of-the-mill, nondescript outfits?" Fig asks, to set me up.

"Thrift shops," I say.

Woody glares.

"Thrift shops?" he says. "Where did you come up with that stupid idea?"

Flower and Blossom break out laughing.

"This girl is a chameleon," I say, slowly. "First, she decides who she wants to be, then she morphs into that person! After that, she goes out and shops. She doesn't want to stand out, so she shops in thrift stores. She buys ordinary clothes that have been worn by ordinary people. She doesn't want you to remember her! She is not on a stage; this girl wants to walk into your life, and then she wants to walk out of your life. She wants you to forget what she looks like the second after you've seen her.

"We need to find a person who's met our friendly deaf girl."

"Let's start a massive search in every thrift shop, second-hand store, and Goodwill in Seattle. Let's ask if they remember anyone who was lip reading. Let's ask around about a girl who has that disability.

"Here's what I am thinking. Let's narrow this down. She may be within walking distance of a bus route. She lip reads or signs, but otherwise she is probably not too different from ordinary people.

"We suspect she hitchhiked all across the country. In Boulder, she changed her looks, her story, and her personality. Now she is in Seattle. We know how she got here.

"Taxis and Uber keep records, so I think she avoids those services. She moves around on public transportation. Buses would be the best bet. We need to create a grid of all bus lines that go to the scenes of the four killings.

"From that point we can create a perimeter where she might live and move around with a combination of walking and bus travel. Then we can comb those neighborhoods. Flower and Blossom can help with the canvassing."

The chief recaps our conversation. "Okay, we are finally making some progress over here! The suggestions you made today, Jesse, are a turning point in our case. Thank you, thank you!"

Woody glares at me. If looks could kill, I'd be dead meat!

The chief slowly looks around the room and stares at everyone of us, one person at a time.

He stands up. "Okay, Mister. You, too, Missies. Listen up. This conversation is confidential. I don't want anyone learning about the decisions we have made here today. I don't want to tip-off this chameleon. Don't tell your spouse, your kids, or your puppy. And definitely do not, do not, do not, leak this information to any media outlets."

After the meeting, Woody is the first to leave. He storms out of the room and slams the door behind him.

The next day, the headlines scream:

The Seattle Killer Is a Chameleon!

The chief calls Woody into his office and slams the door. There is yelling and screaming.

139.

Business at Bad Boy Burgers is slowly returning to normal.

"Fig," I say. "I am amused and confused. I am waiting for the next damn shoe to drop. It's been a month since we've seen any activity."

"Is she still out there," he asks, "or has she hitchhiked to another city? Maybe we should just give up."

"We are halfway through our list of thrift shops. Someone has seen this killer. We need to find her. We shouldn't give up. Please, don't give up. I won't give up!"

140.

FLOWER'S PHONE VOICE SOUNDS MORE ANIMATED than it's been in a long time. She is breathless and restless. "Jesse, I found a thrift shop that caters to the Muslim population. It's called Finders Keepers. It's right near the Islamic Center of North Seattle."

She is excited, and I try to feel her heat, but it's hard to pay attention. I visualize her pacing back and forth, holding onto the phone as she talks.

"It's a nonprofit."

"That's nice."

I take the phone from my ear and stare at it. I am already getting impatient. My hand starts rotating as if I was directing traffic. I am waving big, come-along movements in the air. Since we are on the phone, she can't see my hand.

I fade out while Flower continues. I close my eyes and think about the Muslim population. The town is divided, and I have seen hundreds of handmade "Just Say No to Burqas" signs.

"There are a lot of volunteers at this thrift shop," Flower goes on.

"That's special." I grit my teeth. She seems to notice my negative energy.

"What?" she asks.

"Flower, how will this help our investigation?"

"Shut up," she says. "The manager told me that one of her volunteers was talking with a deaf girl a week ago. They spent a lot of time together. I am going back to Finders Keepers after lunch to meet with the volunteer. Maybe you should be in the store, too. You could use some new clothes."

I am such a jerk. I was trying to cut her off in the middle of her conversation. Flower has made more headway into this case today than all the rest of us have in a month.

I arrive at Finders Keepers early and settle into the men's department.

When Flower starts talking to the volunteer, the two girls become friendly and warm. As they are talking, they seem to be using a bit of sign language.

I realize that most of us already know sign language. We tap our wrist to ask the time. We extend our thumb and pinky to our ear to say *call me*. We hold our thumb up when things are good. We hold our palms up and raise our eyebrows to signify that we don't understand. We all use sign language every day.

Flower thanks the manager and gives the volunteer a long, friendly hug. She walks out, and I follow her to a coffee shop down the street.

"Here's the good part," she says. "The volunteer told me that a deaf girl, maybe Kiki, was looking for a new outfit. The customer said she was going to a costume party and wanted to go as a Muslim woman. The deaf girl had already been there twice."

"Holy crap!" My eyes slam into red-alert mode. I raise my eyebrows. My head leans forward toward Flower, and I kiss her on the cheek. My pulse quickens.

"Jesse, two days ago, the deaf girl bought a complete outfit. A Hijab cap, a traditional, white, Abaya robe, and white pants."

I grab my phone and make an urgent call.

"Upchuck, please!"

"Sir?"

"I need to talk to Upchuck, now, please." I speak louder.

"I am sorry, sir. We have no one here by that name." It's the new switchboard operator.

"Upchuck. Chief Charles Upton! Now!" I shout.

"May I tell him who is calling?"

"No! Just get him! Please. Now. Emergency!"

"Sir, your emergency is not my emergency. Nothing is so important that you need to verbally demean someone else."

"Upchuck! Now! Please! Upchuck! Urgent!"

Upchuck fumbles with the phone. He drops it, and I hear the noise of metal smashing on metal. There are more fumbles as he picks up the phone.

"Upton!" he says. He is out of breath.

"Upchuck. It's Jesse."

"Jesse! She just hit again!"

My lips move again, but no sound comes out. My eyes open as wide as they can. I stand up. I slam back down and slump into the chair.

"Jesse. Did you hear me?"

"Fuck!" I shout.

People in the coffee shop stare.

"Fuck!" I shout again. "Was she dressed as a Muslim?"

There is long silence.

"Jesse, If you knew, why didn't you call me?"

141.

IT'S BEEN THREE MONTHS SINCE THE last murder. We are working harder and getting less information. There is nothing new from Kiki.

Is she hiding in town?

Has she moved away?

Did she kill herself?

Kiki has fallen from the face of the earth. We all are beginning to think Kiki's killing streak has ended. We had her focused in our sights, but we didn't get to pull the trigger. Nothing changes, but everything has changed.

Fig and I are having lunch at Poquito's Mexican Restaurant in Capitol Hill. The waitress says they have a hundred brands of tequila for our fresh, frosty, luncheon margarita. Since I quit drinking, I can't even count to a hundred. It's been a long time since I have had a fresh, frosty margarita. My problem now is that I have too much blood in my alcohol system. But life is good.

As we are seated, we pass the kitchen door. We see the Mexican tortilla ladies making tacos by hand. We find a quiet booth in the back and Fig orders a seven-layer taco. I order a steak-and-cheese fajita.

"I've gotta take a leak," he says

"Will you go for me?"

When he comes back I check his progress.

"Did you go for me?" I ask.

"You didn't have to go."

After we order, Chief Upchuck calls. This is another speaker moment. Fig hits a few buttons, and we both listen in.

"Guys. Something just came up. There was a house fire a few weeks ago. Two girls were torched beyond recognition."

"Why do we need to know this?" Upchuck and I have a good enough relationship to banter.

"You need to know this, because you may get a stiffy."

"Now you have my undivided attention."

"Okay, mister," he says. "Picture this. Two girls in a small house. Owner's name was Candice. The other girl, probably a renter, had no identification. Gas covered everything. The explosion happened in the middle of the night. They were each in bed. Separate rooms. Totally trashed. Ashes to ashes. No recognition."

"You are breaking my heart!" I say.

"Here's the good part. Here's the fun part, if a fire that kills two people can be fun. Something interesting has happened after the fact."

"After the fact. What does that mean, after the fact?"

"We track mail to any address that had a suspicious death. Since the fire, a lot of mail was going to be delivered to the house where the two girls lived. Or died."

"I am waiting for my stiffy."

"Here's the part that might excite you. Most of the mail was addressed to someone named Kiki Sullivan."

"Say what?"

"Incredible amount of mail to the girl of your dreams. One Ms. Kiki Sullivan. Normally this stuff would go to the dead letter office, but since this was a murder scene, it is being diverted to me. Right here."

"Mail from where?"

"There are mailings from work programs and travel sites. Hotel chains looking for employees and vacation companies that need help. There is an envelope from the Cape Cod Chamber of Commerce. Also, there are mailings offering volunteer opportunities from around the world. A few different packages from the Peace Corps. There was a letter from a Colorado Dude Ranch. Tons of mail to Kiki."

Upchuck forwards the mail to us. Fig and I spend an evening sorting through the pile.

"Companies still mail stuff instead of just putting posts up on a website?" I ask.

"Many of the work-stay programs send mail to people who don't have a computer. Or a smart phone. Or a library card."

"So Kiki is officially gone," Fig says. "Someone poured gallons of gas throughout a house in the middle of the night. Two girls sleeping. A match. Flicker to a flame. Two seconds flat."

142.

AGENT WOODBURY IS DISMISSED. HE GOES to another assignment without publishing his best-selling novel.

Life is back to normal, but normal is only a setting on the dryer.

It's the end of the day. Fig and I are sitting at a small beach bar. At least fifty neon beer signs are covering the walls. Instead of being in the electric glow of the lounge, we sit on the outside deck.

"So, she's history?" I say. "I always have trouble with endings."

"I'm out of ideas. What've you got?"

"I got nothing. I guess it's official."

"Deader than a doornail."

"Done deal."

"Down and out."

"One and done!"

We shake hands.

Flower and I head back to San Diego, and she moves in with me. We go to meetings, we take long walks with Mia, and we talk about everything. There are no secrets. This may be the closest to being in love I have ever been.

At Jaspers, Flower takes more of a leadership role. I start working there, too. I can sweep the floor as well as the next guy. I wash dishes and bus tables. I am a slow learner, but they have faith in me.

In Seattle, Blossom and Jeb are working at rebuilding Bad Boy Burgers. The sisters talk almost every day, and they visit each other once a month.

The phone rings, and Flower beams as she looks at caller ID.

"Blossom," she whispers.

I hear one side of the conversation.

"Oh, I am so excited for you," she says.

"Of course we can make it! Whatever day it is. We are free that day!"

"No hamburgers?" She laughs.

"Sure, we will bring her. Aunt Carrie would love it!"

When she gets off the phone, I don't ask. I just wait.

"Jeb is finally having a wedding reception," Blossom says. "It's what he promised her a year ago. Right at Bad Boy Burgers. Closing for the night.

"Inviting the Mayor and the police chief. Professionally catered. Real food. Not a hamburger in the joint.

"Blossom is such a business woman. Even at a time like this, she is thinking about the chain. She said that since her party will be in all the papers, it will be like free advertising."

143.

THE WEDDING CELEBRATION COULDN'T BE MORE festive. A huge blue-and-white-striped tent covers the parking lot. Small lanterns are hung over tables, and it looks magical. The music is upbeat and perky. The buffet is spectacular.

Telegrams, congratulation cards, and gifts are all displayed on a corner table. During the evening, more presents are delivered and added to the pile.

As people are settling in to enjoy the buffet, a huge batch of poinsettias is brought up to the gift table.

The delivery girl carrying the bouquet is wearing a white cutaway tuxedo jacket with tails, a pink blouse, and an oversized red bow tie. Her makeup could be on the cover of *Vogue* magazine. She wears ruby-red lipstick, light-blue eyeliner, and bright-pink rouge. She has the longest eyelashes I have ever seen.

Her vivid blond wig has been sprayed with glitter, and she is wearing a huge pair of square, mirror glasses. Her white gloves are shoulder length. Her legs look very long in her sheer, black tights. Her long legs are the showpiece of her outfit.

"Her outfit is outrageous," Fig says.

"Something is wrong," I say to Fig. "I feel like I have seen that delivery girl before. She is making me dizzy. She is trying too hard.

"I know that girl," I say again.

Blossom hears me and quietly walks up behind the girl with the poinsettias. She steps out of her heels.

The delivery girl holds the bouquet in front of her with both hands as she looks around the room.

A loud detonation comes from nowhere. The tent explodes with an apocalyptic sound and Jeb screams. He falls backwards and crumples to the floor.

Blossom instantly spins and executes a perfect round-house kick. As her foot smashes into the delivery girl's head, it jerks her forward. Her head snaps, and she goes down on the floor. Blossom jumps as high as she can and lands on the shooter's back. The scream is horrendous, and then there is nothing.

The police take the delivery girl into custody. The ambulance takes Jeb to the hospital.

144.

"How do you figure?" Fig says.

"Figure what?"

"The girls who were charbroiled in the house fire. The crispy girls. I thought that it was Kiki in the fire. The mail was all to Kiki."

"Bingo."

"Bingo what?"

"Bingo cards."

"What are you talking about?" he says again.

"People fill out those little pain-in-the-ass cards that are stuffed into magazines. "They're called Bingo Cards. Pretty efficient, except they take months to process. Six months sometimes. Maybe even a year. Kiki probably submitted those cards a long time ago. Long before the fire."

"You think that was her exit plan?"

"Bingo."

145.

Dear Diary _____

As I sit in solitary confinement, I am in shock. My living conditions, allotments, and the rudeness of the staff are not what I expected.

My prison-issue, one-piece jumpsuit is two sizes too large. The suit is boxy in shape and was made from heavy-weight cotton. It is stiff from starch. The jumpsuit has a full-length Velcro closure that is uncomfortable and has already started to cause a rash. I had to roll the pant legs up to keep from tripping and I had to roll the sleeves up so I could feed myself. My shower slippers are too big. One size fits all.

The orange suits that were given to us new fish were designed to make us stand out from the senior inmates. Wearing the prison uniform has caused a crazy unsettling psychological feeling. I have lost my individuality. I feel like I have lost my mind.

I can't stop crying. My life keeps flashing in front of me.

That was supposed to my wedding! My dress! My shoes! Jeb was supposed to be my husband.

146.

Dear Diary

After my first month in prison, a public defender came to visit. He introduced himself as Michael McGillicuddy.

"My friends call me Mickey." He laughed. "Actually, in college, they called me Mickey's Big Mouth.

"I have been appointed by the court to make sure you get a fair trial," he explained. "Many attorneys start their careers as a public defender. I was the oldest guy in grad school. I just got out of school, and I owe a half million dollars in student loans, so this is a good start for me. It is good for you, too, because I am not too busy, yet."

Mickey is handsome, outgoing, and has an infectious smile. His muscles bulge under his oxford dress shirt. He seems to be genuinely interested in my case. He says he can spend as much time with me as I want. When he walks into my cell, he greets me with a warm smile and a firm hand shake. He holds on a little too long. I let him. After a few visits, we share a hug.

We met every week for a few months, and one day Mickey had some good news.

"They have zero clues," he says. "A nothing case. All charges are speculative, hypothetical, and abstract. A bogus case.

"No one has been identified in any of the surveillance footage. The gunshot on the night of the wedding party didn't end up in any videotape. No one saw you holding a weapon. The gun that fell to the floor after you were kicked could have come from anyone. There were no fingerprints.

"I am petitioning the judge to release you from jail and reduce the rest of your sentence to personal recognizance. You can live at home while we work on your appeal. When you are home, you and I can spend as much time on this case as you would like.

Mickey is working so hard for me. Maybe we could be friends.

Maybe we could become lovers.

I might have one more opportunity to change my life.

One more, that's it!

The end?

Made in the USA
Columbia, SC
21 February 2020

Text design by Jillian Downey
Typesetting by Delmastype, Ann Arbor, Michigan
Text font: Janson
Display fonts: Gothic 13 and ITC Stone Sans

Although designed by the Hungarian Nicholas Kis in about 1690, the model for Janson Text was mistakenly attributed to the Dutch printer Anton Janson. Kis' original matrices were found in Germany and acquired by the Stempel foundry in 1919. This version of Janson comes from the Stempel foundry and was designed from the original type; it was issued by Linotype in digital form in 1985.
                                                    —courtesy www.adobe.com

Gothic 13 is a Linotype font, designed by Robert Hunter Middleton. It is a traditional American condensed gothic design, often used for headlines in newspapers and magazines.
                                                    —courtesy www.fonts.com

In 1987, Sumner Stone completed his designs for the Stone type family, which consists of three subfamilies, Serif, Sans, and Informal. In 1992, John Renner finished designing phonetic companion faces for ITC Stone Sans and ITC Stone Serif. The result is a font palette that can be combined successfully over a broad spectrum of typographic applications.
                                                    —courtesy www.adobe.com